Emma watched in shock as Brant moved like he was Justin Freaking Timberlake. Why was he torturing her like this? She had wanted him to impress her friends as a good piece of arm candy, but she hadn't actually wanted them to admire him enough to follow him like the Pied Piper.

If the looks he was receiving were any indication, the women loved him and the men hated him. Her Mr. December had taken the reunion by storm, and she didn't think there was anyone in the room who wasn't affected by him in some way. Had she created a monster?

Emma moved up behind him, sliding her arm around his waist as she moved her hips against his. *That's right, baby. I saw* Dirty Dancing *at least a dozen times.* He stiffened against her for a moment until he recognized her. He turned, pulling her against him, chest to chest. He whispered in her ear as they danced together, "I only want your hand on my ass, baby. I think Jill knows that now."

The desire she had been battling all evening came surging back, and she felt with certainty that if she didn't have him soon, she would explode.

Also by Sydney Landon

The Danvers Novels
Weekends Required
Not Planning on You
Fall for Me
Fighting for You
Betting on You (Penguin digital special)

NO DENYING YOU

YOU

A DANVERS NOVEL

SYDNEY LANDON

A SIGNET ECLIPSE BOOK

SIGNET ECLIPSE
Published by the Penguin Group
Penguin Group (USA) LLC, 375 Hudson Street,
New York, New York 10014

USA | Canada | UK | Ireland | Australia | New Zealand | India | South Africa | China
penguin.com
A Penguin Random House Company

First published by Signet Eclipse, an imprint of New American Library,
a division of Penguin Group (USA) LLC

First Printing, December 2014

Copyright © Sydney Landon, 2014

SIGNET ECLIPSE and logo are trademarks of Penguin Group (USA) LLC.

ISBN 978-0-451-47278-6

Printed in the United States of America
10 9 8 7 6 5 4 3 2 1

As always, this book is dedicated to my husband and children. They handle the world of make-believe that I live in half the time without complaint.

A special note of thanks to Scott and Ida Cash. I am so grateful for your tireless support of my books.

To my friends Donnie and Lisa (the Breakfast Club). Sometimes in this world, you are lucky enough to form bonds that last for a lifetime, and I'm blessed to have you in my life.

Chapter One

"Honey, have you given any more thought to getting some bigger tits?"

Emma rolled her eyes and dropped her head onto her desk. Why couldn't her mother bake cookies, knit sweaters or do any of that other Betty Crocker shit? No-o-o, she couldn't be that lucky. Katrina Davis—or Kat, as she liked to be called—had always wanted to be the cool mom on the block. Heck, most of Emma's childhood friends still called her mother for advice. The woman didn't pull any punches. "God, Mom, can we please not talk about my tits today? Or lack of them?"

"Em, it's for your own good. You're too attractive to sit at home all the time. Men are visual creatures, so maybe a new rack is exactly what you need. Your father can't keep his hands off mine. And you're not getting any younger. You don't want to wake up one day and have them fall out of bed before you do."

"Gross, Mom. This whole conversation is really gross. I don't want to hear anything about your sex life with Daddy. Ever. I'd like to be able to look him in the eyes just once without the constant stream of images in my head of the things you feel the need to confide to me. Maybe you should just go Catholic—then you could confess to someone with a more professional opinion."

"Oh, Em, get over it. I'm just trying to help. You know what? I'll even pay if I can pick them out. I'll e-mail you some information and you can let me know what you think."

"Mom, for the last time, I like my tits just fine!" As soon as she shouted that last bit, Emma froze at the sound of a throat clearing behind her. *Please tell me that the asswipe isn't behind me, ple-e-ease.* As she swiveled slowly in her chair, she groaned. Fate definitely wasn't on her side. Her boss, Brant Stone, stood behind her with his usual condescending smirk. She quickly said her good-byes to her mother although she could hear her still speaking as she gingerly placed the receiver back in the cradle. Determined not to give him the satisfaction of seeing her rattled, she raised a brow, asking as politely as she could manage, "Did you need something?"

"Apparently not as badly as you do, Emma."

Oh great, here it comes, another jab at my work performance. I wonder how much jail time I would get if I choked him with the paisley tie he's wearing. Turning her back to nonchalantly pick up her coffee cup, she said, "Pardon?"

"I am positively riveted by your plight," he replied. *More obscure code to unravel.* She spent half of her time trying to figure out what in the hell he was talking about. She knew he did it on purpose, the sneaky bastard. "I bet you are, considering you cause most of my misery." She knew it was unprofessional as well as career suicide to talk to her boss this way, but she kept hoping he would have her transferred to another department so that he could find someone more suitable for his assistant. So far, that hadn't happened. She had even started dropping hints, but, like every suggestion she made, he seemed to completely ignore it.

"That's flattering, Emma, but I don't think I can accept responsibility for your . . . shortcomings."

Her coffee cup fell from her suddenly limp fingers and crashed to the floor. Then she plowed into him as she jumped back to avoid the hot liquid. "Shit!" The carnage continued as they both fell backward like dominoes. When she managed to get her bearings, she was horrified to realize that Brant was laid out on the floor underneath her, and her butt was nestled firmly near his crotch. Coffee stains were splattered all over his perfectly creased slacks, and it took her a moment to realize why her legs seemed so bare as they lay tangled with his. Her short skirt had blown up during their fall and was now resting well above the level considered legal in most states. Was that . . . ? No, it couldn't be. . . .

Without thinking, she wiggled around experimentally. *No way!* Her boss, the spawn from hell, was not growing hard against her bottom. *Oh my God, he was!*

"I didn't realize that ruining my clothing also came with a lap dance." When she froze, he chuckled. "Oh, by all means, don't stop now. Even someone with small tits is a turn-on when she's grinding against your lap."

Emma jumped up as if she were on fire. "You are such an asshole. I should file sexual harassment charges against you. I'm pretty sure there are rules in the *Danvers Handbook* against discussing my tits."

Brant snorted as he rose to his feet. "I'm pretty sure there are also rules in there about talking about said tits on a company telephone on company time, and I'm even more sure there is a section about job performance."

If she didn't hate the man so much, she would be impressed by the way he excelled at sarcasm. She had worked for Brant Stone for about six months at the communications company Danvers International. Jason Danvers, owner of the company, had bought out the family company that was previously run by Brant and his sister, Ava. They had both come to work at Danvers in vice presidential roles after the merger.

Brant's younger brother, Declan, also worked for Danvers, although he hadn't been involved in the Stone family business. He had recently married Ella Webber, a receptionist on the fourth floor who had become a good friend of Emma's. It was the most recent wedding in a string of couplings at the company. Jason had married his secretary, Claire, and the Merimon brothers, Grayson and Nick, had also settled down. Gray was married to Suzy, who handled the special events for Danvers; Nick was married to Beth, Suzy's sister and assistant. They had recently had a new baby.

As far as romance was concerned, Danvers seemed to be the place to work if you were looking to find a significant other. So far it hadn't helped her, though. Instead, she was stuck with a shit head for a boss and a vibrator for date night. Life sucked in that area.

When Brant snapped his fingers in front of her face to get her attention, she stuck her tongue out at him. She simply couldn't resist, although she did refrain from giving him the verbal slapdown he so richly deserved. She settled for muttering, "Yeah, yeah, whatever." He actually looked disappointed before he turned and stalked off to his office.

When her phone rang yet again, she groaned, praying it wasn't her mother. "Brant Stone's office."

"You sound like someone pissed in your corn flakes."

Emma released a sigh of relief as she heard her friend Suzy's voice on the line. They may not have known each other for very long, but recognizing fellow smart-asses in each other, they had bonded pretty quickly. "Ugh . . . just the usual kind of morning nonsense with Mr. Sunshine. Maybe a little worse than usual."

"You'll have to tell me more; I could use a laugh. How about lunch today? Claire, Beth and Ella are going to the mall for some baby stuff and I'd really like to pass on that."

"I hear you, girl," Emma agreed. "I'll meet you downstairs around noon if that works for you?"

"Sounds good; stay out of trouble."

Emma did manage to work with Brant the rest of the morning without incident until he came out of his office as she was preparing to go to lunch. "Where are you eating? You don't mind if I go, do you?"

For a minute Emma stood there gaping at him. "Are you kidding?"

"Actually, yes. Going to Taco Bell and watching you drip your taco fixings all over the table isn't my idea of a relaxing lunch. I would like you to pick me up something at the deli around the corner, though, on your way back in."

Emma huffed in dramatic fashion. She didn't bother telling him that she was having lunch with Suzy there. "I guess it's asking too much that you get your own lunch. Who runs all of your errands in the evening? Do you have a maid that you keep chained up in your kitchen?"

Brant perched on the corner of her desk, grinning. "What a great idea; are you looking for a second job? If you were on the clock for twenty-four hours, I might be able to get eight hours of actual work out of you."

She gave him a sympathetic look before saying, "You've really got it bad. You deserve so much better than me."

Brant gave her a wary look before saying, "True."

"How about I bring you back a nice lunch and then we fill out the paperwork to have me transferred to another department. Somewhere in this building is the uptight assistant of your dreams. Just think, by Monday you could both be boring each other to death. Just say the word."

He was already shaking his head before she finished speaking. "I don't think so, Miss Davis. If you would like to quit, that is your choice, but I won't be transferring you. If you're going to work at Danvers, then you are going to be working here."

Emma looked at him, truly puzzled. "I really don't get it, you know. You hate everything about me. Our personalities don't mesh at all and you'd be much happier with someone else in this position, but you won't sign the transfer request. Why? Are you like one of those guys who enjoy being tortured? Do you have mommy issues? What gives?"

He gave her that superior look that he did so well and said, "I have no idea what you're talking about." Walking straight back into his office, he tossed out, "Don't forget my lunch," before he shut the door behind him.

She knew it was childish, but she flipped the bird toward his door before going to meet Suzy for lunch.

If there was one person at Danvers who made her feel normal, it was Suzy. She was brash, loud and irreverent, but those qualities were tempered with an eye-catching beauty that basically gave her a free pass. Emma found her standing in the lobby waiting for her. Her long red hair was loose and she was twirling a lock around her finger as she stood on impossibly high heels that matched her black leather skirt.

Emma had always felt her long brown hair was unremarkable, and it resurfaced every time she admired

Suzy's hair. She had started having blond highlights added to it a few years back, which had helped. Her fashion sense was similar to Suzy's, although Suzy probably carried it off better. They both preferred trendy clothes over the tailored business professional look. Today Emma was wearing a short plaid skirt with black chunky heels and a black blouse. She and Suzy both seemed to veer toward black.

They headed out the door and around the corner to the deli. Suzy rolled her eyes as they passed by a crew of workers patching a hole in the road. The wolf whistles from the men continued until they were inside. Apparently, the lack of encouragement wasn't a deterrent. Once they were seated, Suzy took a sip of her water with lemon while Emma tried to keep herself from drinking her entire sweet tea in one gulp. "So how are things with Mr. Sunshine today?" Suzy smirked.

Scowling, Emma shook her head. "You know, every day I promise myself I'll do better, but within a few hours, I've blown that promise all to hell and lost my religion along the way. Even I'm horrified over some of the things that come out of my mouth when I'm around him—but I can't seem to stop. If Claire or Jason really knew what we said to each other every day, I'd be fired for sure."

"Well, it takes two, and from what you've told me, Brant gives as good as he gets. I don't see him waving the white flag and getting rid of you, so maybe he gets off on it. Some guys like a little verbal spanking."

Emma shuddered. "Please don't say the words *spank-*

ing and *Brant* together; it gives me hives. Even Ajax couldn't scrub that image from my mind."

Suzy snickered at the look of distaste Emma was sure she was sporting. "Don't knock the spanking part. Gray loves it when I've been a bad girl. I would never have thought that someone as seemingly straitlaced as my hubby could be such a freak when he wants to be." Sighing, she added, "God, I love that man."

"All right, no more. I already hate you for having a husband that sexy. Telling me he's some kind of sex god only makes me want to unfriend you on Facebook and walk away when I see you at the office." Anyone else might have been offended by her statement, but Suzy only threw her head back and laughed.

"That's pretty good. Maybe you should apply that ambition to your boss."

"You're just mean," Emma said. "Can't you pull some strings and have me moved?"

"Sorry, chick. No can do. I don't think your strategy is working for you, though. Maybe you should try crying when he says something mean. You've tried the incompetence approach and so far, nada. Have you thought about the emotional wreck approach instead?"

Sticking her finger to her chin, Emma said, "Hmmm, no I haven't. My first inclination is violence when he says something snarky, so crying hasn't even entered my mind. I don't know if I could pull off full-fledged tears, but I could at least hang my head and look upset. I might not even feel as guilty about that as I do about snapping back at him, which just goes against everything I've ever been taught about respecting authority."

"Yeah, that's rough when you don't jive with someone. I don't know why he's so resistant to transferring you. Somewhere out there must be someone more . . . suited to his particular personality?"

"You mean, like a Mrs. Sunshine?" Emma laughed.

"Exactly!"

"He needs someone more like Mrs. Doubtfire. She would kick his ass." Their food arrived as they were both throwing out ideas for new assistants for Brant. When she ran out of ideas, Emma asked, "So the others were doing baby shopping today, huh?"

Suzy visibly winced before saying, "I didn't think I could take that again. I love little Hermie and all, but with Claire and Beth both having babies and Ella pregnant, that's all they talk about."

Emma had to smile over Suzy's refusal to call her sister Beth's baby Henry. She was sticking with Hermie. When Beth had found out she was having a boy, Nick, her husband, had insisted on naming their baby after his grandfather, who had died while Nick was a child. Apparently, his nickname was Herman and that's what the kids had always called him. Beth had freaked out about it, at which point Nick's mother had finally admitted that her father's real name was actually Henry. Suzy liked the original name better. "It is a little strange. We seem to be the only ones in our group now who don't have babies on the brain."

When Suzy looked away, an awkward silence settled over their table. Emma was afraid that she had offended her. "Suzy, I didn't mean anything bad by that. You know I love Beth, Claire and Ella."

Suzy took a deep breath and then ran a hand through her long hair. "It's not that," she said quietly. "It's just . . . I do . . . have babies on the brain."

Shocked, Emma sat back in her seat with a thud. "Are you pregnant?" That question only seemed to upset her friend further, and she was clueless as to what was going on. Was this an unwanted pregnancy?

"I'm not pregnant. Please don't mention this to the others."

Emma took her hand and said, "You can talk to me. I would never repeat anything you tell me in confidence."

"Gray and I have been trying to get pregnant for a while now. I know I don't seem like much of a kid person, but you have to understand that was how I was raised." Emma knew from previous conversations that Suzy and Beth were not particularly close to their parents, who were more committed to their jobs than to their daughters. They had been particularly critical of Beth due to the weight problem she had fought for years.

"I think you'll be a great mother. You would have the coolest kid on the block for sure."

"I thought it would be so easy," Suzy continued. "Everyone around us seemed to get pregnant at the drop of a hat. But each month I stare at that white stick, waiting to see two pink lines. I have grown to hate that damned thing as month after month, there is only one freaking pink line."

Emma squeezed her friend's hand tighter. "Oh Suzy, I'm so sorry. I had no idea. All of these babies and pregnancies around you must be hell for you right now."

"Yeah, and I feel like shit over it. I just let them assume I don't like or want kids because it's easier than explaining that I can't get pregnant. I'm happy for everyone, but I feel like such a failure. Why is it easy for them and not for me? The worst part is seeing the disappointment on Gray's face every month. He tries to hide it, and he's always encouraging, saying just the right thing, but I know he wonders the same thing. Why not us? Don't *we* deserve to be parents?"

The longing in Suzy's voice made Emma's own eyes fill with tears. "Of course you deserve it. Have you talked to your doctor? Aren't there some medications that you can take to, you know, jump-start things?"

"Yes, there are other things we can try. We have another appointment next week with the reproductive doctor. They say that medically there is no reason that we aren't, you know, making a baby. Next we're going to try a procedure called an intrauterine insemination. That's a fancy way of saying they are going to help the swimmers in case they are blind or lazy. Poor Gray just got over the anxiety of worrying about his sperm count when they mentioned the term 'lazy swimmers.' He looked at me when we came out of the appointment and said, 'My boys are getting fucked over.' "

Emma laughed. It was hard to imagine a man like

Gray worrying about anything concerning his body, much less his sperm potency, but hey, everyone had problems. "I guess you guys have tried all of those different baby-making positions, right?"

Suzy shuddered. "Ugh, we've had so much sex in the last six months that my vagina is threatening to strike if we don't take a day off. We've even gone home during lunch to do the mambo when I'm ovulating."

Impressed, Emma asked, "You know when you're ovulating?"

"Oh, honey, they make a test to tell you everything now. When that sucker gives us the green light, we go at it like jackrabbits for the next several days. Some men might crack under that kind of pressure, but Gray can perform anytime, anywhere, without fail."

"I already hate you, bitch; must you keep making it worse?" Emma tried to joke to lighten the mood.

"You know, you're kind of cranky today," Suzy said. "Are the batteries dead in your vibrator again? One word, *rechargeables*."

"My batteries are fine. I just have a wicked case of PMS, and my boss is a turd." Emma was happy to see Suzy joking around after looking so upset earlier.

"You know," Suzy began, "I hate to be the one to point this out *again*, but Brant is kind of a stud. I'll grant you, he's all over the place personality-wise, but in the ass department, he has got it going on. You could bounce a quarter off those firm cheeks of his."

"My God, Suzy, no! Stay away from the light! Just hang on; I'll call nine-one-one and get help for you right away. Do you feel dizzy? How do you treat a stroke brought on by bad taste in men?"

Suzy roared, causing heads all around the deli to turn in their direction. "Honey, my taste is just fine. Everyone else agrees with me. If you guys would just have angry office sex, you would both feel better. He works so much that I bet he hasn't gotten laid in ages. A bad case of blue balls will make a man cranky as hell."

Emma dropped her head in her hands. "You did not just say that. My lunch is about to climb back up my throat. Ugh! It's hard enough to work with Mr. Sunshine without thinking of him with ball issues or even worse, having sex with him. NEVER GONNA HAPPEN!"

Suzy raised an eyebrow, clearly skeptical over her denial. "Never say never, my friend. I pretty much said the same thing about Gray, and then I went and married him. He seemed just as uptight as Brant in the beginning, but nothing could be further from the truth."

"That's not the only problem Brant has, though," Emma protested. "He annoys me in so many ways that I spend part of every day fantasizing about ways to kill him and dispose of his body so I don't get caught. This is bad, but I've even wished he didn't have a brother or sister so there would be no one to miss him if he did disappear."

Suzy gave her an admiring look. "You're kind of a scary person sometimes, Em, but I like it. I had a few thoughts of choking Gray in the beginning, too, but never seriously pondered ways to hide his body." Pointing to the to-go box on their table, she added, "That's probably cold and soggy by now. I told you to order it after we were finished."

Emma gave her friend an evil smile and said, "People who don't get their own lunch don't have much say in how their food arrives. He'll just send me down the hall to the microwave anyway."

"Knock, knock." Looking up, Brant was surprised to see his sister, Ava, standing in the doorway. "Where's Emma? You didn't run her off, did you?"

"No such luck. She's gone on one of her usual long lunches. She should be back in about three hours, give or take a few minutes." When Ava settled into one of the chairs facing him, he knew this wasn't just casual chitchat. Ava was more of a pacer and she generally got right to the point. The fact that she seemed nervous made his stomach roll. It was his job as her older brother to worry about her.

"What's wrong?" he asked, unable to hide the concern in his voice.

Ava sighed. "It's Alexia."

He looked at her blankly for a moment. There hadn't been any mention of that name in a couple of years, and it hit him hard to hear it now. Had something happened to her? Almost afraid to ask, he said, "What about her?"

"She's getting married, Brant."

For a moment, he was back to that day two years

ago when his world was rocked to its foundation. Alexia Shaw had been the daughter of a business associate. They had met at a party, and he had immediately been drawn to the shy beauty. After spending years avoiding any serious involvement with the opposite sex, he was officially smitten. Alexia had been home-schooled and a naive twenty-one-year-old when they met. They had started out as friends, but after the first few months things had progressed quickly and they had sex for the first time.

Alexia had brought out a softer, more relaxed side of him that he showed very few people. After dating for a year, he had proposed and she had tearfully accepted. Their wedding was three months away when she made a new friend at the office, Josie. At first, he was glad. Her family had been so protective that she didn't have any close friends, and he thought it would be good for her.

Things had started off innocently enough: a movie here and there or a shopping trip. Unfortunately, under Josie's tutelage, things progressed into trips to clubs, bars and God knows what else. Suddenly, his sweet Alexia was staying out all night or coming to his apartment drunk so that her parents wouldn't know. Sometimes he would go for days without hearing from her. She stopped returning calls and when he did catch her, she was vague and distant. Of course he had tried talking to her, but she didn't seem to care about his feelings.

Things came to a head one evening. Several times

during dinner, she had texted someone. When he asked, she said that it was Josie. She excused herself near the end of the meal to use the restroom. He quickly paid the check, more than ready to leave. He saw Alexia propped against the wall outside the bathroom talking on her phone. As he approached her quietly from behind, he heard enough to know that she was talking to a man. The sexual elements of the conversation were still seared in his head to this day. She finished the call and turned around. He saw a momentary flash of guilt before her expression turned defiant. He motioned her in front of him and they walked outside. When they neared his car, she whirled around, almost shouting, "Go ahead, say something!" When he just looked at her in shock over the scene unfolding, she sneered. "Ohhh no, Brant Stone would never air his dirty laundry in public. What would it take, *honey*, for you to lose control?"

He had put his hand on her shoulder, trying to calm her down. But her eyes were wild and her movements jerky. "Alexia, take it easy."

Her laughter was shrill enough to make his hair stand on end. "I think you're calm enough for both of us. I've had to live like that my whole life, and I don't want to do it anymore." Brant was even more unnerved that her manic behavior had settled into something almost sad but resigned.

When he protested, trying to convince her to get in the car so that they could return home to talk, she had put her hand on his cheek and smiled at him affectionately. Her anger had evaporated quickly, leaving only sadness in its wake. "It never will be the place." She took off her engagement ring and handed it back to him. "You're a good man, Brant, a much better one than I deserve. I never would have gotten out from under my father's thumb without you. Because of you, I can finally be me."

He'd felt his world collapsing when Josie's car pulled up beside them and, ignoring his pleas, she simply shook her head and opened the passenger door to her friend's car. He'd stood rooted to the spot long after the taillights had faded away. In the days to come, he had tried to reach her, but she had officially severed ties with him. It appeared that she had cut her family out of her life as well. In the blink of an eye, his entire future had changed—and he had had no idea what had caused the landslide.

From then on, he kept to himself and licked his wounds in private. After all, Alexia was right—he did not lose control . . . ever. His grandfather had drummed that into them from an early age. Always control the situation and those involved.

Maybe it was a lesson he had learned too well, but he didn't know how to change now . . . it seemed safer not to. He ended his business relationship with her father, which was a relief to them both, and moved on. He was a survivor; he always had been.

"Brant . . . Brant, did you hear me?"

He jerked, shaking off the memories that Alexia's name had brought rushing back. "I . . . How do you know that?"

Ava gave him a wry smile. "How do I know everything? Mac, of course. His company still handles security for her father's company. I guess Alexia is back in the family fold again and getting married. Word is that her parents approve of her choice. I just didn't want you to be caught by surprise if the announcement shows up in the paper."

His head was spinning and his sister knew him well enough to recognize it. Hell, he, Ava, and Declan were all masters at hiding their feelings. When their parents had been killed in a plane crash, they had been raised by their grandfather. It wasn't that he was unkind to them; he was just rather indifferent for the most part. His business was his life and if you were looking for affection, you were out of luck.

Wearily, he ran a hand through his hair. "Thanks for letting me know, but it was a long time ago. Of course Alexia would have moved on, just as I have." Ava gave him a look and he knew she was dying to comment on his last statement, but she let it go. She was never one to press the point on past pain because she damn sure didn't want anyone doing that to her.

"All right, just letting you know." Looking at her watch, she stood up. "I've got to get back to work. I'm watching Evan tonight for Declan and I have a ton of work to get out of the way before I go over there."

Brant looked at her in surprise. "You're babysitting?" Not that he thought Ava wasn't capable—she just had a tendency to distance herself from long interactions with anyone, even family.

He had expected an insult in return but was surprised when she said, "It's the closest I'll ever get to having a child." With that, she turned and left his office as quickly as she had entered.

What a day. It was barely lunchtime and he had already been hit by two things. His ex was getting married, and his sister was still being ruled by her painful past. The first was a sucker punch to the gut; the second was disheartening but not surprising. He knew he needed to talk to Declan about Ava. As for Alexia, he resolved to bury the information that his sister had given him down deep inside. After all, what had really changed? She didn't want him then and she didn't now. He refused to be ruled by his heart again. That part of his life was over.

With a grimace, Brant threw his half-eaten sandwich in the trash. He had no doubt that Emma had made sure it was as inedible as possible. He opened his bottom desk drawer and looked at his junk food collection. His snack consumption had gone through the roof since Emma had started working for him. He wasn't sure why he continued to ask her to bring him lunch every day when he rarely ever ate it. He suspected it was just his perverse need to see those plump lips tighten in annoyance and to watch her green eyes roll dramatically as she snapped off a reply. She was a spitfire, and he had grown to enjoy getting burned by her. It was the liveliest part of his day.

Since he had a few minutes left between calls, he

decided to get her blood pumping for the afternoon. Ignoring the phone, he yelled for her to come into his office. He knew she hated that. She never failed to mention it. When she walked into his office, he felt his physical response to her almost immediately. No matter how much he hated to admit it, his cock jumped to attention anytime she was near.

"You wanted to see me?"

Pointing to his lunch in the trash, he asked, "Did you just leave that sitting somewhere while you read *Cosmopolitan* or did you also drag the sandwich over the sidewalk on your way back to the office?" Settling back in his chair, he waited for the verbal tongue-lashing. Hell, yeah, he got off on it; there was no reason anymore to admit that he didn't. He was momentarily speechless, then horrified when her bottom lip started to tremble and something that looked suspiciously like tears glistened on her thick lashes. Uncertain, he asked, "Emma?" When she turned and rushed from his office, he sat there a moment longer, stunned. What in the hell had just happened?

He hesitated before going to find her. Her desk was vacant and the door was ajar leading to the hallway. As he walked farther down the hall, he couldn't believe that he was actually considering going into the ladies' restroom. He had truly lost his mind. Even as he thought it, he was lightly knocking on the door. "Emma? Are you in there?"

Brant heard a muffled "Go away."

He took a deep breath and wondered why it was so

hard for him to apologize to her. "Emma, I'm . . . sorry. I . . . didn't mean to upset you." When she didn't answer, he felt compelled to add, "My lunch was good, and I was just kidding, really." A woman a few doors down stuck her head out to see what was going on and then gave him a look of disgust. Okay, now everyone in the surrounding area knew he was an asshole.

Finally, Emma said, "I need a little time. I'll be back at my desk soon."

Brant was so grateful to hear her speaking that he said, "Take all the time you need, no rush at all, and, Emma . . . I really am sorry." When she didn't reply, he turned and walked back into his office, shaking his head in confusion.

When Emma had first started as his assistant, he had been desperate to replace her by the end of the first week. She had shattered his perfectly organized routine, and he was a disheveled wreck as a result. She messed up his papers, had some strange, color-coded filing system instead of an alphabetical one, booked him on the wrong flights, and almost killed him by putting dairy in his coffee. At times he couldn't believe he was still alive or employed. Yet as much as he had wanted to throttle her, there was also something about her that he connected with. Even when his brother had teased him about getting rid of Emma, he had been determined not to. There was something about her that he enjoyed, no matter how much she constantly got on his nerves.

He had no idea what he had said today to upset her

so much. He had said far worse to her before and it had never seemed to faze her. Something else must have happened during lunch. Maybe a fight with a boyfriend? Wait. Did she even have one? He wasn't sure why it bothered him to think of her with a man. It was probably just pity for the poor bastard. He might enjoy her antics at the office most of the time now, but he couldn't imagine being romantically involved with such a pain in the ass. Fuck, this day just kept getting better and better.

Emma tried desperately to smother her laughter until she was certain that Brant had walked away. *I can't believe that shit actually worked.* Who would have ever imagined that the asswipe could be brought to his knees by a few well-placed tears and a couple of sniffles—unbelievable! When Suzy had suggested the crying approach, she had been completely skeptical. She figured that every assistant Brant had ever had must have ended up in tears more often than not, and he probably got a big kick out of it. So she was in shock that he had completely dissolved after her first whimper. When he followed her to the bathroom, she had been floored. Luckily, some nice soul who apparently spent a great deal more time in the restroom than she did had left a copy of *Star* magazine. She settled back on the countertop and ignored the few people who knocked on the door trying to get in. She thought about updating her Facebook status, but decided that might be going overboard.

When thirty minutes had passed, she figured she had drawn it out long enough. Someone was getting really anxious to use the bathroom, and she was tired of hearing the handle jiggle. She threw some water on her face and rubbed her eyes a few times. Yep, she looked suitably wiped out. As she walked down the hall back to her office, she wondered how long she could pull this off. The chances of her not snapping Brant's head off when he made another stupid remark were slim to none. She'd give it at best the rest of the day, maybe two if he was out of the office a lot.

When she walked back inside, she saw a Starbucks Frappuccino on her desk. She found herself circling it like a bomb-sniffing dog. Someone cleared his throat behind her, and she turned to find Brant standing there looking unusually nervous. "I . . . I got your favorite."

It was on the tip of her tongue to ask him how he knew her favorite when he was never the one getting the coffee, but she managed to rein it in at the last second. *Look pathetic. Just imagine yourself married to the man.* "Thank you, it looks great. I'm sorry for running out like that." *Oh hell, there is no way I can carry this off all day, no matter how amusing. I'm dying already.*

Raising a hand to rub her temple, she added, "I think it's just this headache I've had all day. Maybe I'm coming down with something." A few moments later, Brant had gathered her purse and ushered her through the door, assuring her that things would be fine there until she felt better. It was amazing—she probably could even push this fake illness to a couple of days if she wanted to because the guilt monkey was riding him heavily. If she had gone home sick any other time, he would have bitched and moaned like the world was coming to an end. Having an afternoon off with his blessing was a rare treat and one she intended to enjoy. She would go home, grab her bikini, and spend the rest of the day at the beach. Life was good. . . .

Chapter Two

Brant slammed the door to his beach house and walked straight to the liquor cabinet. The afternoon had been chaos. When Emma had gone home sick, he had been grateful. He couldn't handle the guilt of making her cry, so running the office alone for the afternoon had seemed like a small price to pay. Who would have thought that the phone would be ringing every five minutes? Then he couldn't find the contract he needed from Emma's wacky filing system. His damn computer had somehow eaten his e-mails and wouldn't spit them back out, no matter how many buttons he pushed. He was completely wiped out. First, the bomb from Ava and then Emma crying.

He poured a generous measure of whiskey and walked out onto his deck to enjoy the view with his hard-earned drink. He had just taken the last sip when someone on the beach a few feet down caught his attention. His house was next to a public-access area, so there was never a shortage of beach lovers coming and going. He wasn't sure what made her stand out from any of the other dark-haired females in the area. Maybe the skimpy cut of the string bikini bottoms. When she finally turned fully toward him, he sucked in a deep breath. That little witch! He'd thought something about the woman on the beach looked familiar. She sure didn't look weepy or sick now. He was off the deck and striding across the sand within moments.

When he reached Emma, she had her pert little bottom in the air while she bent over packing up her beach bag. He cleared his throat at the same time she noticed the shadow falling across the sand in front of her. She whirled, crouching into a defensive posture that impressed the hell out of him. The play of emotions across her face was downright amusing. "Well, well," he drawled, "it certainly looks like you're feeling better."

Barely missing a beat, she smiled, saying, "I thought some sun would help."

Nodding, Brant said, "Yeah, the sun usually works miracles for a headache; that is the first thing I would have done."

"My headache was better after taking some Tylenol. I was still having the chills, though, so I thought the sun would warm me up."

Brant had to give her credit for thinking fast on her feet, but he still moved in for the kill. He took a leisurely look down her barely covered body, smirking as he said, "Your case of the chills must be a lot better since you are wearing next to nothing. I know anytime I'm sick, I come straight to the beach practically naked and bake in the sun for hours. Ahhh, does a body good, right?"

She gave him a dirty look before flopping down on the towel in front of her. When she started rubbing her eyes like she was crying, he threw back his head and laughed. He might have been taken in again had it not been for that look she'd given him before turning on the waterworks.

She looked up at him, dropping all pretenses of sobbing, and deadpanned, "You're a total asshole."

If anything, that just made him laugh harder. He plopped down onto the sand beside her and nudged her shoulder. "That was some performance today. I admit, I fell for it hook, line and sinker."

Emma snickered beside him. "That was pretty priceless. The great and powerful Brant Stone, in the hallway pleading with his lowly assistant to come out of the bathroom. You almost sounded human."

"You stayed in there forever; what were you doing? Updating your Facebook status?"

"Don't flatter yourself. I'd never give you airtime on my social media. I don't want any of my friends to know who I work for . . . meaning you. My high school reunion is coming up and I don't need that kind of embarrassment. If you must know, I read *Star* magazine from cover to cover and slept for the last ten minutes. I would have stayed longer but someone on that floor has a bladder the size of a pea. I guess it was asking too much that she go to another floor. There's no way I would have been that persistent about trying to get into a bathroom someone had been in for half an hour."

Beside her, Brant chuckled in agreement. "So do you

live around here? You must if you're using the beach in this area."

Emma ignored his question, instead asking, "What are you doing here? Why in the world would you be walking on the beach in your suit? That seems uptight even for you."

Brant pointed to his house. "Unfortunately for you, I live over there. It looks like fate brought you to my stretch of beach."

Emma snorted. "Fate, huh? I could think of a few words to describe it, but that isn't one of them." Then she seemed to notice that he looked completely wiped out. "Bad day at the office, Mr. Stone?"

His easy smile turned to a scowl. "You have no idea. It started off badly when my assistant played me and then went to hell in a handbasket when said assistant went home because she was . . . sick. Everyone in the world needed something immediately today, and I couldn't find anything in her complicated filing system."

"Good grief, Brant, what is so hard about organizing by colors? Didn't you learn your primary colors in school? You surely went somewhere like Yale or Harvard for kindergarten, so you must be a fairly intelligent man. Think outside the box for once."

"Think outside the box, huh? I've seen you struggling to find files as well. We both know you only do it to piss me off."

Emma gave him her best innocent look. "I don't know what you are talking about." She rolled over on her stomach and shut her eyes. Brant knew she was just trying to ignore him but damn, did she have any idea what seeing those firm butt cheeks peeking out of her black swimsuit was doing to him? He hated like hell that she turned him on more during an argument at the office than most women did in bed.

He had to battle the urge to lean over and swat her sweet ass. It would almost be worth the slap he would suffer to see the stunned expression on her face. He dug his fingers into the sand before he could give in to the urge. If she wiggled just one more time, though, all bets were off.

She could only figure she had been born under an unlucky star. First, her mother had started the day off by urging her to get a boob job; Suzy had encouraged her to torture Brant by crying when he said something sarcastic, which had worked like a charm; and then, out of the entire Myrtle Beach area, she had picked the patch of sand in front of his house to play hooky. What were the odds of that happening? Now she was lying on the sand beside him in a bikini that she had outgrown years ago and trying her best to wish him away. The bastard even looked pretty freaking hot sitting next to her in his expensive suit and Italian loafers. She could barely admit it, but in some strange and totally wrong way, he turned her on. She would have to have been blind not to notice the size of his cock as it rested against the leg of his dress pants in the office. She had almost swallowed her tongue the first time she saw the outline when he was leaning back in his chair. Once something like that had been brought to your attention, it was damn tough not to look again . . . and again.

The man looked like Christian Bale and had the body of Channing Tatum; how could she be expected to resist admiring a man like that? The fact that she made it through every day without going to the restroom to masturbate was something she was rather proud of. If he would just sit there and look good, they would get along great. But whenever he opened his mouth, things went bad in a hurry. She would deny it with her last breath, but there were days that he made her so hot, she wanted to put a strip of duct tape over his mouth and screw his brains out. One of the big things that had stopped her so far besides common sense was imagining that morning-after scene. He would probably roll over, give her that sarcastic smirk that he wore so well and start listing everything she needed to improve upon in bed. She would then completely lose it, finally kill the man, and hope that her years of watching CSI would pay off.

"I can practically hear the wheels in your mind spinning from here," Brant said.

She groaned before saying, "Are you still here? Please go away; I'm on my own time now."

"Awww, what's wrong, cupcake? Are you still upset over your telephone call this morning?"

She flipped over on her side. "What are you talking about?"

Brant looked pointedly at her chest before giving her

that familiar smirk. "You know, the issue with your asset size."

"Oh my God," she groaned, "isn't this sexual harassment?"

Not looking the least bit alarmed, he said, "I think the amount of harassment that goes on between us is decidedly heavier on your end."

"I'm not the one sitting here talking about your 'size.'"

Grinning, Brant said, "Touché, Miss Davis."

She knew it was childish, but she scooped up a handful of sand and dropped it all over the top of his expensive shoes. She knew that some of it had to be running down the inside of his shoe. She watched for his reaction and was surprised when he continued to smile at her, almost indulgently. What was wrong with him today? He was a lot more relaxed than usual, almost like nothing could get to him. Maybe he was high.

As she looked at his wavy, brown hair blowing in the breeze, she again had the feeling that she knew him from another place or time. Since the first moment they had met, she had been racking her brain trying to figure out where their paths could have possibly crossed before she started working for him at Danvers. So far, she hadn't come up with anything. She was born and raised in Florida and, as far as she knew, he had always been a South Carolina guy. It drove her nuts when she felt like something was on the tip of her tongue and she couldn't come up with it. He sure didn't look like any of the guys she had dated. Fate hadn't been that kind to her in the romance department. It had to be that he reminded her of someone she had met in passing. She decided to ignore his reference to her breasts and instead swatted at him with her hands. "Shoo, go on back home, boy. I'm sure there are more people you need to torture somewhere. Call Declan or Ava. They have to talk to you since they're family."

"But you're so much more fun. I was stuck at the office all afternoon in near hell. You owe me."

"Oh brother, is this where you demand that I walk to your house and fix you dinner? Maybe make your bed and clean the house?"

Emma tried not to stare when he stretched, pulling his shirt tightly across his broad chest. He jumped smoothly to his feet and extended a hand to her. "It's time for you to call it a day."

"I wasn't serious," she snapped.

"Cool your jets, sweetheart. I'm not asking you to come home with me. I try to avoid verbal abuse in my home. It's getting late, though, and you don't need to be on the beach alone."

Emma opened her mouth to argue before noticing how much the traffic had thinned out around her. She hated to admit it, but he was right. She didn't usually linger on the beach alone at night. She ignored his hand and got to her feet much less gracefully than he had. She grabbed her cover-up and thought she must be imagining things when Brant's eyes seemed to linger on her body. "How about another day off . . ."

Before she could finish her sentence, Brant said,

"Don't even think about it. I'll expect you in the office at the regular time in the morning. I think you owe me a cup of Starbucks, too. Make sure you leave the cream out, though."

Refusing to dignify that comment with a reply, she turned and stomped away from him toward the car. *Asshole.* The traffic was light since rush hour was over, so she made it home in record time to her small apartment in Surfside Beach. It was much quieter than the other heavy tourist areas of Myrtle Beach. It was only a two-bedroom, two-bath unit, but since she seldom had overnight guests, it worked well for her. When her parents visited from Florida, they preferred one of the luxury hotels in the area.

She dropped her beach bag on the kitchen floor and went straight to the refrigerator. Why hadn't she stopped for a sandwich on the way home? Being stuck on the beach with Brant had thrown her whole evening off. She grabbed the container of leftover spaghetti from the previous night and popped it in the microwave to heat while she showered off.

After her shower, Emma threw on a long T-shirt and panties and towel-dried her hair. As much as she loved the beach, it always felt good to get the sand off. She couldn't stand having it on her furniture. Before settling down to eat her leftovers, she rummaged in her bookcase and found her senior yearbook. With her ten-year high school reunion coming up, she thought she would take a trip down memory lane while she ate.

As she flipped through the pages and saw pictures

of friends she hadn't talked to in years, she turned the page and noticed a booklet nestled there. Flipping it over, she saw the caption STUDS OF SUMMER. Emma started laughing, recognizing the college calendar that her friend Madison's boyfriend, Paul, had been featured in. The fraternity that had the calendar printed had been raising money for a big graduation trip to Hawaii. Each month, a different fraternity brother was listed with some mindless list of his likes. She thumbed through the pages laughing as she passed Paul's pose as Mr. September. When she got to the last page, she wasn't sure what made her pause to study Mr. December. He was dark and sexy. His hair was rumpled in an "I'm too sexy to care" kind of way. He appeared completely nude, but a clever crossing of his legs covered the family jewels. He was lying on what looked like a black silk-covered bed with an arm thrown back propping up his head. He was giving the camera his best smoldering look. The caption read "Mr. December has been a very naughty boy. This bad boy would love to deck your halls with his boughs of holly . . ." Emma rolled her eyes at the poor attempt to defile Christmas. She took one last look and suddenly it hit her. No fucking way! It couldn't be, could it? She finally knew why Brant had looked familiar to her from their first meeting. Her uptight, sarcastic, arrogant ass of a boss was freaking Mr. December!

Emma gripped her sides as she rolled with laughter. She hadn't been this excited since Macy's put the pair of platform pumps she'd been eyeing for months on clearance. Man, that had been an awesome day, but this was better, way better. Oh, the things she would do to him with this information! Suddenly the thought of going back to work tomorrow didn't bother her. She couldn't wait to get in there and start baiting him. How many hints would she have to drop and how long would it take for him to connect the dots? She was going to deck his halls all right, and she didn't need boughs of holly to do it.

Chapter Three

Emma arrived for work fifteen minutes early the next day with the Starbucks coffee that Brant had suggested. He was already at his desk when she gently placed the cup in front of him. He leaned slightly back, looking at the cup as if it might explode at any moment. He didn't look any more encouraged when she graced him with her brightest smile. "Here's your coffee as requested. Don't worry; it doesn't contain any dairy product."

"Er . . . thank you. I appreciate it." Then, clearing his throat, he said, "I trust you're feeling better today after your headache yesterday."

Emma knew he was trying to bait her to get things back on normal ground, but she refused to rise to the occasion. He deserved to sweat it out for a bit longer. "Oh yes, after getting all 'decked' out for work this morning, I felt much better."

Obviously confused, Brant studied her for a moment before handing her a file. "Could you please fax this for me and then finish the presentation for Gray by this afternoon?"

"Of course, Brant, I'll get right on it." She smiled as she walked back to her desk. The rest of the morning was busy and she didn't have another chance to heckle him until later on.

"Emma, you inverted the last two numbers on this report; could you please correct it?"

As he was walking away from her desk, Emma snickered to herself. "Whoops, that wasn't nice at all. In fact, it was very naughty of me, wasn't it?"

Brant stopped and turned back to her. "Did you do it on purpose or something?"

Shaking her head, Emma said, "No, of course not. Just give me a second and I will fix it for you." He didn't say anything else as he walked back into his office. She gave herself a mental pat on the back for managing to insert the words *naughty* and *nice* into the conversation. But the boughs of holly were going to be more difficult. Why couldn't it be December now instead of July?

When she stuck her head in his office before lunch, he was on a call and just waved her away. She gave him another bright smile and walked out the door whistling. She had a mission during her lunch hour, and she had never been more grateful that Myrtle Beach had a year-round Christmas store. She wanted to hug the kind saleslady when she showed her the rack of Santa hats in the back of the store.

She grabbed a quick burger to eat in the car on her way back to the office. Her cell phone rang and seeing her mother's name on the caller ID made her bite off a curse. The woman always seemed to know when she had five extra minutes, and Kat Davis hated for anyone to have idle time. Emma debated letting it go to voice mail but decided it was better to get it over with in the privacy of her own car. Clicking the answer button, she said sarcastically, "Yes, Mommy."

Her mother chuckled. "I assume you're on your lunch hour?"

"Mmm, yes, but would it bother you if I weren't?"

"Probably not, dear, but I thought I would check. So anyway, I was in Belk's this morning looking for a new swimsuit because your father says I should get a bikini. I found a fabulous one with a metal ring in the middle of the top, which calls a lot of attention to the girls. The bottoms have those drawstrings on the side like you wear. It looks amazing!"

"Um, okay. I'm happy for you, Mom."

As if she hadn't said anything, her mother continued on, almost in the same breath. "So, that isn't why I called. While I was at the mall, I ran into Cindy Hogan. You remember David, who went to school with you, don't you? I know he didn't have much going on upstairs, but the boy was hot and still is. I saw him last year at a barbecue. Cindy said he's going to the reunion next month and doesn't have a girlfriend. I think I can get you in with him. It doesn't matter if he is dumb as a box of rocks as long as he looks good on your arm, right?"

Emma laid her phone down in the passenger seat while she beat her head against the steering wheel. When would she learn to use her voice mail more and answer her phone less? Taking a deep breath, she picked the phone back up, saying, "Good grief, Mom, I don't want you getting me 'in' with anyone. I can find my own date and, for the record, David bats for the other team. He isn't between girlfriends; he has never had a date who didn't have a penis!"

But if Emma had thought she would shock her mom into silence, she should have known better. "Em, I know that. I think he swings both ways, though. Even if you can't talk him into bed, he would probably still escort you."

"Mom, I don't need a date!" Emma could blame the next words out of her mouth only on her mother's continued insistence on fixing her up with David Hogan. "I already have a date!" Of course it turned out *that* would be the one thing her mother chose to hear since the start of the phone call.

"You have a date? Who is it?"

"It's no one you know, Mom. Just a guy I've been out with a few times."

"Honey, that's great. I don't know why you haven't mentioned him, but I shouldn't look a gift horse in the mouth, right? I'll have your room all ready. You know your father and I aren't prudes, so he can share your room. Never let it be said that I cock-blocked my daughter. I'll give Cindy a call and let her know we won't be needing David after all."

"God, Mom, women your age shouldn't talk like that!"

Her mother laughed. "I admit I've picked up a few things from my new book club."

"Geez, what kind of book club is it, porn?"

"We call ourselves the Smut-Loving Wenches," her mother replied proudly.

As far as Emma was concerned, that explained a lot of her mother's new vocabulary. She could just imagine what those meetings were like. She only hoped she'd never meet any of the other members. "What does Daddy say about your club?"

"Pffft, you know he doesn't care about stuff like that. He does enjoy the new . . . ideas it gives me, though." Just as she was prepared to disconnect the call for fear of hearing what those ideas were, her mother made a smooching sound and said, "Kiss, kiss, darling. I've got to go. We'll talk soon."

Emma's head was spinning. Had her mother just promised not to cock-block her? Had she really said that she had a date she was bringing home for her reunion? Her life was starting to resemble an episode of *Jersey Shore*. Now she had to figure out how to find a date willing to travel to Florida with her—and she had less than a month to do it. If she didn't show up with a man in tow, her mother would have David Hogan at the house in the blink of an eye.

She thought briefly of calling her sister, Robyn, and begging for help, but she knew how that would go. There was no way in hell that Robyn would divert their mother's attention onto her. She discounted her brother as well as soon as she thought of him. He played their mother like a fiddle. He was the baby boy and had learned long ago to stay in Mom's good graces. There would be no help from that side either. She was well and truly screwed.

Chapter Four

Emma flopped back in her chair. She just couldn't do it. No matter how desperate she was, an escort service was out. She would have to go home with no boy-friend and put up with her mother's matchmaking. Sure, it was likely to be embarrassing and uncomfort-able, but what family visit wasn't? She could live with being fixed up with David, but having to admit to her mother that she had lied about the boyfriend was go-ing to be hell. There were bound to be more talks about her sexual technique and what she was doing wrong. And what if her mother invited some of her new book club friends over to give her some advice on finding and keeping a man? Emma shuddered at the thought.

"Problem?"

She jerked around to see Brant sitting on the edge of her desk looking at her with equal parts amusement and curiosity. "Yeah, you could say that. I need a date for my high school reunion."

Brant tried unsuccessfully to cover the smirk on his

face. "I can't imagine why that would be a problem. You're such a . . . joy to be around."

She had no idea where it came from, but the words were out of her mouth before she could take them back. "I'm glad you feel that way, because I'm going to need you to fill in for me. There are no available men in my life right now."

It was fairly amusing to see her normally standoffish boss floundering around, clearly at a loss. "Wh-what?"

Before she could reply, Declan Stone walked in for his three o'clock appointment with his brother. Emma stood, giving both men a bright smile. She ushered him into his brother's office and then had to give Brant a little shove to get him moving. She knew this was not an ideal place to have this conversation, but she was also aware that Brant wouldn't let it go, which was fine with her. She stopped him before he crossed the threshold and said, "Let's meet at the bar around the corner at six." Without waiting for an answer, she shut the door softly and took her seat.

The more she thought of her plan, the better it sounded. Sure, Brant was a pain in her ass, but better the pain you know, right? And what he didn't know was that she had an ace in the hole that pretty much assured her that he wouldn't say no. Well, unless Mr. December wanted Christmas to come early to Danvers.

Brant had no idea why he was setting off to meet with Emma. He had no intention of going anywhere with her socially, much less as a date to her reunion. Was she crazy? It wouldn't take people long to pick up on the lack of love or affection between them. They couldn't even have a simple conversation without insulting each other. Regardless of what she said, he didn't doubt for a minute that Emma could find a date if she wanted to. She was a very attractive woman—much to his discomfort at times. Luckily, on the occasions when he found himself admiring her, she invariably opened her mouth and the moment was gone. But the hard-on remained for a while.

He walked into the bar and quickly scanned the room. There was no sign of Emma. What a shock. He strongly suspected she stood out in the hallway at work in the mornings just because she knew it irritated him for her to arrive late. He walked over to an empty table in the corner and smiled as the busty blond waitress approached to take his order. "Hey, sugar, whatcha having tonight?"

"I'll have a Heineken, thanks." He saw the name Daisy on her name tag when she returned with his beer. Yeah, okay, he ogled her tits. He had never claimed to be a saint. He was just pondering striking up a conversation with her when a familiar, irritating voice sounded over his shoulder.

"Ugh, do you have to be such a guy?"

He swung around and damn it, he could feel the guilty expression on his face, even though he had no reason to feel guilty. Daisy gave in to the urge to cut and run when faced with Emma's sarcastic tone. He decided the safest course of action would be to change the subject. "Glad you finally decided to join me. Don't tell me you were working late because I know better."

"You really missed your calling. You'd kill as a comedian." When she pulled out the seat next to him, he forced his gaze away from the miles of legs revealed by the short skirt she wore. This was one of those times when he needed her to continue being a bitch before his cock snapped to attention.

Clearing his throat and trying to focus, he asked, "So . . . um, why exactly are we here? I think we already covered the fact that you're dateless for your reunion, and I'm not even remotely interested in bailing you out of that dilemma. There is nothing you could do that's gonna change my mind, honey, but go ahead and amuse me anyway."

He settled back in his chair with a grin, suddenly interested to see where this would go. He had to give her credit: She was always inventive. If nothing else, he would have a good laugh and a drink before he headed home. Hell, if he played his cards right, maybe Daisy the server would be up for some company later. When Emma remained calm and confident instead of getting upset, he started to feel the first trickle of unease. What was he missing here?

She appeared to be studying her nails as she asked, "Are you sure about that, boss? There is nothing in the world that would convince you to help me out? Nothing at all?"

"No?" Shit, even he heard his statement come out more like a question. "Just spit it out, Emma, I'm tired of this. I can't imagine where all of this is going." *Great, now I sound like some kind of pussy. She's probably expecting me to start crying next.*

She continued to stare him down for another minute before pulling what looked like a calendar out of her purse and plopping it on the table before them. When she swung it open to the month of December, he still had no idea what was going on. He had thought she needed a date now, not months ahead. She looked up at him and then slowly unfolded the calendar to its full length, displaying the picture that had been hidden. He felt the blood drain from his face. She had the nerve to pat his lifeless hand almost sympathetically before saying, "Ah, now it looks like we are on the same page."

"Where . . . how?" he stuttered.

"It was quite by accident, I assure you, or something I like to call divine intervention. Mr. September dated my friend and I ended up with her calendar. A chance look through my old yearbook led to this moment."

"You haven't shown that to anyone, have you?"

Emma smiled at the strain in her usually unflappable boss's voice. Yeah, he was shaken up. It was a little surprising because she suspected most men would be proud for a woman to see such an impressive picture. She might hate the man, but even she had to admit he was smoking hot on the calendar. Of course, most people weren't as uptight as Brant, which was what she was banking on. "Nope, your secret is safe with me. I mean, that's what friends do, right? They help each other out. You would do the same for me if I needed you, I'm sure."

Her mouth fell open in shock when he quickly responded, "What I would really love to do is spank your ass until it shines, but I guess I'm fucked."

"I don't think you're supposed to say stuff like that to your assistant unless you're working in a brothel or something."

Brant quirked a brow at her. "Since when have we ever been concerned with what we say to each other? I don't think you should say stuff to your boss like 'blow me' either, but that has never stopped you before."

Emma nodded. "Yeah, I guess you've got me there. So-o-o, back to my original plan. I'm going to need you to accompany me to Pensacola, Florida, for my class reunion in two weeks. I checked our schedule and, as luck would have it, you have a trip scheduled for Miami in a month. I'm confident that we could move that up and kill two birds with one stone. We'd fly into Miami, take care of business and then catch a plane up to Pensacola. The reunion is on a Saturday night, so we can fly back home on Sunday afternoon and not miss much work."

"Wow," he chastised, "if you put that much thought into your daily work, you would be an unstoppable force at Danvers."

"You know, it's funny. I seem to get a lot accomplished when I don't have someone interrupting me with stuff like 'can you get me some lunch' or 'did you steal my number two pencils again?' Stuff like that tends to suck the motivation right out of you."

*   *   *

Brant couldn't hold back a grin. Sometimes he thought that sparring with her was better than sex. That would explain the wood that he sported at the office when she was around for any length of time. He was a competitive man by nature and succumbing to blackmail over the calendar was not an easy thing for him. On the other hand, he didn't want people at the office laughing over something he did back in college for his fraternity either. How bad could it be? He would stay at a hotel and she could stay with her family. They would really need to see each other only during their travel time and for a few hours at the reunion. If she weren't so damn difficult most of the time, he would have offered to help her out anyway. This didn't have to be a big deal. Knowing her, she would book them seats on the plane as far away from each other as possible. You had to love how predictable she was sometimes.

Chapter Five

Most people might be able to leave on a trip without having a root canal first, but Emma should have learned by now that she wasn't most people. They had been putting in some long hours over the past couple of weeks to prepare for being away from the office for a few days. Now their flight was scheduled for this afternoon and she'd discovered she needed an emergency root canal just hours before they left for the airport.

The nagging discomfort that she had been feeling on and off for a month had turned into a full-fledged throbbing, at which point she finally broke down and went to her dentist. They had scheduled her procedure for today and she had little choice but to keep it. She couldn't risk going out of town and having the pain become unbearable. She might have bent the truth a bit when she assured them that her traveling companion would be taking care of her. But she had already arranged for a car to pick her up at her apartment and drop her at the airport. She knew her mouth would probably be numb for the entire flight. After they arrived in Miami, she would crash for the evening and sleep in the next day while Brant went to his meeting. No problem, right?

Hours later, she knew she might have underestimated the whole thing. Despite the Novocain, her mouth was throbbing when she left the dentist's office. They had given her a prescription for pain medication and advised her to take a pill as soon as possible. Maybe someone with a better pain tolerance could have avoided it altogether; unfortunately, she wasn't that person, so she stumbled into the pharmacy before heading home. She had never taken any prescription pain medication before, but she assumed that if she took a pill right before she left for the airport, it would kick in during the flight and give her a pain-free trip.

Damn it—of course she should have packed earlier, but as usual she had left it to the last minute. She was forced to grab a suitcase and fill it with whatever was clean. It also occurred to her that she should probably change into a pair of jeans, but her short skirt would have to do. She couldn't seem to remove the hand that cradled her jaw for more than a few seconds. Maybe she was a baby, but it hurt like hell.

Five minutes before her taxi was due, she poured a glass of water and took the white pill from the dentist, cursing as she tossed the medication bottle in her carry-on bag and the pills inside spilled out everywhere. She had just grabbed the bottle intending to put them back in when a horn sounded. Shit. Throwing the bottle in the cabinet, she grabbed her bags and was hurrying to the door when it hit her. She had forgotten to pack underwear; she debated just buying some in Miami, but knowing her luck, she would never get away from Brant to do it. Running back into the bedroom as the taxi horn sounded again, she pulled her lingerie drawer completely out and dumped it in the top of her bag— no time to pick out her favorites today. The last thing she needed was to miss her ride to the airport. She could just imagine the smirk on Brant's face if she missed the plane she was blackmailing him into taking. Not going to happen.

Brant had arrived at the airport a couple of hours early as he always did. Emma was right—he did have some hang-ups. When you were forced to rush, things got overlooked and mistakes were made. If you planned things carefully, there were fewer problems in life. He closed his laptop and looked at his watch again. The plane would start boarding in fifteen minutes and Emma hadn't arrived yet. By this point he should have known better than to be surprised. If she didn't show, he would fly to Miami, attend his meeting and arrange a flight home for the next day.

Before he could ponder the strange feeling of disappointment that had crept in at that thought, he saw Emma racing toward him with a huge smile on her face. He rose to his feet, rooted in place. She reserved that genuine smile for her friends. Any smile bestowed on him was of the sarcastic variety. He had never been the recipient of the real thing from her. He cleared his throat, ready to launch the first verbal bullet when she threw her arms around him. What the fuck?

"Oh my God, I made it! My taxi driver almost left me because I forgot my panties and someone hit someone else and we got stuck in traffic. Whewwww!"

Brant stood frozen in shock with her in his arms. She had her body curved tightly to his with no sign of letting go. When she started making sniffing noises against his neck, he pulled back.

"Mmmm, you smell so good. You always do. I could just eat you up."

What had gotten into her? He didn't know how to react. He may have been frozen in place, but his cock wasn't. It was standing at attention, desperate to get closer to the female curves still pressed against him. "Emma . . . is something . . . are you . . . drunk?"

She finally stepped back out of his embrace, giving him a lopsided, glassy-eyed smile.

" 'Course not, silly. I haven't had anything but water today. My dentist told me, nothing cold or hot." Looking adorably confused, she added, "So what am I supposed to do? That covers everything."

He was starting to feel as confused as she looked. He knew she had had a dental appointment, but had assumed it was for a cleaning. "What exactly did you have done today? Emma . . . Emma, can you focus for a minute?" She looked up from her inspection of the buttons on his shirt. "Did you have a cleaning appointment today?"

"Nope." She shook her head vigorously for extra emphasis. "I got a root thingie done." Then tears gathered in her eyes as she added, "It really hurt."

He was starting to get the picture now. Just how much nitrous oxide had they given her? Shouldn't it have worn off by now? She looked like she was as high as a kite. God, he was glad she had called a taxi. "Emma, maybe we should cancel this trip and get you home. I don't think you're in any condition to fly."

The tears that had gathered in her eyes before now started flooding down and he placed both of his hands on her shoulders for support. "Please don't leave me. I already told everyone that you're coming. If you don't, I'll have to deal with my family on my own."

As he prepared to convince her, the PA system announced the final boarding for their flight. Apparently, he had missed the first announcements. In surprise, he watched the tears stop and her head come up in determination. She waved her ticket in her hand and wobbled toward the attendant. Shit, if he didn't go with her, she would probably get thrown off the damn plane by an air marshal.

He reached her, sliding an arm around her shoulders to steady her. "Are you sure about this?"

Giving him a blinding smile, she said, "Yep. Let's do this." Really, if he had any sense he would listen to the voice in his head screaming a protest, and he would have turned and run the other way. Instead, the protective instinct he was born with reared its head and he found himself walking down the corridor toward the door of the plane with her securely under his arm. Once she put her head on his shoulder, he felt something unfamiliar inside of him flicker. *Get a grip, man. This is no different from helping Ava would be. You don't feel anything for Emma. Remember all of the ways she chaps your ass on a daily basis. . . .*

His pep talk was a miserable failure. There was no way he could convince his body that the woman beside him was like a sister to him. His cock wasn't buying into it. The little fucker was a lot smarter than he gave him credit for being.

Even after being blackmailed into the trip, Brant had still grudgingly let Emma use his frequent-flier miles to book seats in first class. He had never been more grateful to have a few more inches to put between himself and another person. If they were in the three side-by-side seats in coach, she would probably either be in his lap the entire flight or worse yet, some stranger's lap on her other side. He led her to the window seat and, after a moment's pause, leaned down to fasten her seat belt. He stored both their carry-ons in the overhead bin before buckling in beside her.

She grabbed his hand as soon as he was seated. "Takeoffs always makes me nervous."

So, he sat stiffly next to her until they were in the air. For two people who had never touched, they were certainly making up for lost time today. He was surprised she had even booked their seats together.

As soon as he could, he stood to get his laptop, intent on putting some distance between them, even if it was only mentally. But as he tried to study some spread-sheets, he felt her eyes on him as if they were burning into him. He tried his best to ignore it until she said, "You're so hot. Really. Even when you're being an ass-hole, which is most of the time, you still rock those suits."

His head jerked toward hers, his mouth falling open in surprise. Still she kept on as if discussing the weather. "We've all talked about it and agreed. You are com-pletely fuckable until you open your mouth." Her last sentence seemed to echo around them within the small confines of the airplane. He quickly looked around to see if anyone had overheard her. The lady across the aisle flashed him a disapproving look.

Turning back to Emma, he cleared his throat and asked, "I . . . um . . . thanks, I guess. I rather hate to ask this, but who is 'we'?"

She put her hand up in front of him and started counting on her fingers.

"Beth, Ella, Claire and Suzy." Hell, this was worse than he thought. Why would they be discussing him? Sure, maybe it was a little bit of an ego boost to be con-sidered fuckable—at least until he considered the part about him opening his mouth. As he was floundering for a reply, she put her hand on his thigh and his thoughts scattered all to hell. "I need to go pee; can you help me?"

Fuck! Just when he thought things couldn't get more uncomfortable. "Emma . . . I don't . . . Er, can't you hold it? I don't think it's a great idea for you to be up walking around."

When she cupped herself like a child, he felt himself go light-headed. "I can't wait. I'll hold your hand, I promise."

Of course, the damn bathroom was several rows away. He didn't relish the thought of her wobbling around, but he could also live without being peed on.

On a loud sigh of resignation, he unbuckled his seat belt and then turned to do hers as well. He extended a hand to her as he stood, pulling her gently into the aisle in front of him. When she stood there looking around in confusion, he put a hand on either side of her hips and pushed her gently down the aisle. She stopped once to compliment a woman on her shirt and another time to introduce herself to a small boy who was playing with a plastic car. When he finally got her to the restroom door, he opened it and pushed her forward.

Then he stood outside the door for what seemed like an hour before he heard a crash inside. Alarmed, he knocked on the door, "Emma, are you all right?" No answer, so he called her name twice more. When she didn't answer, he was at a loss.

He couldn't just leave her in there. The door lock showed green, meaning that she hadn't locked it. "Emma, if you don't answer, I'm coming in there." This time he heard her say what sounded like "help." That was all he needed. He opened the door and gaped at the sight. Emma was bent over the toilet with no shirt on. His eyes almost popped out of his head as he caught sight of her breasts pushing against the fabric of her lacy black bra. "What the . . ."

He finally took his eyes off her chest long enough to notice her trying to pull something that looked like her shirt from the toilet. "Help me! I took my shirt off to wash a stain out of it, and I accidentally dropped it in the toilet. I don't know what happened, but it started flushing and now it's trying to eat my shirt!"

"Emma . . . drop the shirt."

She jerked up to look at him, and the thin silk top flew from her hand, sucked loudly down the toilet. They both stood staring down for a full minute as if the shirt would magically reappear. He finally realized that he was standing in the doorway where anyone could come by and see Emma half-dressed. Shit, what was he supposed to do now? "Do you have another shirt in your carry-on?"

Shaking her head, she said, "No, just panties." Yeah, that's exactly the mental picture he needed to go along with the tits he was now trying hard not to stare at. He pushed the door shut behind them, wedging against her in the small space. Not a good idea, but he didn't want anyone looking at her. He expected a flight attendant to come by at any moment and accuse them of trying to join the Mile High club; in his freaking dreams, maybe. He started unbuttoning his shirt and she giggled nervously.

"You'd better be careful; that toilet is dangerous," she warned.

As far as he was concerned, the only danger in the bathroom was of his cock exploding through the zipper it was uncomfortably pressed against. He got the last button on his shirt undone and struggled to pull the shirt loose from his slacks. Finally, he unbuckled his belt and managed to free the material. He pulled off his button-down shirt and then started easing his undershirt off. He was damned grateful to be wearing layers today, because otherwise the men on the plane would be in for a real visual treat.

Next he handed her the white T-shirt, saying, "Put that on." It was a testament to how out of it she was from the medication that she stood holding it in confusion. "Honey, if you don't put that on, you're going to have to march back down the aisle and spend the rest of the flight in that skimpy bra."

He wanted to fall to his knees and offer up a prayer of thanks when she said, "Ohhh, I gotcha." He started pulling his shirt back on while she wiggled against him, pressing her breasts into his chest as she maneuvered his T-shirt over her head. They were both breathing heavily by the time she finished. Probably for two completely different reasons, though. He was starting to feel like the only thing missing in the bathroom was a stripper pole and a stack of ones. When he opened the door to leave, an elderly woman was tapping her foot while giving him a disapproving scowl.

"I . . . um, was just helping my wife. She lost her shirt." *Shit! Yeah, that sounds so much better.* Behind him, Emma giggled as he took her arm and pulled her in front of him. "Hush," he whispered in her hair. The situation already looked bad enough. Was it his imagination or was everyone on the damned plane grinning at them? He pushed her into her seat, wanting to escape the scrutiny as quickly as possible.

He had just taken a deep breath and started to relax when Emma leaned against him. "Why are your pants unbuckled?" He looked down in horror to see his pants hanging open. In all of the confusion, he had tucked his shirt back in his pants but had failed to button them and buckle the belt. No wonder everyone on the plane had been looking at them. He might as well have been high-fiving as he walked back to his seat. My God, they had barely been flying for thirty minutes and he had already managed to embarrass himself more on board than he had in a lifetime.

He buckled his pants knowing his face was flaming red. Emma's hand landed on his thigh as she started randomly talking about every topic from this month's *Cosmo* to the dog she had when she was a child. When she started drawing circles on his leg that were coming dangerously close to his cock, he clamped a hand over hers, stilling the motion. She propped her chin on his shoulder and asked, "Why don't you have a girlfriend? Is it because you're so . . . uptight?"

He turned to her, finding that he had to scramble to keep up with her rapid-fire subject changes. "Uptight? I have women in my life." He hated that he sounded so defensive. Did everyone at Danvers think he was such an asshole? Since when was it a crime to have a good work ethic? He was courteous and considerate to everyone—well, except Emma. With her, he tended to give as good as he got.

Her eyes rounded as if he had just admitted to having the formula for world peace. "You do?" she gasped. "Who? Wait—you're not talking about your sister, Ava, are you?"

So maybe he had been going to mention Ava, but now there was no way he could. "Just different women, okay? No one you would know." When she gave him a disbelieving look, he added, "I have a lot of sex, Emma, more than you do, I'm betting!" And . . . all eyes in the seats around them were trained on them again. He had managed to make an ass of himself while Emma sat beside him looking like an innocent angel. When she opened her mouth, he said, "Enough. Don't say anything else. Just go to sleep, stare off into space or anything that doesn't require us talking." To drive his point home, he leaned his head back on the headrest and closed his eyes. He didn't intend to open his mouth until they landed in Miami, no matter what she said.

Chapter Six

Brant was absurdly grateful to feel the plane touch down at the Miami International airport. Beside him, Emma yawned, stretching her arms above her head. *Eyes off the tits; nothing good can come of that.* "Feeling better?" he asked her.

She gave him a sleepy smile that still appeared a bit loopy, but he thought she may finally be coming down from the laughing gas that the dentist had given her. "Yeah, just a little tired."

He stood, grabbing both their carry-on bags. She made a halfhearted attempt to take hers from his hand, but he assured her that he would carry it. He didn't think she was steady enough yet to add anything else to the mix. He stepped back in the aisle of the plane and motioned for her to precede him out. What happened next was something he would look back on for the rest of his life with equal parts confusion, horror and amusement—when he was able to remember it without shuddering.

Emma stumbled a few times on the way up the jet

bridge, so his focus was primarily on making sure she didn't fall on her face. There were several police officers and a dog standing at the end of the bridge as the passengers walked by. Brant knew it was standard procedure at many airports to have drug-sniffing dogs stationed where new passengers entered the airport facility. He barely spared them a glance as he steered Emma toward the terminal. When the dog suddenly started barking frantically, he looked around to see what was going on. He was shocked immobile when the dog stopped at his feet, still barking urgently. What the hell? He was so shaken up that he dropped both carry-on bags. Emma's hard-shell bag dropped to the floor with a loud pop and seemed to explode open.

He looked down practically in a daze as skimpy panties covered every inch of the floor around his feet. He could barely hear the chaos around him over the roaring in his ears. Suddenly, he was being pulled off to the side and asked repeatedly if he had a prescription for the medication he was carrying. What the hell were they talking about? He wasn't carrying medication! When he shook his head, struggling to answer and confused by what they were asking, they seemed to take his response as an admission of guilt. He felt hands on his shoulders and cuffs snapping around his wrists. Through the haze, he thought he was probably hallucinating because he was sure he saw Emma on the ground trying to wrestle something from the dog's mouth. The police were shouting at her, but she persisted. Was that? No, surely not. There was no way his assistant was wrestling with a narcotics detection dog for a . . . pink penis?

"Emma," he yelled.

As the police pulled her away from the dog, she gave one final jerk and held up a bright pink, phallus-shaped object in her hands. He knew it was a vibrator because the buzzing sound coming from it was unmistakable. As she waved it in victory, he noticed white things that appeared to be pills sticking to the sides of it. "Fuck!" This was a damn bad time to learn that your assistant had a drug problem.

Necks craned as they were led in handcuffs toward the security office in a back hall of the airport. Their bags were deposited on a table and the police started sifting through them. One of the officers pointed to Emma's bag, asking, "Whose bag is this?"

Emma stuck her hand up as if she were in school. "It's mine. I'm sorry about the mess, but I had to pack in a hurry."

The officer held up one of the white pills that were scattered in the bag. "What kind of pills are these?"

Emma looked at him, clearly puzzled. "I don't know the name of them. I just got them before I left home."

The officer called the numbers off one of the pills to the other officer, who entered them into a computer. "Miss, these are Vicodin. Do you have a prescription?"

Brant wanted to cry when she shook her head no. "I gave it to the man at Walgreens and he gave me these. He said take one or two and I took two . . . I think. My mouth was hurting really bad; I had a root canal this morning." Shit, that explained a lot. She had taken pain medication. Apparently, it was some strong stuff. She still seemed half out of it, even after fighting with a dog.

"Miss, where is your prescription bottle? We need to verify that you were legally prescribed these narcotics."

Big tears flooded her eyes and trickled down her cheeks. She seemed to be thinking the same thing he was now: cavity search and incarceration. "I . . . I think I left it at home. The top came off and they spilled everywhere. The cab horn was blaring outside so I threw my whole drawer in the bag and ran."

Yeah, thanks, baby. That really helped our case a lot. Brant averted his gaze from the huge, pill-covered vibrator that seemed to be staring him in the face. Apparently, the jellylike consistency of the vibrator was like Velcro for pills . . . just their luck. "Emma, can you give them the name of your dentist? Maybe they could give him a call to confirm the prescription." Luckily, she had the receipt in her purse and the officers were able to get the confirmation they needed. They gave her a plastic baggie for her medication along with a copy of the prescription that the dentist had faxed over. He had to give them credit for mostly being able to control the smirks he saw hints of on their faces. The vibrator and the pills stuck to it were left behind to be disposed of. He was sure that they would be kept for weeks as the airport police laughed their asses off.

Emma stayed quiet as they picked up their luggage from the baggage claim and settled into the back of a taxi. He really needed a few moments alone to process everything that had just happened. He wasn't used to being a public spectacle, so this was a new and unwelcome feeling.

When they reached the hotel, it didn't even surprise him to learn that instead of two rooms, there was only one reservation. Of course, the hotel was booked to capacity with several conventions in progress. Perhaps he should consider himself lucky that the room had two double beds. At least it was only for one night, right? Surely they now had covered every possible disaster for this trip. He could lock himself in the bathroom for a while if he needed privacy. On second thought, as soon as he dropped off his bag, he was hitting the hotel bar . . . alone.

Emma woke in a strange room completely disoriented. The sun streamed in, causing her vision to blur as her eyes adjusted to the light.

"Well, good morning, sunshine, I see you finally decided to join the land of the living."

She almost panicked until she felt the fabric of her clothing against the palm of her hand. For a moment, she had been afraid that they'd . . . God, no. She'd never been more grateful to wake up in her old T-shirt. Miami . . . room mix-up, check.

"Ugh," she groaned, "what time is it?"

"It's a little after eight. Why don't you pull yourself together and we'll go have some breakfast?" He gave her a look that indicated he wasn't sure it was possible.

She pulled the covers over her head and waved him toward the door. "You go on. I think I'll pass."

Suddenly the comforter was jerked from her hands and Brant loomed over her. "Oh no, sweetheart, you're not getting off that easy. I have gone through hell for you on this trip and you owe me. You have ten minutes. Do what you can and meet me downstairs in the lobby."

"Good grief, when did you turn into such a drama queen?"

Giving her a disbelieving look, he snarled, "Drama queen? You almost got me fucking strip-searched yesterday at the airport. Did you expect that we would sit around today and have a good laugh over the whole thing?"

She was still a bit hazy on the events of the previous day, but she refused to let him one-up her. "Well, I'm sure a strip search would have been a thrill for you. Perhaps the highlight of your whole year. You should be thanking me instead of whining." She barely had time to think *Uh-oh, maybe I went a little too far* before she was jerked from the bed and held tightly against his broad chest.

"If I'm so lacking in female company, maybe you should help me out. Why don't you show me what I've been missing? I believe you called me fuckable yesterday." She barely had time to gasp in surprise before his lips swooped down to claim hers. Her hands landed on his shoulders to push him away, but instead she found herself gripping the fabric of his suit jacket in her hands, holding on for dear life. His lips plundered and claimed, seeking to both punish and assert dominance. She was surprised to hear the throaty moan and realize that it was coming from her. Almost against her will, she slid closer to him, instinctively seeking the warmth of his hard body against hers. She felt him jerk against her as her tongue rose to meet his, desperate for a taste of his heat. Her mouth protested the activity, still tender from her root canal, but she didn't care. What had begun, she knew, as a punishment was now rapidly spiraling into something that neither of them had been expecting.

Emma felt his hard-on against her stomach and she stretched to run her hands through his hair, desperate to anchor him to her. When his mouth moved from her lips to her neck, she moaned, "Brant . . ." It was as if a dam had collapsed between them. All of the usual animosity they felt for each other was being channeled in another direction and she was powerless to resist . . . she had no desire to resist him. His jacket hit the floor, followed shortly by his shirt and tie. She barely had time to run her hands up the velvety skin of his chest before he was ripping the thin T-shirt she had slept in over her head. She didn't consider herself the most athletic person in the world but when Brant settled his big hands on her ass, she gripped his arms and jumped against him, wrapping her legs around his narrow, muscled waist. God, he felt good against her damp heat.

Brant ground his cock against her as she nibbled and

sucked on his neck. A growl rumbled up through his chest before he dropped her backward onto the bed. She propped her head on her arms to appreciate the masculine beauty before her. His eyes, almost black with desire, caught and held hers as his hands went to his belt. She could see the outline of his cock pushing against the fabric of his slacks. He finished unbuckling his belt and had his slacks hanging open before she could blink. The bulge in his black boxer briefs was threatening to break loose as he kicked his feet free of both his shoes and pants.

She rose on her knees, desperate to touch him. His breath caught as her hand stroked him through the cotton of his briefs. She didn't think either of them was going to make it long, so she pulled the waistband of his briefs down, causing his big cock to spring free. She wrapped one hand around the base while she used her other hand to rub the precum that glistened on the tip along his shaft.

"Emma . . . can't take much more," he groaned before pulling her hand away. He grabbed a condom from his wallet and deftly rolled it on. She felt her sex clenching in anticipation as his big body settled over hers. She had never felt the need to be in control during sex, but something about the dynamics of her relationship with Brant had brought that need to the fore. Before he could penetrate her, she pushed against his shoulder until he was lying on his back. He looked at her in surprise before giving her a knowing grin. He settled a hand around the base of his cock.

"Take it any way you want to, baby." Emma didn't need to be told twice. She had never wanted anyone this much. Any second thoughts that she may have had were quickly discarded and she moved up Brant's big body. She hovered, looking down at his large shaft with both anticipation and trepidation. He was so big and, in this position, he would go deep. Almost as if he understood her fear, Brant's hands settled against her ass, giving her the support to take him as slowly as she needed.

When his tip breached her entrance, she threw her head back, moaning at the incredible feeling. Brant's eyes stayed locked with hers as she continued to take him slowly, inch by inch. She could feel his hands shaking and his breathing grow shallow, but he never rushed her. He let her set the pace until, with a gasp of surprise, he was buried to the hilt inside of her. Emma had a fleeting moment to wonder if all of their needling of each other had been leading up to this moment all along. Had this been the inevitable outcome between two people so hell-bent on getting the best of the other?

Then all rational thought fled as Brant surged deep while she slammed her hips down to meet him. She had never been one to climax from intercourse alone, so she was shocked to feel her body climbing quickly toward release. When he reached up to pinch her pebbled nipples, she felt her control slipping away. The pleasure was so great, it bordered on pain. She felt a momentary panic as her senses were completely overloaded by him.

"Brant . . . I . . . ahhh . . . it's too much."

Brant seemed to sense what she was feeling and he slid an arm up her thigh reassuringly. "It's okay, Em, just let go. I promise I'll be right there with you." At his words, her body came completely apart in his arms. She screamed his name and saw stars behind her tightly closed lids. Her core clenched and shuddered around Brant's hard cock. When she started to sag, completely wiped out, he braced her with his powerful arms as he pumped deep inside her one more time and joined her in release. His big body shook as he growled his pleasure.

"Holy fuck," he moaned as she collapsed against his chest. She could still feel his cock hard inside her and marveled at his stamina. Neither of them had the will nor the strength to move until the ringing of the bed-side phone caused them to jump apart. Brant cursed under his breath before grabbing it. She heard what was obviously a wake-up call on the other end of the line before he dropped it back in the cradle. "I set that last night just in case."

Emma yawned against his chest. "Good idea. I guess you don't have time for that breakfast now, do you? I'll just take a nap while you're gone."

Brant swatted her butt. "Maybe I need my assistant along today."

"Ouch!" She tweaked one of his nipples in retalia-tion. As the afterglow began to fade, Emma started to fidget. Suddenly it felt awkward to be lying on Brant's chest with his cock now nestled between them. The room had gone silent as if they were both lost in thought. She was more than ready for him to leave so that she could have some time alone to process what had just happened. Damn, what time was that meeting again?

Almost as if reading her thoughts, Brant looked over at the bedside clock and groaned. "I've got to get going. A car is supposed to pick me up downstairs in fifteen minutes." They both stared at each other in silence for a moment. Normally, this would be the point where there would be a good-bye kiss or something after what they had just shared. She wondered if a fist bump would be acceptable.

She knew it was probably the coward's way out, but she decided to let them off easy. She rolled off him and did a dramatic yawn before pulling the covers over her. "Have a good day, dear." Brant remained where he was for a moment before she felt the bed dip as he stood. He had very little time left to do anything other than grab a quick shower and throw his clothes back on.

As he was leaving the room, she felt him pause next to her side of the bed. She kept her eyes carefully closed. "Emma . . ."

Damn, he wasn't going to just go away, was he? She held her breath, part of her hoping he would go . . . another part of her wanting to see that he wanted to stay. "Hmmm?"

"I . . ." She tensed as he paused, seeming to struggle for his next words. Finally after what seemed like minutes but was probably only seconds, he said, "Our flight leaves at three. I'll have the car swing by and pick you up on the way to the airport. I don't think I'll be back before then." She nodded her head and held her breath. *Hopefully he'd leave it at that.* After another long pause, she finally heard the door open and close.

Once she was alone she sagged against the mattress in relief. The morning after had never felt so weird. The verdict was in, her uptight boss was a sex god. Her toes curled just thinking about what had happened between them. What a body all of those suits hid! Brant was ripped and seriously blessed in the equipment department. She would never admit it to him, but he had rocked her world.

He was confident, sensual and surprisingly accommodating. He had let her be on top when she had insisted, but she had little doubt who had actually held the power between them. She would have followed him off a cliff had he asked. The problem was, how did you handle having the best sex of your life knowing it should never happen again? Ever. Could she go back to her usual relationship with Brant knowing that just one look from him was likely to send her up in flames? She rubbed her jaw, still feeling the effects of her root canal. She wished she could blame her lack of judgment this morning on pain medication, but desire alone had clouded her mind.

Brant stepped inside the rental car gratefully and shut the door. After giving the driver the address of his destination, he settled back against the leather seat. Fuck, what had just happened? Even after the explosive orgasm less than thirty minutes ago, he was still throbbing with desire. He had only himself to blame. He had been so furious with Emma this morning that it had taken only a few smart comments from her to push him over the edge of rational thinking. Once he felt her mouth against his, he lost all sense. It was like pouring gasoline on glowing embers.

He had admitted to himself more than once that Emma was a very attractive woman—and sure, he had admired her often in a more than professional capacity. But their battle of wills had always kept things from getting out of hand. He might be looking at her ass one minute and then wanting to choke her the next. It had always been all about checks and balances with them. Her attitude usually checked his desire and kept their relationship in some kind of twisted balance. Today, everything had worked just the opposite. He had completely lost control and there hadn't been a damn thing he could do about it. As soon as he had touched her creamy skin, kissed and licked the rosy peaks of her breasts, it had been all over for him. Nothing short of her telling him to stop would have worked—and that hadn't happened. They had both been completely swept up in the moment. It wasn't until she was lying on top of him and some of the haze had cleared that he had started to panic. Immediately he had wanted to grab his clothes and run, something he never did. He wasn't that kind of guy. It wasn't even that he wanted to get away from Emma; it was exactly the opposite.

The question now was where to go from here. Was he capable of acting as if it had never happened? Did he even want to? He knew how it felt to be inside of her now; it was seared on his brain and would be hard to ignore. Damn, it had been the hottest experience he could ever remember having. Why did it have to be with someone he worked with? Hell, he could maybe handle that, but not with his assistant. It just felt so wrong to him. He had been half afraid that Emma would chop his cock off this morning when reality set in. Feeling no closer to an answer, he decided he would take his cues from her. If she didn't mention what had happened, then he would follow her lead and not bring it up. Somehow, he would keep his hands off her, if that was truly what she wanted. If only they were heading back to the office today, things would be easier, but instead he was going to be pushed into even closer quarters with her and with her family. He could only hope that he didn't look guilty and that her dad wasn't a big man.

Chapter Seven

Emma gave a quiet sigh of relief as she followed Brant through the airport in Pensacola. After their awful airport experience in Miami, she was grateful there were no dogs in the vicinity. "Emma!" a familiar voice called out. Uh-oh, maybe her relief had come too soon. Her mother, dressed in formfitting jeans and a white V-neck T-shirt, was bearing down on them. Shit, she had told her that they would take a taxi. She should have known she couldn't count on her mother to listen to anything she said.

Brant gave her a questioning look. She rolled her eyes. "You might want to go ahead and brace yourself; that's my mom." She barely had time to finish speaking before her mother launched herself into his arms. Emma couldn't contain her chuckle at his deer-in-the-headlights look.

"Well, hello there, handsome!" Her mother finally peeled herself off of him long enough to say, "I'm Kat Davis; what's your name, hon?"

Brant gave her a nervous smile. "Great to meet you, Kat. I'm Brant Stone."

Her mother's mouth seemed to drop to the floor before she blurted, "You're the asshole that Em works with?"

Oh my God! Why hadn't she thought of that? Of course she would have mentioned Brant by name to her mother when she was raging about him. The thought had never occurred to her that her mother would make the connection. On the plane ride into Pensacola, she and Brant had decided to say that they had been introduced by a mutual friend. That wasn't technically a lie. The lady from Human Resources had introduced them when Emma was hired. Now that whole story was useless. As they stood there gaping at each other, her mother suddenly pulled Brant back into her arms, slapping him on the back while laughing hysterically. "I love it! I should have known all of that arguing was just some kind of foreplay between you two."

"Mom," she groaned. This was just getting worse and worse. She needed to shut her mother up before this escalated further. "It's all kind of new between us, so we haven't really told anyone yet."

Her mother finally released Brant again and gave them both a wink. "Ahhh, gotcha. Well, come on, you two, let's grab your bags and head home. Your father is firing up the grill tonight."

"I think we both need to shower before dinner.

Could you drop us at our hotel first? They're supposed to have our rental car there."

Her mother gave a shake of her head. "No hotels, honey. You know that's not how we roll. The house has plenty of room. I have your room already made up for you two. Your father and I are hip to how things are now. Robyn and Boston can't wait to see you."

She was scrambling to come up with an argument to get them out of the hell that her mother was proposing when Brant did something that completely floored her. He put an arm around her mother, saying, "That sounds wonderful, Kat. I can't wait to meet the rest of the family."

Emma shot him a look that would have felled a lesser man. He only smiled at her in return. "Right, honey? I know you want to spend as much time as possible with your family while we're here."

That was it. He had officially lost his freaking mind. Was he just trying to get to her for some reason or had he not thought this through? She had to wonder if he even understood that her mom was planning to put them both in a room together for several days. Her room was a good size, but it had a queen-size bed and that was it. Giving him an evil smile, she decided that if he could live with sleeping on the floor all weekend, then who was she to argue?

That's right, honey. Game on.

She was more than a little pissed at him anyway. When he picked her up at the hotel, he had made no mention of what had happened between them that morning. She kept waiting for him to broach the topic, but nada, nothing. It wasn't as if she'd thought he would come back and declare his love, but come on, shouldn't they at least talk about it? Was such an earth-shattering experience that easily dismissed for him? Not wanting him to see how much his actions were bothering her, she reverted to what she knew best: sarcasm. If he could act like nothing ever happened, then so could she. Just because he had given her the best orgasm of her life didn't mean she had to lose her head. She could do casual one-nighters, right?

A few steps ahead of her, Brant continued to talk to her mother like they were old friends.

"Mom, we need to at least stop and pick up our rental car."

"I've got that covered, too. Your father gave your old car a once-over and you can use it while you're here. It will be good for the thing to get some use." Just as Emma started to argue, it suddenly hit her. Yeah, Brant would be horrified by her old car. She could picture his muscular frame folding into her purple Mustang. Not that it thrilled her to drive it either. What was once a cool car back in high school was now considered a vintage Barney reject. Still, she could handle some embarrassment if it bothered Mr. Freshly Pressed even a little.

She smiled sweetly at Brant's questioning look before turning back to her mother. "That's a great idea. I'll cancel our rental car." Soon they were settled into her mother's black Tahoe and she had insisted that Brant take the front seat. He could continue the bonding that he had going on more easily from there. As they approached her childhood home of Pensacola Beach on the Santa Rosa Island, she felt the same old familiar pang. When her friend Madison had decided to attend college at the University of South Carolina, Emma had let her talk her into applying there as well. As luck would have it, they were both accepted and Emma had moved from her home in Florida to South Carolina. Her parents had not been thrilled, which had made her that much more determined to spread her wings. She had mostly lost touch with Madison after graduation. The last she heard, she was in Georgia. Her parents had urged her to move back home, but she enjoyed her independence too much and, quite frankly, long periods of time around her mother were exhausting. South Carolina kept her close to the ocean that she loved, but allowed her the much needed privacy that she had never had growing up with a loving but meddling mother.

When they pulled into the driveway, Emma smiled. The big two-story house looked the same as she remembered. It was comfortable and roomy with a full basement, three-car garage and an infinity pool out back. Some people took living on the coast for granted, but she had always felt like she was on an extended vacation. No matter how bad the day, a good swim in the ocean always made things better. Her father had actually built their house along with many others in the area. He was a highly sought-after builder who didn't believe in constructing the same house twice. If you

asked for a house like your neighbor's, he would re-
fuse. Something had to be different. He said that no
two people had the same personality, so why should
two houses be identical?

It was obvious from the delicious aroma in the air
that her father was already hard at work on the barbecue grill. Beside her, she saw Brant's nose twitch in ap-
preciation. "Come on, you two, let's get you settled in
before dinner. Brant, please tell me you aren't one of
those people who don't eat meat."

Brant gave his most charming smile. "You don't
have to worry about that, Kat. I'm a loyal carnivore."

"Honey, I knew there was more to you than a hard
body." As Emma started to choke, her mother continued. "We'll eat in an hour. Robyn and Boston and the
girls should be here by then."

With a trickle of unease, Emma asked, "The girls?"

As they all started upstairs, her mother looked over
her shoulder to say, "My book club friends. It was my
turn to host tonight so I just invited them over for dinner as well."

Shit! This was starting to sound like some kind of
three-ring circus. "I thought this was just a family dinner. Maybe you should have your club meeting later.
I'm sure they don't want to be stuck with us."

"Nah, they're looking forward to meeting you. I told
them you finally had a boyfriend."

*Zing-g-g. How many embarrassing comments in front of
Brant does that make so far?*

"God, Mom."

As if she hadn't spoken, her mother continued. "You two should sit in with us tonight. We finally read the *Fifty Shades of Grey* trilogy and it was smoking hot. I highly recommend that you both read it. It will change your world. Brant, do you own a gray tie?"

No-o-o-o, she didn't just ask my boss that. Emma knew well what her mother was talking about since she had read the series. Brant, however, looked adorably clueless. She almost laughed when he replied that he had several ties in that shade. The smile fell off her face, though, about thirty seconds later when Brant said: "I think we will sit in with you tonight, Kat. I really enjoy books that are informative and entertaining."

He turned to give Emma a triumphant smile. So the little shit thought he was getting to her, did he? That was just priceless. He had no idea that he had just agreed to join her mother's perverted book club while they discussed bondage, spankings and kinky sex. Had the man been living under a rock? How could he not have heard of that book? He looked a little uneasy when she gave him a big smile in return. "Baby, I think that's a great idea. I'm always trying to get you to try new things. We need to break free of our chains and get tied up . . . er . . . caught up in something new."

When they stopped in the doorway of her old room, her mother stood there beaming at both of them. "Oh, this is so exciting. It will be great to have some new blood." Brant shot her a desperate look over her mother's head. She shrugged her shoulders and walked into the room they would be sharing for the next few nights.

Other than the ragged brown bear in the center of the bed, nothing else stood out as embarrassing. The bed was covered in white eyelet, giving the room a clean, beachy look. There was a bay window dominating one wall with a window seat running the length of it. She had spent many hours sitting there reading while listening to the waves crash against the shore. Her desk sat against the wall in the other corner with an outdated desktop on it. No doubt it was capable of only dial-up Internet. Luckily, she had brought her laptop along.

Her bedroom had its own attached bath complete with double sinks. The thought of having to use the bathroom for anything other than showering with Brant so close was something that she preferred not to dwell on.

Her mother announced, "All right, I'm going to head back downstairs and get everything ready. I'll see you both soon."

As soon as her mother left the room, Emma collapsed on the bed behind her. Just picturing Brant sitting with the book club tonight sent her off into peals of uncontrollable giggles. The more he frowned at her, the harder she laughed. "For God's sake," he grumbled, "what is wrong with you?"

"Nothing . . ." she managed to gasp. He shook his head at her and walked over to look out the window. When she noticed the way the material of his pants stretched across his tight ass, her laughter dried up and her body started to hum. *What is wrong with me? He couldn't have made it any clearer that this morning meant nothing to him. Stop staring at the enemy's ass!*

She really tried to listen to her own pep talk, but he was so gorgeous. She'd always thought he was gorgeous, but now that she knew him intimately, it was proving hard to go back to snarky business as usual. She wanted nothing more than for him to lower his body on top of hers and pound her into next Sunday. Okay, maybe that was the wrong thing to wish for in her parents' home, but still . . .

Brant settled back on the edge of the window seat, thankfully moving said nice ass from her view and asked, "So tell me about the rest of your family."

She gave a grimace thinking of her siblings. Like most brothers and sisters, they spent their early years fighting over toys and most of their later ones ratting one another out to their parents. "Well, I'm the oldest." She held her hand up when he opened his mouth. "Please reserve your comments on that. Anyway, Robyn is the middle child, and she is twenty-three years old and a hairstylist. Boston is the baby of the family and he's twenty. He's attending the University of Florida for a degree in botany. I secretly think it's so he can learn to grow his own marijuana, but that's a whole other story."

Looking confused, Brant said, "Wait a minute. I thought Boston was the family dog or something. Who names their kid that?"

Emma shuddered. "Please, under no circumstances are you to ask my mother about it unless you want some really graphic details. I'll just say that my mother swears he was conceived there after a particularly great weekend. She felt like she needed a permanent reminder so . . . Boston. Thank God he was the only one who inspired that; otherwise, I would probably be named Tampa or Daytona."

Brant started chuckling. "Man, I thought my family was nuts; yours is really something else. When she's not scaring the hell out of me, I kind of like your mother. She's a horrible driver, though. I'm afraid the indentations from the safety handles in the front seat are permanently etched in my hands."

Smiling, she nodded in agreement. The tension in her body had slowly drained away during their conversation, and she felt better able to control the feelings that he aroused in her. She didn't, however, think she should test that theory by staying in the room with him for extended periods of time other than to sleep. She reluctantly pulled herself from the bed, saying, "I'm going to shower and change before dinner." Looking at the suit he still wore, she added, "You might want to find something a bit more . . . casual as well." Did the man even have any casual clothing? He just gave her a nod in response, and she pulled her suitcase behind her into the bathroom. She could do this, right? It was only a few days. *Yeah, you slept with your boss on the very first day; what else could possibly happen?*

Brant breathed a sigh of relief when the bathroom door closed behind Emma. Man, what a long day! He was about ready to climb a wall. Spending time like this with her after what had happened that morning had been hell. The ache in his crotch was approaching near epic levels. No matter how many times he tried to tell himself that it didn't mean anything and couldn't happen again, his body didn't seem to agree. Instead, he had walked around sweating bullets with a near constant hard-on. His usual control had deserted him and he was now more like a damn dog in heat. Hell, he was afraid he would be humping her leg soon enough.

He had followed her cue and acted like nothing had happened, but it was killing him. The only thing that kept him from approaching the subject was the fear that she would cut him off at the knees. The whole masculine pride thing was no myth. No man wanted to be rejected or made to feel he didn't matter, and that was the vibe that he was getting from Emma. It was damn humbling to have what he considered a knock-your-head-off sexual experience and then find out that the other person didn't seem anywhere near as awed. He wasn't vain, but he had never had any complaints in that department. Could he have missed something with her? He wasn't an inexperienced schoolboy; he knew she had come. He still had the marks on his shoulders to prove it. So why the indifference?

Except shouldn't he be happy that things hadn't gotten complicated? Out of nowhere, he remembered the sensitive, supportive advice that he had given his brother when he had been tied up in knots over a woman at work who was now his wife: Never shit where you sleep or work; it always turns out badly. Well, apparently that applied only to him because things had turned out fine for Declan, Jason, Gray and Nick. Hell, he was the only one having a problem with it.

He decided to skip the cold shower that he so desperately needed since Emma had claimed the bathroom and settled instead for a change of clothes. Emma was right; he did look a little overdressed. Going downstairs and making a run for the beach was better than sitting in the room imagining Emma naked in the next room, water lapping over her firm, high breasts. *Fuck.* Pulling open his suitcase, he grabbed a pair of cargo shorts and a University of South Carolina T-shirt. They were both a little wrinkled but it couldn't be helped. He refused to give Emma the pleasure of asking her to use an iron. Regardless of what she said, he could do casual. He quickly changed, pulling on a pair of Nike flip-flops that he usually threw on after a shower. He heard the water stop in the bathroom and took off at top speed. He couldn't handle any more naked images in his head right now.

He made it down the stairs to the front door. Freedom was but a few steps away when the door handle beneath his hands started turning without his help. Uh-oh. He stepped back in surprise just as a group of women literally burst through the door.

The leader of the group stopped mere inches away from him. He tried not to stare at the tank top pulled tightly across her rather large chest that said Smut-Lov-

ING WENCHES DO IT ALL NIGHT, and then in smaller print, READ BETWEEN THE LINES. As he was trying to sort that out in his mind, the proud owner of the shirt gave something that sounded suspiciously like a wolf whistle and said, "Ladies, we have just hit pay dirt. Look at this yummy piece of man-candy." Brant watched in frozen shock as the group of women spread out and looked him up and down.

His mouth felt like it was working, but nothing seemed to be coming out. This was his first real episode of being objectified, and he had to admit it didn't feel that great. Instead, he wanted to run back upstairs and hide behind Emma. Surely, she had clothes on by now. "Er . . . hello," he stuttered.

Just as he was trying to figure out an escape path, Emma's mother walked in from the other room. He was damned glad to see her. Her enthusiasm and ability to jump from one subject to the next in the blink of an eye was a little scary, but he liked her. Emma's father was a lucky man because Kat Davis was a knockout. She reminded him a lot of the actress Andie MacDowell. He had noticed in the airport that Emma strongly resembled her mother and, in his book, that made her lucky. Mother Nature definitely had a soft spot for the Davis women.

She walked up to him and tucked her arm through his. "Down, girls. Don't scare the poor man away or Emma will kill us. This is my daughter's new boyfriend who I was telling you about. Isn't he delish?"

Delish? Good grief, he had at least ten women staring at him now as if he were a prime piece of meat while Kat stood beside him looking proudly on. "Maybe I should run back upstairs and check on Emma."

As he turned to make his escape, Emma walked down the last step, landing beside him. "Oh, no need, honey, I'm right here. I see you've met the girls." Then turning toward the group, she offered them a bright smile. "Brant and I can't wait to sit in on your book club meeting tonight. It's all he's been talking about since Mom invited us."

He gave her a forced smile that he hoped adequately conveyed his feelings of murderous intent. "You know, since there are no other men in the group, maybe we should sit this one out, dear. I wouldn't want to impose." As everyone rushed to assure him that they couldn't wait to have a male opinion in the group, he knew he was screwed. How bad could discussing some book about shades of gray be? He was relieved that the name indicated that it wasn't any type of romance book. God, that was a relief.

Everyone fell in line behind Kat as she led them out the patio doors off the kitchen. Brant took a deep breath, smelling the ocean along with the mouth-watering scents of the grill. Beside him, Emma suddenly squealed and flew across the patio into a man's arms. "Daddy!"

"My Emmie!" Emma's father was a tall, muscular man with a head of thick dark hair just beginning to gray at the tips. It was obvious from his tanned skin that he spent a lot of time outdoors. Brant remembered her telling him once that her dad was a builder and his athletic frame supported that. Her father kept one arm around Emma while stepping forward to extend his other hand to him. "I'm Ken Davis, father to this handful."

Brant tried to keep a blank expression as he thought that his interpretation of "handful" and Emma's father's where she was concerned were probably very different. "Nice to meet you, Ken, I'm Brant Stone, Emma's . . . boyfriend." God, that seemed weird to say at his age. Of course, what else was there? Lover? Yeah, that would go over well with her daddy. "This is a beautiful place you have here. Did you build this house?"

Nodding his head, Ken said, "I sure did. Of course, Kat changed her mind about every damn day, but I finally made her happy. You know, if your woman isn't happy, your life is hell, right?"

He might not actually have a woman, but Brant knew a true statement when he heard it. Emma's mom handed him a cold beer and he took it gratefully. Wait. Should he pretend that he didn't drink to impress them? Looking at the group of book club women still gathered behind him making no attempt to hide the fact that they were looking at his ass, he decided, screw it. If they wanted to judge him, then at least he would be slightly more relaxed about the experience with a few beers.

When her mother asked, "So, Brant, honey, are you from South Carolina?" Emma tensed beside him.

"Yes, Kat, I am." He had already made the mistake of calling her ma'am earlier and he now knew to avoid that.

"What do your parents do?" It had been so long that he didn't even flinch when he said, "They passed away when I was young." Everyone seemed to be waiting for him to explain, so he added, "They died in a plane crash near the Florida Keys, actually."

Emma gave him a look of sympathy even though he knew that she was already aware of the story. Kat stepped forward and gave him a hug. "Oh, honey, I'm so sorry to hear that. I'm sure they would be proud of how well you turned out." Emma found herself nodding in agreement. There was really no debating that. Brant was one big walking accomplishment.

At that moment, her brother came striding out, gaining everyone's attention toward him. The baby of the family always took center stage. She took a little whiff as he drew closer, thinking he had probably been practicing his "botany" before he came in. She gave him a hug when he finally managed to escape from their mother.

"Hey, Emmie-Lou."

"Hey, Brat," she fired back fondly. "How's school?"

"Not bad; the class load is kicking my ass, though."

Emma quickly introduced Brant, who asked, "How many classes are you taking this semester?"

Wrinkling his nose, Boston said, "Three. I usually try to stick with two. You know . . . to have more time for other things."

Brant, oblivious to Boston's surfer-dude attitude, said, "Oh, you work and go to school part-time?"

Boston looked confused. "No, man, I go full-time. It's pretty rough, too."

Emma was grateful when their father interrupted the conversation to say that Robyn had to work late and would have to drop by the next day. By that time, Brant would have already gathered that her brother was a slacker, but why make it worse? Boston walked off to sneak some food off the table, leaving her alone with Brant for the first time since coming downstairs.

"Your brother is quite a character."

Emma smiled. "Yeah, he's the go-to guy for all leisure activities." She took a minute to study him. "You look pretty leisurely yourself. I didn't think you owned anything besides suits."

His eyes drifted over her white shorts and turquoise off-the-shoulder top. "You look pretty laid-back yourself, I like the top. A lot." Emma felt her face flush at his unexpectedly flirtatious words.

"I . . . um . . . thanks." Oh no, she could feel her nipples start to harden at his continued attention. She could tell by the slight widening of his eyes that her body's betrayal was obvious to him. Suddenly it was as if their usual insults had turned into come-ons. Frankly, the whole thing had her off center. She didn't know how to act in a world where her words may now be considered foreplay, not only by Brant but herself as well.

She jerked when Brant settled an arm around her

shoulders and nuzzled her neck. Was that his tongue? "I guess we need to look the part, right?" he whispered in her ear.

"Hmmm?" she croaked out, barely able to think with his body this close to hers.

"You know . . . boyfriend, girlfriend, lovers. That's what we are playing at, right?"

"Oh, yes, right, of course."

Her mother beamed her approval as Brant led Emma toward a chair. "You go ahead and sit if you want. I'm going to grab a Coke," she said. In truth, she just needed a few minutes away from his amorous attention. She stopped to talk to her dad and then her brother before deciding she couldn't stay away from Brant any longer without it being obvious. Drink in hand, she turned back in his direction and then abruptly stopped. Brant was still seated at the table, but her vacant seat and all of the others next to him had been filled by her mother's book club friends. In fact, Brant was now the center of their attention. Far from looking awkward, he appeared completely at ease as he laughed and joked with the crowd of admiring females.

Her father walked to her side and tracked her line of vision. "Thank Christ, at least I'm off the hook tonight. If there's a male anywhere in the vicinity, they're all over him."

"Daddy!"

"Baby girl, I'm just calling a spade a spade. Your mother loves that group and I like 'em just fine as long as they meet at someone else's house. Most of them are divorced and it doesn't take long to figure out why. Their men probably packed up and ran like hell. They don't bother your brother too much. They probably figure it would go right over his head."

Emma put her hand over her mouth, trying to stifle her giggle. God, she loved her daddy.

"It looks like I'll be able to enjoy my beer and my burger tonight, though, since they have their hooks firmly in your new man."

"Yeah, I see that and it's only just begun. He accepted their invitation to the book club meeting tonight to discuss *Fifty Shades of Grey*."

Emma laughed as her father's mouth dropped open. "You're shitting me?"

"Nope. I don't think he knows what it is, though."

"I'd just think it was some painting book if not for your mother trying to read me every other chapter." Emma decided to let him off the hook since he was starting to look uncomfortable. This probably wasn't a book you wanted to discuss with your daughter. "I need to go get the food off the grill and you'd better go rescue Brant." She had been planning to leave him to fend for himself, but she was supposed to be in love with him, and it might look strange if she sat at the other end of the table.

Luckily or unluckily, when she walked up behind him, the line of women automatically shifted down one seat and she slid into the empty chair next to his. He threw an enthusiastic arm around her, pulling her in closer to very tempting warmth. "Hey, baby, I missed you." Everyone at the table gave an *awww* while she tried to tell herself that the pang she felt in her heart wasn't real. Nothing about their rapport was real other than the fact that they worked together and, when this was over, it would be back to business as usual. Sure, they were both physically attracted to each other, but that changed nothing in the end. She was just too different from Brant for things to ever go any farther, wasn't she? After all, the man sitting beside her now was an illusion. He was acting a part and she had to remember that. When they returned home, he would be the same uptight man that he normally was, and she would be back to calling him on it at every opportunity. She couldn't be deceived by how good it felt to be a "we" and not just plain old Emma. Opposites may attract, but in this case, they may also strangle each other.

Chapter Eight

Brant had just finished eating his hamburger and Emma was now curled into his side. The mannerisms of being a couple seemed to be coming more naturally to him than he would have imagined. She had given him a couple of elbow nudges that kept him somewhat grounded in reality. Dinner with her family had been lively and fun. He didn't have to fake his connection to her parents; it was genuine. He had carried on a long conversation with her father on everything from politics and the economy to college football. Her brother had invited him for a stroll on the beach to "burn one," which he politely declined. Her mother and her friends were a constant source of off-color jokes and stories about their husbands, boyfriends and neighbors. As a group they were rather scary, but you had to laugh with them.

Once the food was cleared from the table, he watched in curiosity as one of the women, Doris, pulled a bag from her purse and shook out some jewelry. She passed what appeared to be a necklace to the other women.

Emma held hers up and he could see what looked like a tiny tie, something that looked like a mask and . . . what the . . . handcuffs?

Emma smiled sweetly at his puzzled expression. "Could you fasten this for me, honey?"

"Um, sure, sweetheart."

Her father stood up, saying, "Well, I think that's my cue to head inside."

Kat glanced at her husband, giving him a look that made Brant turn quickly away. The love and passion between them was obvious in every interaction they had with each other. "Honey, you're welcome to stay. We have another man in the group tonight, so you might be more comfortable."

Ken leaned down and gave his wife a lingering kiss before straightening. "I've got some calls to return. I'll see you when your friends leave. Do you want me to open your bottles of wine before I go?"

As Kat nodded, Ken grabbed a couple of wine bottles from the kitchen, returning with one of them open. Brant saw the Sancerre label on the bottle and thought it was a strange pick for a book club meeting, but who was he to say since this was his first time. As Ken walked by him on the way into the house, he clapped a hand on Brant's shoulder, saying under his breath, "Good luck, son."

Twenty minutes into the meeting was all it took for Brant to go from alarmed to traumatized. When Doris was asked her favorite part of the book, she said, "I loved it when Christian took Anna into the red room of pain because nobody wants a vanilla relationship, do they?" He jerked back in alarm so hard that Emma almost tumbled off the seat beside him.

While the others at the table went off into a very long and detailed discussion of floggers and paddles, he pulled Emma closer, whispering in her ear. "What the fuck kind of book is this?"

She gave him an innocent look but couldn't quite keep the mischievous expression off her face. It was there dancing in her eyes, impossible for him to miss. "Why, honey, I thought you knew that *Fifty Shades* was erotica."

He gave her an incredulous look, hardly believing the shitstorm he had walked blindly into. "You set me up. Have you read it?"

Smirking, she admitted, "It's one of my favorites; I've read it twice."

Part of him was still pissed, but another part, mainly the one between his legs, was dying to know what *her* favorite part of the book was. As intrigued as he was, he knew one thing: He had to get the hell out of here before her mother detailed her favorite part and scarred him forever. He couldn't bear the idea of accidentally picturing her and Emma's father re-creating some scene complete with a spanking for the bad girl.

He jumped up from the table, causing all eyes to land on him. "I, er . . . just remembered that I need to call my brother about some business. You ladies go on without me . . . please."

Emma didn't look as amused when she realized she

was being left to have what Brant considered a porn discussion with her mother while he hauled ass. He trailed a finger over her chin, returning the smirk she had given him earlier. "Take your time, precious, I'll be upstairs." Yeah, he might never get the images out of his head, but he had gotten the last laugh and that had to count for something.

When he walked through the family room on the way to the stairs, Emma's father looked like he was having a hard time keeping a straight face. Brant shook his head, saying, "I guess you knew what that book was about."

"Yeah . . . sorry, son. This is far from my first rodeo. Kat makes sure I get a summary of every book she's reading. I don't think there's any such thing as a good old Western anymore. Nowadays, the cowboy would be whipping the girl instead of the damn horse."

Brant burst out laughing. Ken sure had a way with words. "No kidding. If anyone ever mentions a book club to me again, I'll probably start running and never stop."

Ken waved the beer he was holding. "You look like you need a drink. You probably need something stronger than beer, but Boston is never around when you need him."

Apparently, Boston's activities were well known in the family. Ken reminded Brant a lot of the grandfather who had raised them after their parents died. He could be a hard-ass, but the man was the king of one-liners. "Thank you, but I think I'll just go on upstairs and stare at the walls for about ten hours." After a few more pleasantries, he sighed with relief when he closed the bedroom door behind him. He was glad to have a few moments out of the spotlight. Those women needed some kind of professional help. He shuddered, remembering the graphic details of their conversation.

Pretending to be Emma's boyfriend had been the one easy part of the evening. Having her curled against him had felt far too natural. Even though he had been desperate to escape the book sex-talk, he had still been hard-pressed to leave her. Having to keep up appearances in front of her family had ensured her behavior toward him was nothing like it usually was. Gone were the barbs and insults and in their place was nothing but soft, sweet and amazing-smelling Emma. If not for the other women killing his hard-on, it would have been impossible for Emma to miss. Calling a halt to his usual war with her was causing a problem that he had never expected. He actually liked her now, maybe too much. If he had these types of feelings for any other woman he had slept with, he would be pursuing a relationship with her. With Emma, it was all kinds of complicated. They worked together—which, granted, seemed to be how everyone at Danvers found a mate, but he tried damn hard never to complicate his life to that degree.

He was almost desperate enough to call his brother for advice. He knew that calling his sister was out. Although they were close, Ava didn't do relationships and she would flatly tell him to move on. But Declan would understand where he was coming from since his wife also worked for Danvers. Did he want someone to encourage or discourage him? Damned if he knew.

Brant had just stepped out from the shower and was toweling off when the bathroom door opened. Emma's eyes were wide and her breathing seemed just a little heavier than it should have been. She was twisting the hem of her top in her hands, seeming to be filled with a nervous energy. She stared at his groin as if riveted before he wrapped a towel around his waist. "Ever heard of knocking, sweetheart?"

Her face flushed and she opened her mouth as if to say something before suddenly launching herself at him. "Oh my God, it was so bad listening to my mother discuss anal plugs, but the rest of it was just hot . . . Brant?"

With her warm body pressed against his almost naked one, he barely managed to get out, "Hmmm?"

"I'm so horny I can't stand it. Please fuck me . . . now . . . right here."

His cock was rigid, ready to give her anything she wanted. He couldn't believe he had any thoughts of objecting, but still he had to be the voice of reason. "Your parents . . ."

By this time, she had all but climbed him like a tree. "Their bedroom is on the first floor at the other end of the house. They won't hear us."

It still felt wrong, but by that point he no longer cared.

Putting his hands on her ass, he ground himself against her. "I'll fuck you, baby, and I'll even spank you." At her moan of approval, he stripped her clothes off and dropped his towel. He turned the shower back on and backed her inside. He hoped the water would disguise any sounds just in case someone was nearby. He plucked a condom from his shaving kit on the sink and sheathed himself before following her in. He took a moment to appreciate the picture that she made with the water running in rivulets down her beautifully curved body. Her breasts were the perfect-size handful for him, with rosy nipples that looked like raspberries. Lower down, her pubic hair was neatly trimmed and her shapely thighs were moving restlessly. It seemed that neither of them could wait another moment.

He backed against the wall, bracing her. She wrapped her legs around his waist and met his mouth as it came down on hers. Their tongues clashed and he held her hips up before plunging her down onto his cock. "Brant . . ." she moaned. He could feel her nails score his back as they both raced desperately toward the peak. He figured by this point that water was probably flying out of the shower and drenching the bathroom, but he didn't care. All that mattered was the woman wrapped around him. There was no illusion of control left; they had both lost it with his first thrust. He continued to pound into her velvet heat and she ground herself against him. When a strangled cry tore from her throat, he felt her body go stiff and then shudder. She spasmed around his hard cock as her release seemed to go on and on. He held off as long as he could, letting her ride the peak before he erupted inside her.

They both slid to the floor of the shower, letting the water pelt them. When he had recovered enough to move, he juggled the still limp Emma in his arms and managed to step out onto the rug in front of the shower without injuring them both. They quickly dried off without speaking. It was a comfortable silence. He suspected they were both too exhausted after traveling and having shower sex to attempt conversation.

Next Emma dropped her towel and pulled a T-shirt out of her bag before scooting under the bedcovers. She slid to one side and without asking, he slid in behind her. In his experience, it was always easier to ask for forgiveness than permission anyway. He was surprised when she turned and settled against his side, curling around his body like a lazy cat. He stiffened for a moment before pulling her closer. He hadn't slept this intimately with a woman since Alexia, and if he had stopped to think about it, it would have scared the hell out of him. And yet he couldn't resist her.

Emma woke slowly. She was in the middle of a yawn when she noticed the time on the alarm clock. Was it really after eleven already? She rarely slept that late— even on the weekends. As she stretched she noticed that her body ached in all of those long-neglected places from the previous night. Just remembering how she had practically attacked Brant made her groan and bury her head in the pillow. The man never stood a chance.

Reading an erotic book got to her every time, and

last night had been no exception. Even with her mother's book club taking some of the thrill out of it, she had still been turned on from reviewing the hot and heavy scenes of *Fifty Shades of Grey*. If he had been asleep, she might have left him in peace, but there was no way she could stop herself when she saw him standing in the bathroom almost naked. Heck, nothing short of divine intervention could have stopped her at that point. The man had a drool-worthy body and, oh baby, did he know how to use it!

Most of her past orgasms had been at her own hands. With Brant, though, she could feel her orgasm building from the moment he entered her. She had now slept with her boss twice. There was no way this could end well. Their whole relationship was built on mutual disrespect. She was now taking the term *"sleeping with the enemy"* to a whole new level. It had to stop . . . didn't it? So what if he was God's gift to women in bed? He was still the same Brant Stone that she loved to loathe.

She had put in yet another transfer request before they'd left together for Florida. Yeah, it really looked like she wanted out from under him, didn't it? *Ugh, I'm the office slut now.* It felt like everything was catching up to her as she walked dejectedly toward the bathroom to shower and then hunt down the missing Brant. Maybe the situation was still salvageable. She could stop anytime she wanted to, right? She had complete control over her body. There was no way she was going to lose it just because she lusted after him.

Chapter Nine

Her whole pep talk was in danger of going up in flames simply from looking at Brant sitting on the deck with her father reading the morning paper. *Oh yum! Why does casual have to look so good on him?* Emma wanted to turn around, run upstairs and jump back in the shower . . . this time for a cold one. He was in another pair of cargo shorts paired with a black T-shirt. The thin cotton of the shirt showed clearly defined muscles, and she knew from experience that his stomach was a perfect V-shape. He had mentioned previously that he liked to run every morning. Since finding out by accident that he lived on the beach, she now knew where those runs took place.

Her father looked up with a smile. "Good morning, sleepyhead. We all slept in, but I think you and your mother took it a bit too far. Brant here had already been running on the beach and made a pot of coffee when I wandered down." It was obvious from her father's warm tone that Brant had been accepted into the family fold. They were going to be disappointed when she pretend broke up with him.

Brant held up the coffeepot and motioned her to the seat beside him. "Morning, baby, coffee?" When she nodded, he poured her a cup and leaned down to give her a hard kiss on the mouth before putting the pot back. She was momentarily surprised at how natural it felt to be greeted by him in that manner. While Brant had a lively discussion with her father on who was going to win the Florida–South Carolina game that evening, he absently ran a hand up and down her back. It felt too good for her to pull away.

"So, you two ready for the big event tonight?" Emma looked at her father blankly before it registered that he was referring to the reunion.

"Er . . . yeah, I guess." Emma had never felt less enthusiastic about anything—except maybe for her recent root canal. The thought of having to make small talk with people she hadn't seen for years held little appeal now. She would much rather be somewhere alone with Brant and that, she thought dejectedly, was the problem. Just last week, she would have rather been anywhere in the world than with her insufferable boss. Now she couldn't think of anyone else that she would rather spend time with. She knew in her heart that as soon as they returned home, this strange new thing would be over.

But it shocked her to realize that she could hardly stand to think of him going cold on her again. Did he feel anything at all toward her or was he just a good actor? She could have sworn she saw real affection in his gaze this morning. It was probably just for her father's benefit, but it had made her heart beat madly.

"Penny for your thoughts . . ." She looked up flushing as she realized that her father had left the table and Brant was looking at her curiously. "You looked like you were a million miles away."

"I . . . sorry. I think I'm still tired."

He gave her what she could only call a wicked grin. "Something wore you out last night, huh? Maybe a shower would help wake you."

Giving an unladylike snort, she said, "I've already had a shower."

Brant lowered his voice and let his hand slide against the curve of her ass. "I didn't mean alone."

Oh my God, the sexy Brant from the previous night was still very much front and center this morning. He moved her hair aside and nibbled her ear. Shivers raced up her spine and her body caught fire. "Mmmm," she moaned quietly before she could stop herself. Her hand tangled in his hair without conscious thought and next thing she knew she was out of her chair and on his lap. She felt him hard against her bottom as she wrapped her legs around his waist. His eyes blazed into hers for a moment before their mouths met, tongue to tongue, all-consuming. "Brant . . ."

His tongue took control and dominated hers. She was helpless to deny him anything as he plundered her mouth. The voice in her head was screaming loudly, *What are you doing?* It was going to have to come up with something better than that if there was any hope of making her back away from the amazing mouth devouring hers.

"Good morning, kids!"

Yeah, that would do it, Emma thought as she jerked away from Brant. Her mother's loud, chipper greeting was enough to douse the flames that had been consuming her.

To his credit, Brant continued to hold her loosely in his lap as he smiled a greeting at her mother. "Good morning, Kat." Emma was relieved to note that her mother had her purse and keys in her hand. Thank God for small miracles. She wasn't up to a grilling session over her relationship with Brant.

"I have to take Sandra for her laser eye surgery. Her daughter was supposed to take her, but she canceled at the last minute. What time are you leaving tonight? I wanted to be here to take pictures."

"Mom," Emma groaned, "it's a reunion, not the prom. We'll probably leave early so we can have dinner first."

"Honey, I need to capture you and this hunk beside you on film. I have the picture I took of you two last night with my phone, but I need a better one for Facebook."

Emma felt Brant's body shaking as he laughed. She couldn't believe Mr. Conservative wasn't freaking out at the thought of having his image plastered all over Facebook.

"You're no help," she grumbled to him. Then turning back to her mother, she added, "If we don't see you before we leave, I'm sure we will when we get home. Now you'd better hurry so Sandra isn't late to her appointment."

Her mother gave her a hug and a kiss on the fore-head and then surprised her by repeating the gesture on Brant. "Enjoy the beach today. Your father is work-ing for a while, but Robyn said she would stop by sometime."

Emma untangled herself from Brant's lap when her mother left. "I don't know about you, but that was the equivalent of a cold shower." Taking his hand, she pulled him up behind her. "Let's go change and grab a paddleboard."

She smiled when she heard Brant ask warily, "Pad-dleboard?"

Chapter Ten

Brant's breath caught in his throat as Emma made her way down the stairs. She was wearing a white, above-the-knee dress that made her legs look a mile long. The dress hugged her figure and showed off her tanned skin to perfection. Her brown hair cascaded down her back in a jumble of loose curls. He wanted to bury his hands in the soft mass and devour her. He wanted to take her somewhere and just lose himself in her until he could no longer remember all of the reasons that getting involved with her was wrong.

But he had been down this road before and he knew where it led.

Emma was even more of a risk than Alexia. Standing before her in his black suit, he had never felt more unworthy of someone. She was beautiful, sexy, a free spirit . . . and he didn't have the first clue as to what to do with her. If he wasn't enough for his first love, there was no way Emma would ever be seriously interested in him. She would be back to hating him as soon as their play-cation was over. The person he had been pretending to be while they were here wasn't who he really was. In reality, he was the tightass that she had so often accused him of being. The surprising thing about this trip was how much he had enjoyed acting like someone who didn't take everything so seriously. He hadn't even bothered to check his company e-mail this morning, which was a first for him.

He knew their time was coming to a close soon and he wanted to enjoy every moment of being the man that she seemed to want. He took her hand when she reached the last step and pulled her against him. "You're stunning." When he picked up a box from the table beside him, she gave him a questioning look. "I know you said this wasn't the prom, but I decided to cover my bases." In truth, he had called a local florist earlier and bribed the owner to make a late Saturday delivery.

Emma smiled when he opened the box to show a delicate orchid corsage. "Oh, Brant, it's beautiful." She reached up and pressed her lips against his softly. "I love it."

His hands shook slightly as he pinned the flower against the shoulder of her dress. This was unfamiliar territory for him and he was afraid he was going to stick the pin through her delicate skin. God, he could barely remember a time when his life was carefree enough to just be in the moment. Even with Alexia, he had always held a part of himself back. He had loved her but was very aware that bad things could happen to people you loved. In his experience, there was less pain if you kept your heart better insulated. After all, something bad was bound to happen sooner or later. He had thought that Alexia was fine with that until she walked away.

Emma, he knew, would never be content with half of anyone. A relationship with her would mean he'd have to be all in. She didn't do anything in life halfway. She would love hard and completely. He had no clue how to approach something like that. Once she figured out that he was not capable of being more than he was, she would be gone. He could live out the fantasy for the weekend, but things between them had to end when the plane touched down at home. No party could last forever.

The reunion was in full swing when they arrived. Brant had insisted on hiring a car and driver for the evening and, from the looks of the well-stocked bar, Emma thought that was probably a good idea. She figured it was largely due to the fact that he didn't want to take her old car, rather than worrying about alcohol, but she had decided to let it go. She'd already sent Brant off to get her first drink of the evening, needing some time to compose herself. She had been floored when he had produced a corsage earlier. Such thoughtful gestures were something she would have never thought Brant was capable of. Heck, she would have never imagined him capable of all that he had been for the last few days—Mr. December was also Mr. Multi-Orgasm, Mr. Sensitive, Mr. Gentle and Mr. Personality, just to name a few.

On top of that, her parents were completely in love with him and, if she didn't take control of her traitorous heart, she would be right there with them. Her pretend boyfriend was turning out to be the best man she had ever had in her life. She had even taken to chanting under her breath, "It's not real, it's not real." He had actually caught her doing it earlier and she had brushed it away explaining that she was saying, "I need a meal." Yeah, she wasn't a fast thinker on her feet, but he seemed satisfied and had promptly ushered her in for lunch.

They had spent the day on the beach. She had discovered that Brant was possibly part fish because there was nothing he couldn't do in the water. Some of those things would have probably gotten them arrested. He was a natural at paddleboarding although he claimed to have never tried it before. He was also well above average in the surfing department. She, on the other hand, had been so distracted by his gorgeous body in his Nike board shorts that she had tumbled into the waves times and again. She was sure that he knew the effect he was having on her. He never missed an opportunity to touch her whenever he was close. If not for her sister dropping by for a few moments to chat as they were making their way upstairs, she would have surely attacked him in the shower again. Unfortunately, now she was horny and in for a long evening before she could do anything about it.

Yeah, bring on the alcohol; maybe it could cool the flames roaring inside her. She had never felt the need to masturbate in public, but she hadn't ruled it out this evening. Brant had her completely on edge.

Emma jumped when she felt a hand on her lower back. When a fruity drink was pressed in her hand, she looked up to give Brant a grateful smile. His answering sexy grin turned questioning when she immediately drained half of the glass. She couldn't detect any alcohol, and she wondered how bad it would look if she asked him to get her a glass of straight-up vodka.

"You'd better take it easy, baby; drinks like that will bring you to your knees."

Emma could see the exact moment that they both got a visual of just what she could be doing on her knees. As his eyes locked on hers, he pulled her body closer to his, murmuring in her ear, "Well, maybe that wouldn't be such a bad thing."

Her nipples hardened and she clenched her legs together, trying to relieve the pressure there. This conversation so wasn't helping. She was one suggestive comment away from ripping his clothes off in front of the crowd and making this a reunion that no one would ever forget.

"Emma!" That was the only warning she received before someone almost knocked her off her feet. "Oh my freaking God, I can't believe you're here!" She was forced from Brant's arms when her friend Madison pulled her into a rib-breaking hug.

"Maddie! I so hoped you would be here." Emma was thrilled to see her old friend. Other than the hem of her dress being even higher now, Madison had changed very little. Her long blond hair was still the same super-straight style that Emma had always envied and her skin still held that sun-kissed golden glow.

Madison had always been much more outgoing than Emma, especially where the opposite sex was concerned. She knew nothing had changed in that area when Madison said, "Girl, I'm gonna be honest. I have been staring at this stone-cold fox you're with since I got here and hating the tramp plastered all over him. When I finally looked away from his luscious buns long enough to glare daggers at the tramp, I figured out it was you!"

Emma laughed helplessly at her friend's colorful description while beside her Brant had stiffened. She didn't know if he was offended at being called a stone-cold fox or by her being called a tramp. Possibly a little of both. She took his hand, giving it a squeeze for reassurance.

"Brant, this is my friend Madison." And then because she couldn't resist, she added, "I believe you went to college with her old boyfriend Paul." She could see the exact moment that he made the connection in his head.

She fully expected him to excuse himself and head for the door, so she was surprised when he gave Madison a dazzling smile and said, "Paul always was a lucky bastard." As soon as he spoke, it was clear Madison was officially in love with him, and Emma was at a complete loss. As her friend hung all over her fake boyfriend, Emma had to wonder if maybe she didn't miss the usual tightass Brant just a tiny bit. This one was unpredictable. Things that would normally freak him out didn't seem to faze him at all.

Before Emma could blink, there were three more of her old friends, Meg, Tina and Jill, gathered around them. Even David, who her mother had targeted as a possible reunion date, had joined them. Emma had to admit her mother was right—David was a damn nice-looking guy. The problem was, though, he, like her other friends, seemed more interested in Brant's attention than hers. Fifteen minutes later she was sipping her second drink and trying not to stare daggers at her friends. Was this what being jealous felt like? Brant, to his credit, had kept a firm hold on her hand no matter who attempted to squeeze her out. When Jill asked him to dance, she was relieved. Jill was happily married, even though she hadn't seen her husband yet tonight. Brant released Emma's hand and escorted Jill to the dance floor. Emma was floored when Jill put her arms around his neck and plastered herself against Brant. "What the hell?"

Madison stood beside her surveying the scene. "Yeah, I can't believe you let that happen. The girl has turned into a major slut since Dean left her."

Whirling around, Emma gasped in horror. "What? Why I am just hearing about this?"

"I have no idea; your mother must not gossip as much as mine." Yeah, right, Emma thought. Her mother never missed anything . . . so why didn't she know about Jill's divorce? She would have at least warned Brant ahead of time.

"Damn, would you look at that," Madison said. "I can't believe she went there."

Emma shut her eyes and opened them again before she could muster up the strength to look back over at the dance floor. No, it wasn't a dream; her friend had her hand on Brant's ass. She was just fixing to march over there and make a huge scene when Brant took Jill's hand and gently but firmly removed it from his backside. Whatever he said to her must have been effective because her hand stayed where he placed it without roving again.

David had come back from the bar and turned his head to see what they were looking at. With a sigh, he said, "I don't guess he's gay."

"Um, no," Emma grumbled, "he is definitely not." My God, couldn't any of her friends keep their eyes and their hands off her man? Okay, well, maybe he wasn't really her man, but he damn well was tonight— and it was time she staked her claim. As she set her drink down, the room started spinning for a moment. When she had cleared her head enough to proceed, she noticed that Jill was no longer alone with Brant on the dance floor. Madison, Meg and Tina had now joined them as the music changed from a slow song to a faster number. Emma watched in shock as Brant moved like he was Justin Freaking Timberlake. Why was he torturing her like this? She had wanted him to impress her friends as a good piece of arm candy, but she hadn't actually wanted them to admire him enough to follow him like the Pied Piper.

If the looks he was receiving were any indication, the women loved him and the men hated him. Her Mr. December had taken the reunion by storm, and she didn't think there was anyone in the room who wasn't affected by him in some way. Had she created a monster?

Emma moved up behind him, sliding her arm around his waist as she moved her hips against his. *That's right, baby. I saw* Dirty Dancing *at least a dozen times.* He stiffened against her for a moment until he recognized her. He turned, pulling her against him, chest to chest. He whispered in her ear as they danced together, "Interesting friends."

"I didn't see you complaining when Jill grabbed a handful of your ass." Beside her, Madison raised a brow. Whoops, maybe that was a little louder than she had planned. Jill seemed to be oblivious, though.

Brant circled his tongue around the shell of her ear as he replied, "I only want your hand on my ass, baby. I think Jill knows that now."

The desire she had been battling all evening came surging back, and she felt with certainty that if she didn't have him soon, she would explode. She wasn't sure whether a person could actually die of horniness, but it wasn't a risk she was willing to take. Grabbing his hand, she pulled him toward the nearest exit. She heard her friends cheering her on and knew her intentions must be obvious. When they made it into the night air, she took a deep breath. Beside her, Brant put a hand against the small of her back and asked, "What's up? Are you feeling sick?"

Shaking her head, Emma pulled his lips down to hers and started devouring his mouth like the starving, sex-crazed person she had become. Brant moaned against her, backing her into a secluded corner of the building before pulling her tightly against him. As with most of their encounters, slow and sweet wasn't in the cards. It was frantic, hot and bordering on insanity. When Brant ran his hand under her dress and snapped the delicate thread of her thong, she attempted to clamp her legs around his waist. Tonight, though, he had other ideas. He turned her to face the wall behind them and braced her hands against it. The sound of his zipper lowering was magnified in the quiet surrounding them. She heard him curse under his breath as he fumbled with a condom. His fingers probed between her legs. When he was satisfied that she was more than ready, he pushed into her from behind. The angle provided a deep penetration that had her on the verge of orgasm with just one thrust. He held still for a moment, letting her adjust before retreating. She pushed her hips against his, soon meeting him thrust for thrust. His large hands cupped her breasts, squeezing the nipples to the point of pain as his hips slammed into hers over and over.

Emma heard the sound of car doors just as her body started to spasm. Brant put his hand against her mouth, and she bit into his finger to stifle the sounds of her scream as she climaxed. Behind her, she heard Brant's muffled curse as he exploded inside her. He continued to slide his cock in and out of her, slowly bringing them both back from the edge. She collapsed against the wall of his chest, grateful for the support that it offered.

"Fuck, that was off the charts," he murmured as he pressed a kiss against her neck. She nodded her agreement, still too out of breath to reply. He braced her body with one hand, while he pulled his trousers up and zipped them with the other hand. She felt him stroke the curve of her ass before he pulled her dress down. "I think you and I need to find a restroom before we go back in. Right now, it's obvious what we've been up to."

Emma agreed with him even though going inside was the last thing she wanted to do. She would have loved nothing better than to curl up in Brant's arms and spend the rest of the night there. If she did, though, Madison was sure to tell her mother, who would tell Emma's mother, and the gossip would go on and on. She also hated to leave without telling her friend good-bye since she so rarely got to see her anymore. She stifled a giggle as Brant reached down to pick up her ruined underwear and put them in his pocket. He gave her a wolfish grin as they both straightened their clothing to a decent level before walking back in the side door.

Luckily, the restrooms were close to the entrance and mostly deserted. Emma did what she could to restore order to her appearance and walked back out to find

Brant waiting for her. He dropped a kiss onto her forehead before leading her inside. Emma felt almost sad as they rejoined the group of her friends. After believing that she detested Brant for so long, she was now facing the undeniable truth that there was more between them than simple contempt. Standing in front of him, pulled against his chest and anchored there with his arms, she wished more than ever that this was real.

She didn't want to pretend anymore. She wanted whatever had been happening between them this weekend to continue. Her heart was going to break on Monday morning when she walked into the office and Brant treated her like nothing more than his assistant. Shit! This had been a bad idea from the start. Life was so much easier before. They might not have had a great relationship, but it was one that they both understood. He didn't like her and she didn't like him. They both mostly enjoyed their verbal wordplay, but that was it. Truth be told, the arguments with Brant made her job more interesting. Even when he pissed her off, things were never boring. She put in the transfer requests only because she knew he wouldn't approve them. She wasn't sure what she would do if he ever did. Now, though, she was forced to admit the horrible truth that she had been denying, even to herself: She was in love with Brant Stone and had been for a while. He was everything she said that she hated, but it was a lie. She loved him right down to his boring black suits and matching, nondescript ties. She was in *so* much trouble.

*   *   *

Brant discreetly removed Jill's hand as it crept closer to his crotch yet again. He thought he had made himself clear to her earlier when she had grabbed his ass on the dance floor. He had nicely but firmly told her he was involved with Emma and he wasn't interested. She had handled that pretty well until she had tossed back another half-dozen drinks. Actually, the whole crowd was consuming alcohol as if they had just been threatened with Prohibition at midnight.

Emma's friends had settled into a table in the back of the room and, unfortunately, Jill had immediately taken the vacant seat on the other side of him. She told him all about her husband dumping her for another woman. He figured her husband probably got tired of having his cock grabbed in public and packed his bags.

Emma had been quiet after their spontaneous combustion against the side of the building. He had been on the verge of asking her if she was feeling okay when Madison jumped up and pulled Emma out of her seat. Soon they were on the dance floor doing some dirty dancing moves that had him breaking out into a cold sweat. How could he possibly be hard again this soon? It had nothing to do with Jill's wandering hands and everything to do with the siren in the white dress looking at him so provocatively as she danced with her friend. Damn it, she was killing him. He barely recognized who he was at this point. He had torn up the dance floor with a group of strangers, thanking God along the way that he watched *Dancing With the Stars* often enough to function. He had slow danced with a woman with at least five sets of hands, and he had fucked Emma outside against a building for anyone to see. This was not him at all. He wasn't a man led around by his penis or his heart. He felt completely out of control and yet . . . he couldn't remember enjoying anything in recent memory as much as he had enjoyed this weekend with Emma. Could he turn something from make-believe to real? Did he really want to go there with her?

"God, you're gorgeous," Emma's familiar sexy voice purred against his neck. He jerked back in surprise. He had been so lost in thought, he hadn't seen her return from the dance floor. She was flushed and her eyes were bright, possibly with one too many daiquiris.

He pulled her against him, settling her in his lap. His cock was thrilled with her close proximity, although a bit frustrated with the barriers between them. "Hey, baby, I enjoyed your dance, although I would have preferred watching it in private." She wiggled her bottom against his hard ridge, causing shivers to shoot through him. "Behave before I embarrass myself in public."

"Mmm, I'd love that," she teased. He was thrilled when she added, "I'm ready to go whenever you are. I don't think I have another dance left in me." Almost before she could finish that thought, Brant had them up and saying their good-byes to her friends. Another minute later and they were back in the humid night air. His driver and car were parked around the corner, and a quick call had them picked up and settled in the back.

He would love nothing better than to skip going

back to her parents' house and find a nice hotel for the rest of the night. Unfortunately, they had a very early flight home tomorrow and they would have to pick up their luggage. It just wasn't workable. Maybe if they were quiet, though, her parents wouldn't have to know that he was having sex with their daughter under their roof . . . again. Yeah, he could do quiet.

When they pulled up to the house, he helped a sleepy Emma to the door. It took another few minutes to locate the key in her purse. A lamp was on in the foyer, but there was no sign of anyone awake. Things were definitely going his way so far. Emma giggled and groped him all the way up the stairs. He gave her a lingering kiss before making a quick trip to the bathroom. When he returned to the bedroom ready to continue their foreplay, he was brought up short. Emma was sprawled out on the bed, sound asleep and snoring like a sailor. Her dress had ridden up, exposing the tops of her creamy thighs. He tried not to dwell on the fact that she wasn't wearing underwear. Sighing, he dropped to her side and removed her shoes. He lifted her slightly to pull up the bedcovers and then settled her back beneath them. Maybe it was better this way. Sex could only cloud things further between them.

He knew tomorrow was likely to be a difficult and confusing day, and he probably needed all of his wits to make some decisions. He had started to hope that she was as interested as he was in seeing where things might lead between them. There was no way this could have all been an act on her part. He didn't know what he felt for her, but he did know that it was completely foreign to him. He had never been this messed up over Alexia, even when she left him. There was something big happening between them, at least on his part, and he was both anxious and terrified to know how she felt.

The last thought he had before drifting into sleep was that the woman beside him held the long-lost key to his heart.

Chapter Eleven

Emma found herself sitting on the airplane beside Brant not having a clue as to what to do. The morning had passed in a blur. They had been up early for their flight and she barely had time for a good-bye hug from her mother and father before Brant was rushing her out the door and into a taxi. Since they were up late the night before, the ride to the airport was spent in companionable silence as they both dozed lightly. Now, on the plane, the first moment of awkwardness had arrived. She wanted to reach over and take his hand, but she didn't know if that was okay anymore. Was their time officially over now? As she continued to sit quietly, racked by indecision, Brant reached over and took her hand in his, settling them both in his lap. She felt her body relax. Everything was still okay between them. She leaned her head on his shoulder.

"You're quiet this morning," he murmured against the top of her head.

She quickly blinked back tears. God, she had gotten so attached to that voice this weekend. Whereas once a statement like that from him would have pissed her off, now it just made her sad. She wished the plane ride were longer. Here, pressed against his warmth, was where she wanted to stay. Should she just put her feelings out there? The worst that could happen was that he didn't feel the same way. "I'm . . . um . . . just tired from last night, I guess." Shit! She couldn't force the words that she wanted to say past her lips. She just couldn't bear to have it end yet. For the next two hours, he was still hers and, right now, that was something she wasn't willing to risk. "Speaking of last night, where did you get those dance moves? I never would have believed you had it in you." She smiled as he chuckled.

"Some television and a lot of improvising. It helped that everyone was too drunk to notice the times I almost tripped over my own feet. I really enjoyed your friends. Well, with the exception of Jill. She's not easily deterred."

Emma pulled back, looking up into his smiling eyes. "That was a different Jill from the one I knew in school. Madison said she has been going through a divorce and I believe she was a bit desperate to prove that she's still got it. In her defense, you looked pretty hot last night."

Brant gave her a surprised but pleased look. "I . . . really?" It was obvious that he wasn't used to compliments, and she felt a guilty pang that he had certainly not received any from her in the time they had known each other. Most of her comments to him were negative and critical. That he enjoyed finally being on the receiving end of something positive was apparent. Why oh why couldn't they have met under different circumstances? At work they had rubbed each other wrong almost from the start. Would things have been different if they had met somewhere else? He had been so caring, attentive, funny and affectionate all weekend. It was hard to believe that it was all an act. Somewhere inside of him, that man had to exist. Maybe if there hadn't been an underlying attraction between them from the beginning, things would never have escalated to the love/hate, well, mostly hate, relationship that they had. It was never too late to try to change things, was it?

Giving his hand a squeeze, she said, "Oh yeah, you knocked my friends for a loop. Even David couldn't keep his eyes off you."

Pulling their clasped hands to his lips, he kissed her knuckles. "No one held a candle to you. I was the envy of every man there." Emma felt herself doing something she rarely did: blushing. There was no doubting the sincerity of his words. She almost told him how she felt then and there, but the flight attendant picked that moment to start the beverage service and the moment was lost. Instead, she curled against him as much as the small space would allow and enjoyed feeling the steady beat of his heart against her ear as the last moments of the flight passed so much faster than she wanted.

*   *   *

Brant pulled the last of their bags from the baggage carousel and wondered to himself, *What now?* Emma was standing beside him awkwardly. "Did you drive to the airport?" he asked.

"No, root canal, remember? I was too high to attempt that." They both laughed for a moment, remembering all that had taken place after her out-of-it plane ride to Miami. He was secretly relieved to have an excuse to extend their time together. He wanted nothing more than to ask her to come home with him, but he wasn't sure how she would feel about it.

He took her carry-on bag from her. "Come on, baby, I'll give you a ride." Damn, was it okay to call her *baby* now? Should he have just said Emma? She didn't seem uncomfortable over his slip, so he decided to relax and stop overthinking everything. If she jumped out of the car at her apartment without looking back, he would know that she wasn't feeling what he was. Simple, right? Fuck, except why did it feel anything but?

Emma came to an abrupt halt when they reached his car. He popped the trunk of his Mercedes SL550 and stored their luggage inside. She gave him an incredulous look. "You drive a sports car?"

He paused in the act of opening her door. "Why is that a surprise?"

"This is one sexy car, Brant. I always had you figured for more of a car and driver or maybe a Volvo."

He couldn't help it. Rather than take offense, he burst out laughing. "I know there's an insult in there. I find it hard to believe you've never seen my car in all this time since we work at the same place."

Putting her hands on her hips, she smirked up at him. "Honey, there is a bit of distance between the executive parking and the rest of the Danvers staff parking. You guys probably have some kind of protective cover pulled over your vehicles during the day."

"It doesn't get that good. You didn't notice it when you were invading my beach area a few weeks ago?"

"Um . . . no," Emma said. "I was too busy trying to get away from you to peek in your garage." Opening the car door herself, she jumped inside. "I'm not complaining; this car is off the charts!" Brant whistled as he walked around the car to open the driver's door. At least he knew there was one thing of his that impressed her. Maybe he would keep her in the car for the rest of the night. The way she was purring against the leather seats, she probably wouldn't complain.

She gave him her address and it took him a moment to figure out why it sounded familiar. "Isn't that the complex that Nick and Beth live in?"

Nodding, Emma said, "It used to be. They bought a house closer to Suzy a few months ago."

Brant shuddered. "That's one scary lady."

Emma asked, "Suzy?"

"Yeah, Suzy. Don't look so surprised. All of you women may love her, but she makes most of the men at Danvers want to cover their balls and run."

"Oh, come on!" Emma defended her friend. "What has she ever done to you?"

Cringing, Brant said, "It's not what she's done to me; it's how she looks at me. Sort of like I'm a cross between a toad and a cockroach. I feel like I've really disappointed her at some point, but I have no idea when."

Putting her fingers up to form quotation marks, Emma teased, "She thinks you're 'prime man candy,' which is a major compliment."

Brant smirked back at her. "I believe you mentioned something along those lines when you were intoxicated on the plane. If my memory serves me correctly, you also agreed with her." Before she could answer, he added, "Now, I found that very flattering but also a bit disturbing that I was the subject of such an . . . intimate conversation."

Emma slid her hand along his thigh, murmuring, "Oh, honey, you have no idea."

Before their flirtation could escalate, Brant was pulling into the driveway of her apartment complex. A sudden onset of nerves seemed to hold them both speechless. Should he ask to come in or let her make the first move? Wasn't the guy usually expected to do that? Hell, he didn't know and he'd never really cared before. You didn't have these kinds of complications with casual sex. Everything was defined ahead of time. Now he felt like he had been reduced to a teenage boy on his first real date.

This kind of indecision was completely foreign to him. A few days ago, he would have imagined the final leg of this journey being much different. He could think only that if he had been forced to take her home, he would have brought the car to some kind of a rolling stop and asked her to jump out. When she did, he would have peeled out of the parking lot in his haste to finally be free of her after a weekend of complete hell.

The reality now, though, was so different. Just a few days with someone whom he finally admitted to himself that he desired had changed everything. He wanted nothing more than to follow her into her apartment and make love to her until they both passed out from sheer exhaustion. The fact that he thought of it as making love and not having sex was not lost on him. "So . . . do you . . ." They both almost jumped out of their skin when Emma's phone shrilled in the confined space of the car. He thought he heard her mutter a curse under her breath when she looked at the screen.

Brant saw her wage a mental debate before clicking to answer the call. "Hi, Mom, can I call you back in a bit? We just got home." She listened for a minute before exclaiming, "What! Oh crap, are you kidding me?"

Brant laid a hand over hers, quietly asking, "Is something wrong?"

Putting her hand over the phone, she said, "Boston got busted in a campus raid for possession of marijuana."

He fought the urge to ask why they were so surprised by that fact but decided now might not be the best time to point that out.

"Mom, let me get in my apartment and I'll keep trying to reach Uncle Ted." She clicked to end the call and sagged back against the seat. "I so didn't need this to-day." She turned her head to look at him. "I have to go in and try to reach my dad's brother, Ted. He's a lawyer in Destin." Brant did his best to hide a smile when she repeated his earlier thoughts. "Why is any of this surprising? Everyone in the family knows he is high as a kite more often than not. He's studying botany, for God's sake. Not only is he constantly smoking weed, apparently he's growing the stuff as well."

"What can I do to help?" he asked.

"Turn my brother into a scholar and not a pothead?" she asked hopefully.

Kissing her hand, he smiled. "Sorry, baby. That may be a tall order. How about I help you inside with your bags and let you do what you need to do for your family?" He could tell by the longing in her expression that they had both had other ideas about how the evening would end and now that was over. She needed to help her brother and that would be easier for her if he went home and let her concentrate.

He didn't know if it was his imagination, but their pace seemed to drag by mutual consent as they made it up the one flight of stairs to her apartment. She opened the door and he had just a glimpse of the brightly painted wall behind her before she turned in the doorway. He gave her a gentle kiss on the lips, mindful of the fact that neither of them needed to end the night any more frustrated than they already were. "Brant . . ."

He put his finger against her lips. "I know . . . I'll see

you tomorrow. If something comes up and you need the day off, just call me."

With one more brief brush against her lips, he forced himself to turn and retrace his steps. Fuck, his life seemed to be filled with bad timing.

Chapter Twelve

Brant was at the office early the next morning. He tried telling himself it was just to get through the backlog of work waiting for him, but he knew it was to see Emma. They could go to lunch together later on and talk about what was going on between them. He smiled to himself, thinking it would be a better meal than the cold sandwiches she usually brought back on her own for him. As he walked through the lobby of the Danvers International building, he was surprised to see Mac there waiting for the elevator. Mackinley Powers had been a friend of the family for many years. He and Brant's brother, Declan, had enlisted in the marines together and served a couple of tours before coming home. Mac ran a security company with Danvers as one of its clients so it wasn't unusual to see him in the building. Plus, he was a very hands-on boss and didn't leave much to chance. He turned as he heard Brant approach. Mac clapped him on the shoulder. "Hey, good morning, man, didn't know you were back yet."

"Morning, Mac. Yeah, we got in yesterday. This is an early morning for you, isn't it?"

Grimacing, Mac said, "For sure, but I offered to cover for one of my guys today. His mom was having surgery so he needed to be there. I was just going to do a walk-through before things got under way today. I had dinner with Declan, Ella and Evan last night. Shit, that's really hard to adjust to now, but I'm happy for him."

Brant smiled in return. He had similar feelings where his brother was concerned. It was almost surreal to have the wild child of the family married with a new baby on the way and a son. When Declan discovered that he had fathered a child six years ago from a one-night stand, he had stepped up to the plate and was now an active parent to Evan. Coincidentally, a short time later, his new wife, Ella, had found out she was pregnant. It was a huge shift in Declan's life after leaving the military and suffering from post-traumatic stress syndrome over the death of a friend in Afghanistan. Ella had helped him turn it all around and now he was the most content that Brant had ever seen him. "I know what you mean. It's been hard for me to believe as well, but he deserves it. Was Ava also there?"

Mac looked away, obviously uncomfortable with the question. "No, I left before she arrived. It's . . . just different now."

Brant looked at Mac, surprised by his shuttered expression. For as long as he could remember, Mac had been in love with his sister. He knew that she loved him in her own way, but so far that hadn't been enough to make her take a chance, and now maybe that would never happen. "Has something happened between you two?"

Sighing, Mac said, "No, not at all and that's the problem. I told Declan a while back that I needed to move on with my life and Ava shows no signs of wanting to be a part of that." Mac looked at him almost apologetically. "I'm sorry, man. I really am. I'm not abandoning her; I'll always be here if she needs me, but in a different way."

Brant felt a pang for his sister, realizing that she was about to throw away the best thing to ever happen to her, and yet there wasn't anything he could do to stop it. Maybe Ava, like Declan, would have to hit rock bottom in order to come back up for air. Hell, maybe there was something in all this that he needed to be paying attention to. Did he want to be alone and closed off to the world forever like Ava? Holding out a hand to Mac, he shook the other man's hand. "I understand. No one's going to think less of you, Mac. You've always been there for Ava and I know you'll continue to watch over her. Maybe she needs to be forced from her comfort zone."

Mac gave him a skeptical look. "I wish it were that easy. But I've started putting some distance between us and I will talk to her soon. Truthfully, I've been putting that off because I'm not ready to see her indifference about me."

Brant couldn't imagine his sister being indifferent to

Mac moving on and finding love somewhere else, but he couldn't be sure. He may be emotionally reserved, but Ava was emotionally detached, which, in his estimate, was hard to overcome. He and Mac parted ways at the elevator and he walked toward his office even more determined to pursue a relationship with Emma.

Brant looked up from his computer as the sound of movement in the outer office caught his attention. Anticipation filled him as a knock sounded on the door. He was momentarily surprised because Emma usually sailed into his office without bothering to knock. He grinned, yelling out, "Come in."

His surprise turned to shock as the door opened and Alexia Shaw walked hesitantly into his office. It seemed they were both momentarily at a loss for words before he finally remembered his manners and stood. "Alexia?" He knew that his greeting came out more like a question, but he was powerless to stop it. The same shy smile was there, but she looked very different from the last time they had seen each other. She was thinner, bordering on too skinny, and her hair was shorter and pulled back into a ponytail.

Alexia looked nervous as she closed the door behind her. He walked around the desk to greet her. They exchanged an awkward hug before he indicated one of the chairs in front of the desk. Frankly, he was afraid she would fall over if she stood much longer. "Hi, Brant," she said quietly. "It's so good to see you again. I know this must be a bit of a . . . surprise."

He settled back on the corner of his desk, studying her curiously. He knew from Ava that Alexia was back in town and supposedly engaged. He hadn't expected to see her, though, so the surprise was hard to shake. "I am surprised, although it's nice to see you, too. You look . . . well." *Shit, why had he mentioned anything about her appearance?*

A laugh erupted from her at his words and finally he saw a brief glimpse of the woman he once loved. "You're a terrible liar, Brant, you always were. Even when I really didn't want to hear it, you gave it to me straight. I always admired that about you," she added almost absently.

Attempting to lighten the mood, Brant smiled, asking, "Is that the only thing you admired?"

His attempt seemed to have the opposite effect as she shook her head solemnly. "No, it's not. I'm here because I'm counting on your strongest quality . . . loyalty. I know we haven't been involved for years, but I also know you would never turn your back on someone you cared about. I . . . I need help, Brant. I don't have anywhere else to turn." When tears welled in her eyes, Brant grabbed a tissue from the container on his desk and handed it to her.

Fuck, a crying female and it was his ex-fiancée to boot. This morning had officially taken a nosedive from promising to unsettling.

"Alexia . . . what's wrong?" Brant was starting to get nervous. What was going on here? This didn't sound like someone needing a loan or wanting absolution for past sins. He found himself not wanting to ask but really he had no choice. "Tell me what I can do to help you? It can't be as bad as you think."

"Well, let me see," she said. Lifting her fingers, she started ticking off her problems for him. "I'm fresh out of rehab after a drug overdose. I'm engaged to the doctor who helped me get into rehab. My parents, who were thrilled with the whole doctor-engagement thing, just found out that their daughter was a former junkie and are terrified that someone else will find out. And my friends, who are still using, have been calling me every day wanting to get together. I can't seem to get a moment's peace from anyone in my life!"

Still dazed, Brant asked, "Drug abuse?"

Now it was Alexia's turn to look at him in surprise. "Surely you must have known? I mean, I was clean when we started dating, but Josie . . . she got me into things that I couldn't control. It started out with just a few drinks and after a while, those drinks turned into hard alcohol. Finally, it progressed into harder stuff like cocaine, heroin and crystal meth. I . . . knew it was wrong, but I couldn't stop."

Rolling up the sleeve of her shirt, she showed him her arm, covered with dozens of scars that must have been track marks. Taking a deep breath, she added, "By rights, I should already be dead. I woke up more than once in a strange bed, or on the street."

"Where the fuck was Josie during those times?" Brant demanded. When she flinched, he lowered his voice, fighting for control. "Didn't she care what was happening to you?"

"I don't know," Alexia admitted. "I think it was funny to her at first. You know, take the innocent new friend out and loosen her up. I realize now that she liked having me around because I funded the party for her. I received a check from my father's company, plus I had a nice savings account that my parents had set up for me when I was younger. Josie never seemed to have any money, so I automatically paid for everything when we were together, including the drugs. She usually took off with her boyfriend during the evening and I somehow made it home most of the time. After you and I broke up, though, I really went off the rails. Knowing you were there was the only thing that kept me in check until then."

"And your parents? Did they have any clue as to what was going on?"

Alexia shook her head. "Not for a while, or at least I don't think so. I had never been a problem child so they probably overlooked the initial signs. When they found out, they really didn't know how to deal with it."

"How did they find out?" Brant asked quietly.

Alexia dropped her head in her hands. "My mom walked in on me shooting up. The one thing I remember from that moment is how confused she looked. Her mind simply couldn't grasp what she was seeing: her daughter with a rubber band around her arm, injecting something. The sad thing is that I could have probably talked my way out of it had I not panicked. I think at that moment, regardless of what she thought, she would have jumped at any other explanation. I just started blabbering how sorry I was over and over. Unfortunately, my father was walking by at that exact moment and heard the commotion. Unlike my mother's shock, he was livid. He yelled, threatened me and generally went ballistic. He demanded that I pack my bags and get ready to go to a clinic that night. When they left my room, I called Josie and had her pick me up at the end of the driveway. I snuck out of the house and left. Other than making friends with Josie in the first place, that was the worst mistake I ever made."

"What did you do after that? Did your parents look for you?"

Another tear escaped the corner of her eye as she said, "I'm sure they did for a while, but what could they do really? I was an adult. Even making bad decisions, there was nothing they could do to make me come home legally. I had a bank account in my name, which meant they couldn't freeze that either. God, I almost wish they had been able to. Maybe if the money had run out sooner, I'd have been forced to go home before all of this happened."

Curious despite himself, Brant asked, "What made you come back?"

"They say you have to hit rock bottom before you admit that you have a problem and that finally happened to me. I was at a party and overdosed on cocaine. There were a few big names at the party and one of them had a bodyguard with him. If not for him being there and sober, I'd probably be dead. He had medic training and knew the signs. All I remember is feeling like my heart was going to burst from my chest. My body temperature had also risen so high that they had to dip me in an ice water bath at the hospital. The doctor there just gave it to me straight. He said I was damn lucky I hadn't had a heart attack and that if I continued, that was just around the corner. I cried then, while he stood there looking at me. I'm sure he had seen junkies like me before and had long since lost any sympathy for them. He offered me a place in a treatment program he sponsored and I accepted. I don't think either of us really believed I would do it. He looked surprised when I asked him the next morning to be transferred into it."

Brant moved back, giving her room to collect herself. He was reeling from her story. Never in all of this time had he suspected what she had become involved in. He mentally kicked himself, knowing he should have seen the signs. Even though she had broken it off with him, he felt like he had let her down. "Alexia, I'm sorry. . . ."

Shaking her head, she said, "Don't, it's not your fault. There was nothing you or anyone else could have done. I was sheltered for so long that when I finally broke free, I just lost it. Without Carter, I don't know if I would have made it back. . . ."

Quirking a brow, Brant asked, "Carter?"

He didn't miss the soft smile curving Alexia's

mouth. "Carter is the doctor who helped me into treatment. He . . . he was there for me through it all. When I wanted to give up, he pushed me. He saw something in me worth saving. I was terrified I would relapse when I was on my own, but he continued to encourage me, checking in often. We . . . um . . . fell in love. Can you believe that something positive came out of the nightmare my life had become?" Suddenly her hand flew to her mouth. "Oh my God, Brant, I hadn't even thought of how this might make you feel!"

"Alexia, it's fine. I'm happy that you have someone in your life now; you deserve it." Strangely enough, he was happy for her. "So what happened with your parents? You mentioned that they know about your addiction problems."

"Yes, I told them everything yesterday and they asked me to leave. I had told them over the phone a few weeks ago about Carter, but not about my time in rehab and how bad things had gotten before I checked myself in. I wanted to talk to them about that face-to-face. I think they had convinced themselves that my drug usage was just a small act of rebellion. When I told them in detail how bad things had gotten for me, they completely locked down. They were happier not knowing where I had been or what I had been doing." Alexia looked down at her hands. "The sad part though is that for a brief moment, I was their daughter again. They were thrilled to welcome me back with a doctor as a fiancé. I found out that they had been telling their friends that I was away at college and had met a doctor there. They were ready to acknowledge my existence again, but that ended when they found out that their daughter had been a serious addict for the past few years. I've lost what little relationship I had with them and, more important, I may have lost Carter."

Surprised, he asked, "Why would you have lost him?"

"He didn't want me to come see my parents or risk seeing anyone from my past. He felt like it was too soon in my recovery to face such strong emotional triggers. I had told him all about my parents, so he knew they were likely to reject me when they found out the truth. I just . . . didn't want to accept that he was right so we fought and I told him I needed a break. Time apart to think. Of course, when I walked out, I thought I would be staying with my parents for a while, but that's obviously out."

"I'll help you get settled in a hotel," Brant found himself offering, falling right back into his old habit of taking care of her. "You can take a few days or weeks to see where you want to go from here. I'm sure your parents will just be glad to have their daughter back when they have time to think."

He was shocked speechless when she looked at him beseechingly, and said, "Could I please stay with you . . . just for a little while? No one will look for me there. I promise, I won't be any trouble! You're the only person in my life right now that I trust not to push me. I need a place to think and someone to lean on. I just . . . don't have anywhere else to turn."

"Alexia . . . I don't think that's a good idea. We don't know each other anymore. I'll be happy to help you in any way I can, but staying with me just wouldn't work out. You'd be much happier in a hotel." But when she burst out crying, he knew he was screwed. He didn't owe her anything; hell, by rights, he should have tossed her out the door already. But . . . she looked so damn fragile. He couldn't help but remember their past relationship and even though the love was gone, he still cared about what happened to her.

"I'm sorry," she said, wiping her face. "I'm horribly embarrassed to be doing this. My pride seems to have completely deserted me lately. Just please . . . forget I asked. It's crazy that I would expect something like that after all I've done to you."

Brant sighed, knowing that he was probably making a huge mistake, but unable to turn his back on her. He stood up, pulling his house key from his key ring. He had lived in an apartment back when they were together, so she had never been to his new house. He scribbled the address of his house on the back of a business card and handed both to her. "Why don't you go to my place and rest? We can talk more this evening. I . . . This can't be for long though, Alexia, just a few days."

"Thank you, Brant," she whispered tearfully as she stood, giving him a hug. Pulling back, she asked, "Could you please not tell anyone, even your family? I . . . just don't want people looking at me like my parents did."

"Of course." He was just dropping his arms from around her when the door burst open. He saw the smile quickly slipping from Emma's lips as she stood in the doorway. As she started to turn away, he said, "Emma, come on in." She stopped uncertainly as Alexia turned, looking toward the door. "Emma, this is a friend of mine, Alexia, and Alexia, this is my . . ."—*fuck what do I say here?*—"assistant, Emma." Both said hello. Maybe it was his imagination, but the moment seemed awkward as hell to him.

Alexia picked up her handbag. "I'll see you later on, Brant." With a parting smile to Emma, she walked out the door. If he had thought things were awkward before, it was doubly so now. He found himself wanting to squirm under Emma's unwavering stare. *He was just helping a friend. He really hadn't done anything wrong.* Maybe he needed to stop acting so damn guilty then.

"Good morning, Emma." He walked over to shut the door behind her. "I've been waiting for you to get here for hours it seems." *Real good, now it sounds like you're chastising her for being late to work.* "I mean, I got here early, so you're not late." *Yeah, that was much better.*

"It looks like you found something to occupy your time. Did you need anything?" she asked over her shoulder as she turned to leave.

Grabbing her hand, he pulled her back against him. "She's just a friend who came to me because she needs some help." Looking down at her formfitting black dress, he groaned, "God, you look good today." Just as

Emma softened and moved closer to him, the door burst open yet again.

"Bro, was that your ex I just passed in the hallway?" Declan asked. Brant closed his eyes briefly as Emma stiffened and pulled away. Declan grimaced, noticing for the first time his arm around Emma. "Um, shit, sorry about that. I was just . . . surprised to see Alexia. Maybe I was wrong; it didn't look anything like her."

This was just going from bad to worse. He was afraid of what Declan would say next in an effort to pull his foot from his mouth. "It's fine," Brant said, "and, yes, it was Alexia."

Emma pulled her arm away, saying, "I'm going to my desk now," without making any further eye contact.

When she closed the door behind her, Brant turned to his brother. "Thanks for that."

Declan took a seat in front of the desk, giving him a wry grin. "That wasn't one of my smoothest moments. What's going on here? It sure seemed like I walked in on something."

Brant took his seat, running a hand through his hair in frustration. He had never been comfortable talking about his personal life, even with his family. He was sorely in need of some moral support, though, and knew that a newly married Declan was more likely to provide that than his sister. "Things with Emma have gotten . . . interesting."

"Interesting?" Declan asked. "Could you be a little more specific?"

Finally Brant blurted out, "Interesting as in I want her now more than I want to choke her."

Declan's eyes widened before he started chuckling. "I always knew that if you two ever stopped all the bitching, you would probably be all over each other. No one argues that much if they don't give a damn."

"Yeah, well, suffice it to say, I can't get her out of my head. I could probably have saved myself a few stomach ulcers if I had parted ways with her after our first verbal sparring match, but that, as they say, is history. Now thanks to her walking in on me while I was hugging Alexia and you announcing to everyone in a three-block radius that she's my ex, Emma is probably ready to run."

"Sorry about that. Not cool at all on my part. What is Alexia doing here, though? I didn't think you had spoken with her in years."

"I haven't," Brant agreed. "She's in a bit of a bind and needs my help."

"What kind of help?" Declan asked.

Brant shook his head. "It's private and I've promised her not to tell anyone. It's going to make it difficult with Emma though." Before his brother could dig further, he decided to change the subject. "So how's the whole family thing working out for you?"

The old Declan would have cringed over a question like that, but the new one just grinned. "It's all good. Ella almost burned the place down last night when she attempted to make homemade manicotti. Evan and I had to wear towels over our faces for an hour. When the smoke detector went off, she started crying. It was a damn mess there for a while. I told her there was no shame in picking up take-out. Without people like us, restaurants would go out of business. It's a fucking hormonal minefield at our place right now. You make one wrong step and you go from hero to zero in the blink of an eye. Thank fuck that Mac was smart enough not to mention the smell when he got there for his well-done dinner."

Brant chuckled, trying to picture the scene Declan was describing. It sounded absolutely terrifying, but his brother seemed perfectly content. "You've got a few cooking skills; why don't you help Ella out?"

Declan gave him a rueful smile, saying, "I've tried, but she is craving all this stuff right now that is beyond both our skill levels. I usually just have her call in what she wants and I pick it up on the way home. She thinks on the nights that Evan is there, though, that he should have home cooking. I finally had to tell her last night that the kid is better off with McDonald's than smoke inhalation." Looking down at his watch, Declan stood, saying, "Man, I got sidetracked, but I came by to tell you that Jason has called a meeting for ten this morning. He has his eye on another company that he is thinking of acquiring. We need to head out to the fifth-floor conference room."

He followed his brother out on their way to the conference room, with Emma refusing to make eye contact, but Brant heard Declan chuckle under his breath when she called him Mr. Stone on the way out the door. He would take her to lunch today and explain as much as he could without breaking his promise to Alexia. He wished for a moment that they were still in Florida without the stress and interruptions of their everyday life. Things had been simpler then. How could a morning that had seemed so promising only hours ago have gotten off course so fast? Playing the love-struck boyfriend had been like second nature when they were together in Florida. A large part of him knew that it hadn't been acting at all; it had been acceptance of what had always been between them.

Chapter Thirteen

Emma sagged back against her chair as Brant followed his brother out the door. She was extremely grateful to have a moment to herself. In her eagerness to see Brant, she had made it to work ten minutes early, knowing he would already be there. She had burst through the door of his office only to come to an abrupt standstill at the sight of him standing there with a beautiful woman wrapped in his arms. At first, she thought she must have been imagining it. In all the time she had worked for him, Brant had never had a woman in his office who wasn't a business colleague. But something about the familiar way he held this woman had signaled something very different between them.

The woman had been friendly enough. There had been only curiosity in her gaze as she greeted Emma. Brant, though, had looked decidedly uncomfortable. Declan had walked in only minutes later, supplying the missing piece to the puzzle. This woman was Brant's ex. The only question was his ex what? Girlfriend or wife? Had he been married before? She had never heard anything along those lines. Suddenly, though, her position in Brant's life seemed very precarious. Was their time together in Florida truly just a weekend fling? She had always assumed that Brant didn't have a life other than work, but now she knew that he had been involved and that the woman was very much in his life.

She realized there was only one thing you could do when you were in this much turmoil: Call the girls.

Emma walked from the elevator toward the lobby of the main floor of the Danvers building. She was relieved to be meeting her friends for lunch but depressed that Brant hadn't returned before she left. Suzy, ever punctual, was the first to arrive. She embraced her, glad to have a moment alone with her before the others arrived. She pulled back, still holding Suzy's hand while she asked, "How are you? I wanted to call and see how everything went for you with your . . . procedure, but I didn't want to pry. So, yeah, now I'm obviously prying."

Suzy gave a small laugh, squeezing her hand. "Things went just fine. Gray was proud to have thousands of swimmers who had the speed of Olympic champions."

Emma could only imagine that the very suave and handsome Grayson Merimon would have been absolutely appalled to have his sperm count discussed in the lobby of their workplace. Luckily for him, though, they were in a deserted corner with no one in sight.

Emma grinned. "Hey, I wouldn't have expected less.

I don't think there could be anything to do with his body that isn't perfect." Emma wanted to groan as she realized what she had just said. Her friend probably didn't need to know that she had checked out her husband so thoroughly. "Er . . . I mean, he seems to stay in shape."

With a wink, Suzy said, "I gotcha and you are quite right."

Curious, Emma asked, "So when will you know if it worked?"

Suzy looked down, fidgeting with the strap on her purse. "I'm not sure, probably soon. You never know about these things."

Emma was sure that it took only a few weeks to find out if you were pregnant the normal way, but maybe things were different when you went another route. God, she hoped Suzy hadn't had bad news already. She was acting a little evasive about the whole thing. When Claire walked in the door, Emma was grateful to let the subject drop. Better to let Suzy talk if she wanted to and not because she was being badgered.

Claire pulled them both in for a hug. "I'm so glad to see you! I love my daughter, but it's great to escape potty training hell for a few hours. Our washing machine has been running around the clock since I started trying to train Chrissy. Jason says we should just buy stock in Pull-Ups and admit defeat."

As they were laughing, Beth and Ella stepped from the elevator and started waving. They had decided to walk next door to the sandwich shop and avoid having to drive in the Myrtle Beach lunch rush hour. When they settled into their table, Emma noticed Beth pull out an iPad and start watching what appeared to be a video.

"Oh good grief," Suzy grumbled. "Give me that thing. How can we talk about men, sex and whatever else while you're over there stalking your nanny."

Beth held on to the iPad for a moment before grudgingly giving it to her sister. "I can't help it. I'm not used to leaving him at home all day. Janice is great, really. Nick's parents know her family and she comes highly recommended, but still . . ."

Claire put her hand over Beth's in sympathy. "Trust me, honey, I understand. There are times that I'm so ready for a mommy break that I'm standing at the door waiting to hand Chrissy off to the paperboy if it will get me five minutes of peace, but when I do have a sitter other than my mom and Louise, I'm a nervous wreck."

"So wait a minute," Emma asked. "You have a nanny cam?"

"Well, it's not really a nanny cam, since she knows about it. Nick had it installed because we hated to miss so much with Henry while we were gone each day."

"I think the thought was that you would check in occasionally to see what Hermie was up to, not stalk poor Janice every hour of the day," Suzy added. Everyone laughed at Suzy's continued insistence on calling Henry by his nickname of Hermie. Beth and Nick had long ago given up the battle to change it. Emma had even caught Beth calling him that on occasion. Turning to her sister, Beth said, "You just wait until you decide to have one of your own. You will probably terrorize your sitter."

Emma wanted to cringe for her friend. She knew that Beth would be horrified to learn what a blow a casual comment like that was to her sister right now. The smile that Suzy gave in response to Beth's comment looked strained, so Emma jumped in, trying to save Suzy from the current line of conversation. "So, something happened while I was in Florida." *Well, shit, maybe some weather comment would have accomplished the same thing.* All eyes were on her now as she gave a weak smile of her own.

Suzy squeezed her arm briefly in what she suspected was gratitude before asking, "Does this involve sex? God, I hope so!"

Emma now wished she had just kept her mouth shut. Could she really tell them about her weekend without it being blatantly obvious that she was in love with Brant? Maybe if she distracted them with her airline disaster, they might be too busy laughing to pick up on the rest.

"Well, let me start off by saying I ended up getting a last-minute root canal before I left, had a pretty major reaction to the painkillers and accidentally took my vibrator in my carry-on bag." As everyone's eyes bugged out, she continued. "My pain pills spilled out in my bag, stuck to the vibrator, and were detected by a drug-sniffing dog at the Miami International Airport. Brant was almost arrested because he was carrying the bag."

There was nothing but silence at the table for a full minute.

"No fucking way," Claire whispered. Everyone's head swiveled to her since it was rare to hear Claire use the *F* word.

"I couldn't have said it better myself, Claire," Suzy added, while Beth nodded in agreement. "You have got to explain the whole story."

Emma went back from the beginning and by the time she was finished, there wasn't a dry eye at the table. Ella laughed so hard that she finally had to excuse herself; she was terrified that her weak pregnancy bladder was going to cause her to pee on herself.

"Oh my God," Suzy gasped out. "I wonder if we could get a copy of that security footage. I can just picture you on the floor wrestling a dog for your vibrator."

"And can you just imagine Brant's face?" Claire laughed. "I'm surprised he survived the experience."

"The only way this could have possibly been any better was if Brant had ended up on the front page of the paper in cuffs standing next to Fido, the vibrator-sniffing dog!" Beth added.

"So how was the reunion?" Claire asked. "Things must have been pretty anticlimactic after the airport incident."

Emma fidgeted in her seat, trying to decide how best to answer when she noticed Suzy watching her with interest. "Maybe you're a little off on your spelling, Claire. Instead of climactic, maybe it's more climax."

Ella chose that moment to return from the restroom.

"Who had a climax?" she asked. Emma felt her face redden along with Ella's when she realized how loudly she had spoken. "Oh crap," she murmured as she slid into her seat. "I didn't mean for that to come out like that."

"I don't think anyone heard you," Beth offered.

"Oh totally." Suzy smirked. "At least a few people in the kitchen missed it." Turning back toward Emma, she said, "So-o-o . . ."

This was it, Emma thought. She either lied to her friends or admitted the truth. Ah, good grief, she had never been big on hiding things, so why start now? "I slept with Brant a few times while we were gone." There, the Band-Aid was ripped cleanly off; the truth was out there.

"No shit," Suzy drawled. "Well, it's about time! There was so much foreplay going on in that office, I left there hot and bothered a few times. You two should have gotten it on ages ago."

"Boy, is that the truth," Claire agreed. "I don't see how you made it this long. It was obvious you two had some major chemistry. I have never seen two people more opposite, but more perfect for each other."

Emma looked around in surprise to see both Beth and Ella nodding their agreement. "Am I the only one at this table who didn't think I was hot for Brant because I have to say, I just really didn't see it. I mean, I realize now that I have been in some denial about being attracted to him, but it truthfully never hit home until this weekend."

"So . . ." Beth said. "How was it?"

"Freaking amazing," Emma sighed. "The first time was like a fast explosion, the second time, I kind of attacked him and the third time was a joint outdoor venture."

Raising a brow, Suzy said, "So this wasn't a one-ride kind of thing?"

Beside her, Claire giggled. "I'd say there was definitely more than one ride there, Suz."

Emma felt her face flush. She really wasn't used to having her sex life front and center. She did need their advice, though, and to get that, she needed to be honest about what had happened. "It was . . . wow, for someone so reserved, Brant is *amazing* in bed. He throws his whole textbook mentality out the window and just . . . feels. I didn't think he could possibly be any better after the first time, but it just got hotter. He's also so . . . well, tender and adventurous. It wasn't just like a one-night stand kind of sex; he was really caring afterward. Like he couldn't get enough of touching me, even in a small way."

"Oh wow," Ella sighed dreamily. "I just love that. It must run in the family because Declan is the same way. He can be wild during sex, but then so loving afterward. Sometimes it's hard to believe one man can be so many things."

"That's Jason, too," Claire added. "He's so completely focused and intense during, but afterward he just can't stop touching me in some way. I'll be falling asleep and he will still be running his fingertips up and down my arm, my spine and anything he can reach. It's very sensual."

Nodding her head, Suzy agreed. "I have to admit, that used to freak me out about Gray in the beginning. His need to always have some kind of physical contact with me. I never really had that with anyone before. My ex-fiancé just turned over and went to sleep afterward. I thought that was the way it was for everyone. It was almost as if Gray was invading my personal space the first few times. I loved having him close, but at the same time I wasn't truly comfortable being the focus of that much attention. Now, it centers me. I wouldn't know what to do without it."

Raising her hand as if they were in a schoolroom, Beth asked, "Does Nick passing out on top of me afterward count?" Everyone started laughing. "Nick is amazing in bed, but since Henry keeps us up half the night now, instead of the marathon sessions we used to have, we're more into short, hot bursts and then collapsing for an hour before we have to get up again."

Suzy groaned. "Please don't tell me how wonderful Nick is in bed again. I have to look at the man over the dinner table at family gatherings. It's bad enough that Gray's mother never fails to mention what a stud Gray's father is in the bedroom." Laying her head in her hands, she added, "There are just some things you shouldn't know about family . . . like ever."

When their food arrived, Emma let everyone take a few bites before putting down her fork. "I do need some advice about Brant. I thought we were in a good place last night when he dropped me off, but this morning I walked into his office to find him hugging an attractive woman. He introduced her as a friend, but when Declan walked in, he asked Brant what his ex was doing there."

Claire's fork froze on the way to her mouth. "Was it Alexia Shaw?"

"Um . . . yes, I believe so. Why?" asked Emma.

"I . . . Jason mentioned Brant being engaged before to the daughter of a friend of his father's. I was surprised at the time because I just couldn't picture him getting married; he's so . . . reserved. I think it was a while back, though, and I'm not sure what happened."

Always the voice of practicality, Suzy said, "Well, honey, she's old news. You're the here and now. They didn't have their tongues down each other's throats, right?"

"Er . . . no, not when I walked in."

"Did it look like they had at any point?" Suzy asked.

"How would she know that?" Beth asked curiously.

Before Suzy could answer, Claire spoke up. "Oh, you'd know. Men just have that crazy, 'I'm so close to having sex look' that they can't hide, especially with little notice. I agree with Suzy; if he and Alexia had been doing anything other than sharing a platonic hug, you would know it."

Surprisingly, Ella nodded her head in agreement. "Whenever we have unexpected visitors like my mother, she always knows when she's interrupting something. The last time she actually said, 'I'll make this quick since Declan looks feverish.' We all knew she didn't think he was coming down with anything. It was just her way of pointing out that she knew what we had been up to. If my mother can spot something like that, you would have been able to as well."

"Well, crap," Emma sighed. "I guess I should stop acting like such a teenage girl then. I should have known it was innocent. I mean, I've seen Brant . . . excited and that wasn't it."

"Well, either that or you're just way better than this other woman." Beth clapped her hand over her mouth, seeming to realize how wrong her sentence sounded. "Damn, I didn't mean it like that. You are better, of course, but there was nothing there to start with, so . . ."

Suzy interrupted her sister. "Let me put you out of your misery before you dig yourself in any further." Turning to Emma, she said, "So everything is fine and if you want to continue with Brant, then there is no reason why you shouldn't." Then, drilling Beth with a look, she added, "Just please don't do it in anyone else's house like some people . . ." Beth responded with a grimace and Emma had to wonder what she was missing. "Hey, speaking of sex and exes, I have a new and interesting friend, Beth, with ties to one of your exes."

Looking surprised, Beth said, "Really? Heck, I don't have much of a dating past, so who could that be?"

"Well, you only went out with him a few times . . . but you remember Seth Jackson, right?"

"Oh my God," Beth moaned. "That man had a front-row seat to one of the most embarrassing moments in my life. Please tell me he isn't your new best friend now."

"Hardly." Suzy smiled. "But you'll be happy to know he's moved on . . . to someone very close to home."

Beside Suzy, Claire smiled. "Oh yes, that's right. I had forgotten that you went out with Seth."

Holding up her hand, Emma said, "Whoa, let's take this back a little for the benefit of those of us who don't know. Who is Seth and what embarrassing moment did I miss?" Ella was trying to stifle a giggle under her hand, so Emma knew it must be a good one.

Beth took a breath and said, "I met Seth through a dating service. He works at the Oceanix."

"He *owns* the Oceanix," Suzy added. "Big difference."

"Wow," Emma breathed. "I'm impressed." The Oceanix was the most elite resort in Myrtle Beach and that was saying something. Her parents had insisted on taking her there for lunch on their last visit. She probably wouldn't have been able to afford more than a crouton without them paying.

"Yeah, well, I didn't know he owned it at the time. He just said he was the manager there. Not that it would have made any difference to me. Seth was a great guy." And wiggling her eyebrows, she added, "And very easy on the eyes. We had only been out a few times when things with Nick started to . . . heat up. I had a very bad and temporary lapse in judgment and decided I was going to continue dating despite finding out I was pregnant."

Suzy opened and closed her mouth. Emma had to give her credit for holding in whatever comment she had wanted to make.

"So, um, how did that work out?" Emma asked.

Beth started laughing. "Not very well. I met Seth for dinner one evening and Nick showed up. He introduced himself as the father of my child and also let Seth know he was living with me. When Seth asked me if it was true, I had no choice but to tell him that it was. Have you ever had a gorgeous man look at you like you were a complete and total train wreck? Let me tell you, it's not a good feeling. It was completely humiliating and I have prayed that I would never see him face-to-face again."

Ella squeezed her friend's hand in sympathy, saying, "It could happen to any of us."

Suzy laughed out loud before telling Ella, "Unless you are planning to start dating now, it's probably not gonna happen to anyone at this table again."

"I almost hate to ask," Beth said, "but what were you saying about Seth?"

"Believe it or not," Suzy said, "he's dating someone at Danvers . . . again. With a little more success this time, though. She works in installations and her name is Mia Gentry. She's actually pretty cool; I think you'd all like her."

"Small town, small world," Claire offered.

"Should make for a hell of a good Christmas party, though, right?" Suzy smirked.

As the other women gathered their things to leave, Emma was surprised when Ella pulled her aside. Ella gave her a shy smile before saying, "If Brant is what you want, then never stop until you get him. That whole family is so . . . closed off. Declan is better now, but he still has times when he wants to shoulder everything on his own. I've gotten to know Brant a bit since Declan and I got together. I can see that there's a lot more to him than he lets most people see. Ava—she has been a bit tougher. I don't think she's ever gonna call me wanting to have a girls' night. Evan is crazy about both of them, though, and they say kids are the best judge of a person's character."

Emma smiled her gratitude. "Thank you, Ella, and for what it's worth, Declan is damn lucky."

Brant was waiting for her near her desk when she returned from lunch. She looked at him uncertainly for a moment before putting her hands on her hips and breaking the silence. "What? Don't tell me you wanted your slave to bring you back some lunch?"

His eyebrows shot up in surprise before a smile curved his gorgeous lips. "Now why would I want yet another sandwich that you had left sitting on the table for an hour before bringing it back to me? I'm sure you have been sorely disappointed that I haven't succumbed to a bad case of food poisoning yet."

Dropping her purse on the desk, she said, "It hasn't been from a lack of trying on my part." Suddenly Brant gripped her hips, pulling her bottom back against him. She felt his erection nudging against her and wiggled against it, eliciting a groan from him.

"God, you're turning me on. One more nasty comment from you and I'll have you lying on your desk with your panties on the floor and my cock driving hard inside you."

Holy shit! Emma felt the moisture pooling between her thighs as erotic images of the two of them together ran through her mind. As he reached up to pinch her taut nipples, she groaned, "You . . . have . . . an . . . appointment . . . soon."

"Fuck." Brant cursed against her neck. He kissed her ear before stepping unsteadily back.

"Let's go to your place after work," Emma whispered seductively. Was it her imagination or did he suddenly look uncomfortable?

"How about your place? I'm . . . having some work done at mine."

Emma felt herself relax. Things had seemed so awkward for a moment that she had been afraid he was going to turn her down altogether. She knew that her apartment was still a wreck with luggage lying around the living room, but she didn't care in the least. If they had to make out on a pile of laundry, it was something she'd have to live with. "Sure, that sounds good. Do you want to grab some dinner first?"

Brant smacked her sharply on the butt, something

he seemed to love doing, and said, "Have a snack this afternoon to tide you over. I can't sit across from you in a restaurant without wanting to fuck you. After we've released some . . . tension, we'll order a pizza." Emma was more than happy with his plan since she didn't think she could last much longer without feeling him against her. Being this close to him for the rest of the afternoon was going to be hell. She had never been so glad to have a full schedule; otherwise, she would have ended up doing something she never had: beg Brant to meet her in the supply closet before she exploded.

Brant had just walked back into his office when the owner of the company, Jason Danvers, walked in followed by Mark DeSanto, Brant's next appointment. The DeSanto Group had been a partner in some projects with Brant's previous company. Brant had maintained a friendship with Mark and wanted to introduce him to Jason. He thought there were some interesting possibilities for projects between DeSanto and Danvers.

"Emma." Jason smiled, holding out his hand. Emma shook hands, returning the greeting. She had met Jason on only a few occasions and each time she found herself blushing like a schoolgirl. Claire Danvers had hit the jackpot and it had nothing to do with his wealth. He was tall, drool-worthy handsome, and what a body. What Emma found the most attractive, though, was that he didn't use any of that to get what he wanted. He was like a gorgeous geek. After speaking with him on any subject for a few moments, it became apparent that the man was brilliant. With so many attributes to admire, his intelligence had always been what really stood out to Emma.

Mark DeSanto gave her a look that was frankly appraising and appreciative as he dropped a kiss on her hand. Emma smiled at the gesture. There wasn't a lot of hand kissing in Myrtle Beach. Mark had raven-dark hair and reminded her of a younger Andy Garcia.

When Brant walked out of his office to greet his guests, Mark took the opportunity to ask her if she would be interested in joining him for lunch one day. She could tell by the tightening of Brant's mouth that he had also heard the question and didn't like it. She didn't think it would look good to Jason Danvers if he saw her making dates with their business associates. Just as she was trying to phrase her rejection nicely, the telephone rang and she jumped on it like a lifeline. Brant also took advantage of the call to usher Mark away from her desk and lead them all into his office, shutting the door firmly behind them.

As Emma was getting ready to leave for the day, the men finally came out. "Emma, Jason, Mark and I are meeting up with Declan, Nick, Gray and Ava for dinner. Could you possibly make us a reservation at Ivy for seven, please?" Ivy was a favorite among the executives at Danvers and as such, there was always a last-minute table available to them there. Emma smiled at him as Mark and Jason walked into the hallway and she picked up the phone. Brant leaned over her desk to sign some papers and whispered near her ear, "I'll drop by your place after dinner, okay?"

"Er . . . sure," she replied, suddenly feeling like more of a booty call than a date, which she knew was silly. Did she think that Brant was going to announce to the CEO of Danvers that she was his girlfriend and include her in the dinner arrangement? "Will any of the wives be joining you this evening?"

"Ah, yes, Em, thanks—please also include a plus-one for Jason, Gray and Declan. I don't believe Nick's wife can make it." Emma couldn't help but think that if Brant were still with Alexia, he would definitely have a plus-one for the evening. He brushed her hand fleetingly before murmuring, "I'll see you soon."

Emma quickly made the reservation before locking up for the evening. She was walking through the lobby when she saw Brant's sister, Ava, staring at the elevator. Thinking that Brant may not have passed the dinner information along, she approached her. "Hi, Ava, were you looking for Brant?"

Ava gave her a look of surprise before answering. "No, should I be?"

Emma verbally kicked herself. She liked Ava fine, but she was now stuck delivering the required five minutes of small talk when she could have walked out the door and been on her way. "I just thought since you were meeting the rest of the team for dinner tonight that you might be riding together."

"Oh . . . No . . . I'm just . . . I thought Mac would still be here and I was going to walk out with him."

Like most of her friends at Danvers, Emma had wondered more than once about the relationship between Ava and Mac. She knew he was an old friend of the family and that Declan had served in the military with him, but she had always thought there was something else there.

"Do you want me to check and see if he's still in the building?" Emma offered.

Ava looked down at her watch and then back at the elevator as if willing Mac to appear. "No, that's okay, I probably just missed him. Thanks, though."

Emma couldn't help but notice how sad the other woman looked as she walked away. Maybe they had more in common than she thought, because it appeared that they were both waiting on a man.

Chapter Fourteen

When Declan caught him looking down at his watch yet again, Brant tried to hide his guilty expression. It was already after nine and he knew that Emma was expecting him. As if taking mercy on him, his brother cleared his throat. "Ella and I are going to have to get home. She's a bit tired tonight and needs to rest."

Clearly, pregnancy did have its advantages, Brant thought. He shot Declan a grateful smile as the dinner meeting came to an end. He said a quick good-bye to everyone, noting absently that Suzy had been unusually subdued during dinner. She had also left the table several times, so Brant wondered if she was sick. Gray seemed to be thinking the same thing, as he kept a firm arm around his wife, leading her toward the door. When his cell phone rang as he was walking toward his car, Brant was momentarily surprised to see his home number on the caller ID. He had completely forgotten about Alexia.

He hit the CALL button, answering, "Stone."

"Hi, Brant, it's Alexia. I . . . er . . . just wondered when you were going to be home."

He was a little surprised by the question. When he had invited her to stay at his home, he hadn't imagined that he would need to check in with her. Although he supposed it was a common courtesy when you had a houseguest, no matter what the circumstances. It would be rude to burst in during the middle of the night and scare her. "I just finished a dinner meeting and I . . . have plans, so I'll be late. Was there something you needed?" *Oh fuck, was that a sniffle he heard on the other end of the line?* "Is everything okay?"

After a moment's hesitation, she said, "Oh sure, I . . . Carter called tonight and we had a fight. He wants to see me and I refused. I just . . . needed to talk, but it's not important."

Brant closed his eyes as he felt the guilt jumping up to choke him. Alexia was clearly upset and had been waiting for him to come home so that she wouldn't be all alone. Sometimes he really hated his constant sense of responsibility because he felt an overwhelming obligation to go straight home and try to solve Alexia's problems for her. It was nothing to do with love and everything to do with a—misplaced—sense of duty. On the other hand, he wanted nothing more than to be with Emma. All day long he had missed having her in his arms.

It hadn't even been a full day and already the weight of helping Alexia was dragging on him. He needed to tell Emma that she was staying with him, even if he couldn't tell her the reason why. There was nothing going on that he should feel guilty about. He'd give her a call and then head home. "I'll be there soon."

"Really?" He could hear the hope in Alexia's voice as he told her he'd be there in twenty minutes. Next, he dialed Emma's number, putting it on speaker before turning his car toward home. A spark shot through his body when he heard her voice. She sounded so damn close he almost expected to see her in the seat next to him. "Hey, Em."

Before he could go any farther, she said, "You aren't coming, are you?"

He couldn't keep the surprise from his voice when he asked, "How did you know that?"

Sounding tired but faintly amused, she said, "Because you'd be here now and not calling. Did you decide to hit a bar or something with the guys after dinner?"

God, how simple it would be to just agree with her and let it go for the evening. Sadly, though, he didn't often take the easy way out in life and tonight would be no exception. "No, I'm on my way home now from the restaurant." Letting out a breath he hadn't been aware of holding, he said, "Em, I need to tell you something." When there was nothing but silence from her end of the line, he quickly jumped in before he could chicken out. "The woman you met in my office this morning, Alexia, is actually my ex-fiancée and she's staying with me for a few days. That's why I didn't want to meet at my house tonight. She's . . .

having some problems with her current fiancé and asked me for somewhere to stay." The silence continued so long after his revelation that he looked over at his phone to make sure the call was still connected. "Um . . . Em?"

"I'm here," she answered, sounding perfectly normal. "Just out of curiosity, why would she ask her ex-fiancé? Did you stay in contact after your split or was it recent?"

"It was a few years ago and, no, today is the first time I've spoken with her since our relationship ended." Brant thought she sounded more puzzled than anything now and he couldn't blame her. When he thought about it in those terms, it seemed strange to him as well. He wouldn't have sought Alexia out if the circumstances had been reversed. Of course, Emma didn't know the whole story and that made a bit of difference.

"She is dealing with a family situation and doesn't have any friends that she can . . . trust."

"It still seems strange that she would come to you after so long in those circumstances."

Brant was starting to wish he had just kept his mouth shut. This was becoming harder and harder to explain without telling her what was going on and he couldn't do that.

"She has some other problems as well. I guess, due to our history together, she felt she could count on me for support. Our relationship was built on a friendship and she had nowhere else to turn."

Emma's only comment was "Hmmm."

"So, I'll see you tomorrow?" Brant asked.

"Um-hmm," she replied absently.

"And we'll make plans for tomorrow night?" Brant asked almost hesitantly.

"What? Oh sure, yeah, that sounds good. 'Night." With those words, he heard a click. He felt uncomfortable with how the whole conversation had gone. He would have felt better if she had overreacted and accused him of something. As it was, though, she seemed almost distant from the entire subject.

Fuck, now I remember why it was a helluva lot easier to avoid romantic hassles. Right now I don't know my ass from a hole in the ground, and that happens only when a woman is involved.

Emma looked down at her watch and hoped Suzy was still awake. She didn't think she would have had time to make it home from dinner and already be asleep. She quickly found Suzy's name on her phone and texted her: *Old bitch moving in on my man.*

Her phone almost immediately signaled an incoming text: *What???*

As she was typing in her reply, the phone rang. She saw Suzy's name on the caller ID. When she answered, Suzy immediately asked, "What the hell?"

"Er . . . sorry about that. The last time I had man drama, I was a teenager, so I regressed back for a moment."

"All right," Suzy laughed. "So what gives?"

"Well, I found out tonight that Alexia is staying with Brant temporarily since she is fighting or something with her fiancé."

"Pardon?" Suzy asked. "I don't think I heard that right."

"Oh, you did. Trust me, I had the same reaction when he told me. He said that they have been broken up for a few years and in that time have not been in touch with each other. Now, out of the blue, she's back and needs somewhere to stay? Hellooo! Would you call your ex-fiancé if you and Gray were having problems and ask to stay with him?"

"Um, hells-to-the-no," Suzy muttered. "I'd rather sleep in my car."

"Thank you!" Emma exclaimed. "That's pretty much what I thought. The whole thing seems strange to me. Do you . . . do you think she wants him back? Maybe she made up this whole thing about a fiancé and having nowhere to go."

"Well, men are usually suckers for the whole damsel-in-distress act," Suzy admitted, "so I wouldn't rule it out. I think it might be time for a little R and R."

"Rest and Relaxation?" Emma asked, thinking maybe Suzy had been asleep after all.

"Duh, no—Research and Reconnaissance. Know thy enemy and all that. I think it's time to see exactly where Alexia came from and if there is another man in her life. I'll see if I can get some information out of Gray and maybe Ella can talk to Declan discreetly as well. We'll figure out if this is on the up-and-up or if someone wants your man back." They talked for a few more minutes before ending the call.

Emma felt better after talking to Suzy, but she had to fight the urge to kick off Operation R & R right then. She felt the need to do something completely juvenile, like drive by Brant's house and peek in the windows. Didn't they say that eavesdroppers never heard anything good about themselves? That probably went double for Peeping Toms then. To distract herself from doing something stupid, she flipped open her laptop and started on the research end of the mission. Thanks to Google, there were very few secrets in the world anymore.

After fifteen minutes of reading everything she could find on Alexia Shaw, Emma sorely wished she had remained in her ignorant bubble. Her family was mentioned tons of times in the different society pages. A younger Alexia stood next to her parents in many of the older pictures. Strangely enough, she had fallen off the radar in recent years. Her parents were still pictured at various events, but Alexia was nowhere to be seen. As Emma pondered what that could mean, she ran across a picture that caught her attention. It was a charity event for the Children's Hospital and not only were Alexia's parents in one of the photos, Brant stood with his arm around a beaming Alexia and damn it, he looked happy. *Well, what did you expect? They were engaged.*

Maybe a part of her had hoped that the whole engagement thing was a mistake somehow. But if the hug in his office this morning hadn't convinced her, then the picture she was staring at did. It wasn't just a friendly photo-op picture. Brant's whole stance toward Alexia was possessive. He cradled her against his side protectively. Emma could only imagine how a photo of she and Brant as a couple might look. The photographs would probably alternate between one of them having their hands around the other's neck to something a little more sweaty and graphic.

Yeah, researching your new enemy at night: not a good idea. Couldn't Brant's ex have been a homely, poor wallflower who didn't have tons of hits on Google? Just for kicks, she entered her own name and while she got some hits, the only halfway interesting one was a college student named Emma Davis who went by the nickname Emmie-Pie and had quite a talent for tying things in knots with her tongue, as evidenced by all the video clips posted on her site.

Right now, even Emmie-Pie seemed to have a better shot at happiness than Emma did.

Brant rubbed the back of his neck, hoping that the drama with Alexia was going to die down soon. When he arrived home, tired and sexually frustrated as all hell after having to cancel his evening with Emma, he had found Alexia on the phone crying. When he asked her what was wrong, she thrust her phone in his hand and asked him to deal with it for her . . . please? What the hell? He put the phone to his ear, fully expecting to hear either her mother or father on the other end. Instead, he ended up in a lovers' spat. There was a man whom he soon found out was the fiancé, Carter, begging Alexia to listen to reason. "Um, Alexia stepped away for a moment." *Great, that sounded fucking brilliant. Just the type of thing to reassure a man that he can work things out with his woman.*

Dead silence followed before an angry voice boomed, "Who the fuck is this and where's Alexia?" A smarter man would have ended the connection at that point. How screwed up was it that he wanted to help the woman who had dumped him two years ago to save her relationship with the irate man on the other end of the line?

"This is Brant Stone, a friend of Alexia's. She's—"

Before he could finish his sentence, there was what could only be called angry laughter from the other end. Brant could sense no real amusement in the sound. "You're kidding me, right? I'm over here on my knees groveling and begging for forgiveness and she went straight back to you?" Brant didn't know why he was surprised. Of course, if you were serious enough about someone enough to marry him, you would tell him about your past. He was naive to think that Carter didn't know who he was. He actually felt a bit like an asshole for doing this to the guy. There was nothing going on with Alexia, but how was Carter supposed to believe that?

"It's not like that, Carter. Alexia just needed a place to stay. I'm sure she told you that her parents have been less than . . . supportive."

"What?" Carter asked, clearly having no idea what he was talking about. "I gather you know, but she already told her parents as well?" The concern in Carter's voice was real and raw. Brant found himself feeling sorry for him.

Alexia was nowhere to be seen and Brant sat on a barstool in his kitchen faced with a decision. If she was going to place him in the middle of whatever was going on with Carter, then he wasn't going to lie when asked a direct question. "Yeah, she did and it was . . . tough."

Carter's voice rose again as he asked, "What do you mean, tough?"

Sighing, Brant said, "Tough as in don't expect any support from them. I think they pretty much made her feel like an outcast and she left. With things up in the air with you and them cutting her off at the knees, she was desperate. That's the only reason she would have come to me after all this time."

"Damn, she really didn't need that after me being such an asshole about the whole thing."

"I don't really know much about Alexia now, but back when we were together, she had always had a man in her life making the decisions. First, it was her father and then me. I think she almost needs the comfort and familiarity now while she tries to get her life together. Especially if things are unsettled between you two. I suspect that's the biggest reason she turned to me when her parents didn't offer it."

"Yeah," Carter answered absently, "that makes sense.

I guess I have been playing that role in our relationship. I just . . . I'm so afraid of her falling back into that old crowd she was running with. I can't stand to see her relapse after going through so much to get clean. She thinks it means I don't trust her and that she's just a burden to me. I know that she's doubting our whole relationship no matter how much I try to convince her that everything is okay."

Brant was starting to feel like he was a cross between Alexia's father and a host on a dating show, but this stuff happened when you got involved in people's lives—and he was in up to his neck in Alexia's. "Just give her time, Carter. Let her recover from this fallout with her parents and then try again."

Carter insisted on leaving his phone number and grudgingly thanked him for his help. Finally, with assurances that he would call if anything happened with Alexia, Brant gratefully ended the conversation. He wasn't used to dealing with emotional people very often, and it was damned exhausting. Suddenly he remembered the day that Emma had faked a crying spell at work to yank his chain and chuckled. God, he missed her so much in that moment that he felt an actual ache in the area of his heart. He was more determined than ever to get things settled here so he could focus his attention back on the little spitfire who was turning his carefully ordered existence on its ass.

"I'm sorry, Brant." He turned to find Alexia shifting nervously from one foot to the other behind him. "I shouldn't have put that off on you. It's just too . . .

hard." Brant felt a different ache as she started to sob on the last word. This ache he knew was something like heartburn from too much stress. No doubt he had even consumed some type of dairy product without thinking during dinner as well.

"It's okay, Lex, I managed. Carter seems like a nice guy and he obviously cares about you."

The tears started falling harder and Brant thought that maybe he should have suggested they talk in the morning and run for the sanctuary of his room. It was probably never smart to mention anything about feelings to an emotional woman.

"He's . . . great . . . he does . . . love . . . me," Alexia managed to get out between sobs. Brant pulled a tissue from the box on the bar and then thought better of it and handed her the entire box instead. He patted her back awkwardly and for the second time that day she wrapped her arms around him and cried. He rubbed her back and just let her cry. He had a feeling that the upheaval with Carter was just a small part of the upset. Very little time had passed since she had left rehab, and she was no doubt still trying to come to terms with the daily struggle to stay clean. She was scared to be a burden to Carter, but terrified to be alone. He cursed her parents silently for being so insensitive to what their daughter was going through. She needed them and whether they had intended to or not, they had confirmed in her mind that she was nothing but a burden to those she loved now. Brant felt that if things had gone better with them, she would have been more willing to listen to Carter and have hope that their relationship could work.

"He does love you," Brant agreed, "and he's worried about you."

She took a moment to dry her eyes before asking, "Will you come sit with me for a while? Maybe we could watch a movie. You're the only one I feel good around right now." Brant felt warning bells go off inside of him. He could be her friend, regardless of their history, but he couldn't be her savior. That job needed to go to the man who loved her. He would have to step carefully, because he didn't want to drive a wedge between her and Carter.

"Ah, I wish I could. I have some meetings tomorrow." *She must think you're an insensitive prick, but it's for the greater good, right?* "I . . . it's just that I was away for a few days and now things are really backed up at work."

Her smile didn't quite reach her eyes. "It's okay. I grew up with a workaholic father, so I do understand that business usually comes first." Brant winced, but he didn't see any other options. Whether she wanted to admit it or not, Carter was the man she needed to be her rock now.

"If you're all right now, I think I'll head to bed. Do you have everything you need?"

Alexia nodded and turned toward the guest room. Great, Brant thought as he walked toward the master bedroom at the other end of the house. That was the second time in one day that a woman had looked at him like he was an asshole. First, Emma for having her make dinner reservations and now Alexia. He didn't seem to be pleasing any of the women in his life and that stung a lot more than it used to.

Chapter Fifteen

Suzy looked up from her computer as Emma threw herself in the chair in front of her friend's desk. Before she was even seated, she moaned to Suzy, "You aren't going to believe this."

"Oh, go ahead and try me," Suzy said with interest.

"I started on the R and R that we talked about last night and I'm pretty sure I got busted on my first mission."

Suzy waved her hand impatiently as Emma paused to gather her thoughts. "Come on, I've got to hear the rest."

Covering her eyes in shame, Emma admitted, "I decided to do a drive-by of Brant's house on the way to work. I mean, I don't know what I thought I would see at eight o'clock in the morning . . . Maybe Brant and Alexia making out in front of the house for everyone to see?"

Looking curious, Suzy asked, "So what did you see?"

"The bumper of Brant's car," Emma mumbled.

"Come again?" Suzy asked.

"Brant was pulling out of his driveway when I drove slowly by and I think he saw me."

"Nah, that's pretty early and he wouldn't have been expecting you in the area, so I doubt it would have occurred to him."

"But he waved," Emma said.

Suzy shook her head. "Men wave at everyone; he probably thought you were his neighbor. I don't think you have anything to worry about. Even if he did recognize you, he might think it's on your way to work."

"He knows where I live and he would know that his house isn't vaguely on my way. There's another reason I think he saw me." When Suzy raised her brows in question, Emma said, "He pulled up beside me at the red light right up the street from his house and motioned for me to pull over."

"Uh-oh," Suzy muttered. "Well, what excuse did you make when you talked to him?"

"I . . . um . . . didn't stop. I took the next turnoff and went the long way to work. I came straight to your office, so I haven't seen him yet. Shit, what am I going to say?"

"Hmm, well you've already used up one of the guaranteed ways to get a man to leave you alone and that's by crying. Since he probably wouldn't fall for that a second time, use the whole 'it's that time of the month' thing. Trust me, I don't care how much he wants to question you, if you start talking about Aunt Flo coming to town, the man is going to turn tail and run."

"Aunt Flo?" Emma asked.

"It's slang for your period. Also a word of advice: Usually if you decide to stalk someone at home, you borrow a different car. Next time you get the urge to spy on him, let me know and we'll change cars for the evening or I'll just go over and do it for you."

"Really? Wouldn't that be hard to explain to Gray?"

Suzy laughed. "Honey, Gray never asks questions about things that he really doesn't want to hear the answers to. He is still so traumatized by knowing too many details of his brother and Beth's relationship that he can barely be in the room with both of them. He always knew his brother was a bit of a horn-dog, but he never thought it would involve his wife's sister." Suzy shuddered. "Hell, I never thought it would either, come to think of it."

Emma stood up, coming around the desk to give her friend a hug before leaving. She stopped to talk to Ella at the receptionist desk for another few minutes, making her late by the time she made it to her office. Brant was standing in his doorway obviously waiting for her when she opened the door. He leaned against the doorframe and with no preliminaries asked, "Why'd you take off this morning?"

"I . . . er . . ." Shit, she was already stuttering like someone guilty. She might as well admit to teenage stalking and get the humiliation out of the way.

"I wasn't sure it was you until I was next to you at the light. What were you doing out that way?" he asked.

"I was looking for a drugstore," she blurted out.

"Oh . . . isn't there a Walgreens right down the street from your place?" *Damn, she should have known he had his brain wired like Google Maps.* At least he looked puzzled and not suspicious.

Trying to maintain eye contact, she said, "They weren't open yet."

"But there's also a Walgreens near my house, so wouldn't both stores have the same hours?" he asked.

"My God, Judge Judy, can we end the questions! I have PMS! Do you need to know what I bought and if I favor pads or tampons?" Emma watched in fascination as a red flush ran up Brant's neck and settled on his cheeks.

"I . . . shit . . . I'm sorry," he stuttered. "I shouldn't have kept pushing you like that." He turned to go back in his office, then turned back, looking at the floor, "I didn't mean to embarrass you." She sat on the corner of her desk, surprised at how fast the tide had turned. Brant went from twenty questions to running from her. She hadn't seen him move that fast since he figured out what kind of book her mom's book club was discussing. She definitely owed Suzy one. It had saved her from what was potentially a very embarrassing conversation.

Brant leaned back with his feet propped on his desk, taking a moment to relax. The day had been nonstop busy and, truthfully, he had hidden like a coward in his office since embarrassing himself with Emma first thing in the morning. He'd been so surprised to see her near his house on his drive to work and had hoped for a moment that she was stopping by because she wanted to see him. He thought maybe he had imagined the whole thing until he pulled beside her car at the light. She had looked him straight in the eye and turned the other way at a fast clip. He still thought it was kind of strange that she would come to a pharmacy near his house when she lived in a busy area with plenty of stores. He knew, though, that you never questioned a woman about the choices she made at that time of the month. He had only continued to question her because he was disappointed that she hadn't been in the area to see him. Pathetic, but true.

Emma walked into his office carrying a bag. She plopped it on his desk and settled in the chair across from him. "Hey, babe," he said before remembering where they were. She smiled in return, seeming to enjoy his slip of the tongue.

"Hey, yourself. I thought you might be hungry since you haven't had a chance to leave today." She chuckled as he looked at the bag warily.

"Don't worry. I actually picked it up in the cafeteria on my way up so it should be fresh. It's just a bowl of chili and some cornbread. I figured you might like something new," she finished with a smirk. She knew he hated the soggy sandwiches that she usually brought back for him.

Brant opened the lid, inhaling appreciatively. "Wow, this smells great, thanks." He swallowed a bite of the chili as she got up to leave. "Wait, Em. I've barely talked to you since we got back. Do you . . . want to go to dinner or something tonight? I'd love to see you . . . away from here."

Her eyes softened. "I'd like that. How about I cook dinner for us?"

Brant smiled, thinking the evening would sound even more promising if she hadn't admitted to having her period this morning. What the hell, at this point he'd be happy to just spend time with her. They talked while he finished his lunch. He stood to give her a quick kiss of thanks just as Mark DeSanto walked in without warning. "Am I interrupting?" By the leer on his face, Brant could tell that the other man already knew the answer. He was surprised to see Emma looking flustered as she gave Mark a tight smile before walking out and shutting the door behind her.

"Was it something I said?" Mark laughed. Before Brant could answer, he added, "I guess that would be why she wasn't interested in going out with me. I have to admit, I was puzzled."

Brant was taken aback by his sudden desire to throttle his old friend. He had always gotten along well with him, although they had few things other than business in common. The only thing that surpassed Mark's love of women was their love of him. Brant suspected women were probably drawn to the whole emotionally unavailable thing. Mark was rich, a fitness buff, and Brant could grudgingly admit that women probably found his dark looks attractive. In their course of business, he had been out socially with Mark before and while he was completely focused on business when it was important, as soon as the deal was over, he was looking to blow off some steam and that usually came in the form of a woman. Mark worked hard and he played harder.

He'd known him for years and in that time, there had never been a serious relationship in his life that Brant was aware of. Hell, he knew he wasn't much better, but he had never dealt in the sheer quantity of women that his friend seemed to. He decided to ignore the line of questioning concerning Emma and change the subject. "Did we have a meeting today?"

Mark quirked a brow, seeming to notice the subject change. "No, we didn't. I stopped by to drop off some paperwork with Jason and thought I'd see if you were free for lunch. I see you've already eaten, though. I don't guess you're free for a drink tonight either."

Brant knew the last question was a challenge and he didn't give a damn. If this had been business, he would have worked something out, but he wasn't going to change his plans with Emma tonight just to prove something to Mark. He shuffled some papers on his desk, saying, "I'm tied up, sorry." Brant silently cursed his choice of words, knowing exactly what Mark was picturing him doing with Emma now.

Mark was at the door before he turned to ask, "How's Ava been? I was disappointed she couldn't make it to dinner last night."

"She's fine." At that, Mark finally smiled and walked

out. Brant heard him talking to Emma for a few minutes before the outer door clicked shut. The last thing his sister needed was to get mixed up with Mark De-Santo. She didn't need any more trauma in her life, and that was all someone like Mark would offer her. The one man she needed was Mac. Brant just hoped she opened her eyes and realized it before it was too late.

Chapter Sixteen

Emma opened the door to her apartment and felt her jaw drop open at the sight of Brant standing on her doorstep looking like the man she had fallen for in Florida. Gone were his work clothes and in their place were the cargo shorts and T-shirt that showcased his broad chest and muscular arms. In a suit, Brant looked good; in casual clothes, he was beyond handsome . . . incredibly hot. They both stood there uncertainly for a moment before he walked toward her and pushed the door shut behind him. God, she wanted him to kiss her.

It must have been written all over her face because suddenly he was there. His lips were on hers and his arms were encircling her waist. Her heart raced, her toes curled and her body hummed. *Well, hello Mr. Florida, welcome back!* When she felt his fingers pinch her nipple through her bra, she started pulling him toward the bedroom. She was desperate to rip his clothes off and run her hands all over his firmly chiseled body. "Em," he groaned as he pulled her body tightly against his. She felt the firm ridge of his arousal pressed against her. She dropped her hand, palming and lightly squeezing his length. "Fuck," he growled, pushing back against her.

"I need you inside me . . . now," she whispered.

He had just literally ripped the shirt from her body when he froze. "Fuck . . . Damn it! Em, stop! We can't . . . remember. . . ." He was taking deep breaths and trying to get himself back under control. She had no idea why he paused or what he was talking about and she knew she would probably explode if they stopped. She unclipped her bra and let the straps slide from her arms. She lifted Brant's shirt and slowly, deliberately, rubbed her erect nipples against his hairy chest. He shuddered against her as if in physical pain. "Em . . . baby, I've never . . . um . . . you know . . . had sex like this."

His words penetrated her sexual fog and she pulled back to look at him. "What are you talking about? Sex like what?"

He rubbed her shoulder almost consolingly as he shifted around nervously. What the hell was wrong with him? "During . . . that time of the month."

She looked at him blankly before it hit her. Oh shit! She had told him this morning that she had been near his house looking for supplies for her period. Crap! What a tangled web you weave when first you practice to deceive. No kidding! "Oh, that's finished," she said before reaching for him again.

"Whoa, what?" He was clearly confused.

She couldn't meet his gaze as she continued adding

to the lie that had gotten her in this mess in the first place. "It was a false alarm. I was all crampy this morning and I thought it was, you know . . . coming, but nothing ever happened, so I guess I was wrong." He was still giving her a skeptical look, so she decided that a distraction would be the only thing to save her and she went for it in a big way. She lifted the short skirt she was wearing and gave him an eyeful of what she was wearing underneath . . . nothing. She saw his face go blank and no more words were exchanged between them. He pushed her backward until her bed was against her knees. He paused only to strip off the rest of his clothes before following her down. She started to pull her skirt off when his hands stopped her.

"Don't. I want to lift this skirt and fuck you. Do you have a problem with that?" Before she could answer, he grabbed the foil pack he had thrown on the bed and tore it open, rolling the condom down his length.

"God, no," she moaned. With no more preliminaries, he proceeded to lift her skirt, wrap her legs around his waist and push into her, hard and fast. Her breath left in a whoosh as her body stretched to accommodate him. Just when she had settled into the hard rhythm, he put an arm around her, turning them both so that suddenly she was on top. He was even deeper now, hitting against her cervix. She put her hands against his chest, trying to control his thrusts. When he reached a hand out and started rubbing his thumb in circles against her clit, she forgot all about control and rode him hard . . . over and over until she was screaming his name. Her body came apart in an explosion of spasms and with another few quick thrusts into her quivering body, Brant joined her in release.

She collapsed against his sweaty chest, gasping for breath, too spent to separate her body from his. She had no idea how long they lay there, both trying to catch their breath and calm their racing hearts. When Brant's stomach growled against her ear, they both started laughing. He smacked her butt and asked, "Any chance you could feed me now like you promised?"

They took a quick shower together, soaking the bathroom floor as they teased each other. She was surprised by the end of their shower that one of them hadn't slid down and broken a bone. She slipped a short sundress over her head and left off the bra and panties. She thought Brant might enjoy that surprise later. Soon they were both sitting on her couch with bowls of shrimp pasta balanced on their knees. "So how's Alexia? Is she still staying with you?"

The fork that had been going toward Brant's mouth paused in midair before continuing on. He slowly chewed, seeming to drag it out as long as possible before answering. "She's fine and, yes, she is still there."

"Hmm, I see. That all still seems a bit strange to me." When it became obvious that Brant wasn't going to add any additional explanation, she decided to change the subject. Truthfully, she couldn't imagine that any man could make love to her with the intensity that he had exhibited and be having an intimate relationship with someone else at the same time. He definitely hadn't just

been going through the motions. He was just as focused and in the moment as he had been in Florida.
Maybe he did have the desire and stamina to go home
now and do the same thing with Alexia . . . but she just
didn't see it. Sure, she wasn't comfortable with the
other woman living with him and she felt like there
was more to the story than he was saying, but the alarm
bells in her head had dropped to a light ping now. He
still wanted her and that went a long way toward qui-
eting the inner stalker within her, at least for tonight.

Chapter Seventeen

Emma rubbed her temples, trying to soothe the headache pulsing there. To say it had been a hectic day would be a grave understatement. Both Jason and Gray had been called away on some emergency, which meant that many of their meetings and obligations for that day had been shifted to Brant, Declan and Nick. She had spent the morning running back and forth to Gray's and Jason's offices gathering files that Brant needed. They had worked steadily throughout the day with little time for any personal interaction. He had spent the night with her last night and left before dawn to go home for a change of clothes before work. She had given him a huge grin when he left her bed in the early-morning light, thinking of him making the walk of shame that was usually reserved for a woman leaving a man's apartment in the same clothes she had arrived in.

She studied him as she dropped another file on his desk. His eyebrows were furrowed and his jaw was flexed in concentration. He jotted notes in the notebook in front of him as he asked what seemed like a hundred questions. He looked like a perfect picture of every up-tight name she had ever called him. The problem now was that she knew there was more to him than that. He could completely immerse himself in work to the exclusion of all else, but he could also burn hotter than any man she had ever known. He looked up to give her an absent-minded smile, catching her in the middle of staring at him. He was so sexy to her in that moment that she wanted nothing more than to grab him by his paisley tie and drag him on the floor with her. Just one sharp pinch to the nipple like he had given her last night and she would orgasm right here on the beige carpet in front of his desk.

As he continued to study her expression, seeming to know what she was thinking, she was gratified to see his hand shake even though he never stumbled during his telephone conversation. She understood then how it was that he set her body on fire. Brant excelled at everything he touched . . . including her. Just as she was considering doing something drastic to rattle him such as taking off her panties and putting them on his desk, the door opened in the outer room and she turned to see Alexia Shaw standing there smiling shyly.

Emma smiled through clenched teeth even though she wanted to roll her eyes and do something completely juvenile like stick her tongue out at the other woman. Alexia was dressed in understated but obviously expensive clothing, and her hair was perfectly styled without a single hair out of place. In comparison, Emma felt like an underdressed slob in her simple black slacks and baby-doll top. Of all days, she had even worn flats, so Alexia seemed to tower over her.

Brant saw Alexia standing in the doorway and gave her a polite smile that didn't contain any of the heat that it had just moments ago. Thank God, maybe she wouldn't be forced to stab her with a pencil after all. Then Brant finished his call and motioned Alexia into one of the seats in front of his desk. Emma escaped to her office, leaving the door open behind her. She was surprised a few moments later when the door closed quietly. Maybe it was time to start sharpening those pencils after all.

Brant was surprised to see Alexia once again in his office. He had a feeling from the strained look on Emma's face that she was less than thrilled with her reappearance. He had been pondering dragging Emma out of here at five o'clock and into the nearest hotel before Alexia's impromptu visit. "What's up, Alexia?"

Alexia smiled in return, seeming to be more comfortable around him again. He would guess that it would be hard to remain on formal ground when someone knew most of your secrets. "I was hoping I could take you to dinner. I wanted to thank you for the last few days. I wasn't sure if you were . . . planning to come home tonight."

He settled back in his chair, noticing that Alexia seemed calmer today, more relaxed. He hated that he felt guilty about not calling to let her know where he was last night, but truthfully he hadn't wanted to imply an intimacy that wasn't there. She needed to get back to her life with Carter. "That's not necessary, Lex. I am happy to help. Are you feeling okay today? You look great."

She smiled, seeming happy over the compliment. "Thanks, Brant, not just for that, but for everything. I know that I had no right at all to come to you and expect you to solve my problems after what I put you through."

When he started to protest, she held up her hand. "No, just let me finish, please." She took a deep breath and continued. "I was horrible to you. It doesn't matter that I was strung out on drugs. I still knew what I was doing, at least in the beginning. I lied to you, I took money from your wallet on more than one occasion and I . . . God, I cheated on you, too."

Brant shut his eyes briefly, finding that he could still feel a twinge of pain over her confession even though he didn't love her anymore. He had suspected at the end that she was cheating, but hearing her confirm it was still a sucker punch to the gut. No man liked knowing that someone he loved had slept with another man during their time together, regardless of the circumstances. He rubbed the back of his neck, working on the knot of tension that had formed there.

"Lex, that was a long time ago. We've both moved on. Does it bother me? Sure, of course it does. But it's in the past. If you're looking for absolution, then I forgive you."

"I'm not looking for forgiveness, Brant. I guess I just needed to come clean with you. Even though you probably knew what was going on for the most part, I still just walked away from you in a restaurant parking lot."

Brant was afraid that the tears in her eyes would soon turn into full-blown sobbing if he didn't stop the conversation that had left them both so uncomfortable. This wasn't the time or place for this discussion. He leaned forward, getting her attention, and said, "Lex, stop doing this to yourself. It's over now. I don't hate you. You have far too much on your plate right now to rehash the past. If you want to do something for me, then take care of yourself. If you love Carter, then don't waste time second-guessing yourself. Build a life for you and for him."

She gave him a trembling smile. "That was the other thing I wanted to tell you. Carter called again last night and we talked everything out. I . . . still feel like he deserves better, but he promised me that he would let me know if it all became too much for him."

Brant had a feeling that was a conversation that Alexia would never have to have with Carter. He seemed like a good man who was very much in love with the woman sitting in front of him. She took a deep breath and wiped the last moisture from her eyes. "So, back to my original question, would you like to have dinner tonight? Please don't say no. We were friends before we were anything else, Brant, and I'd love one evening to catch up before I leave."

He found himself agreeing for old times' sake, even

though he wasn't completely comfortable with the idea. "Sure, that sounds great." He jotted down the time and place she suggested and walked her to the door as Emma buzzed him for his last conference call of the day.

When he finished his call, Emma was waiting with her handbag to walk out with him. He wanted to take her hand but knew it wasn't advisable to openly advertise their relationship at the office. He settled instead for a quick kiss in the elevator on the way to the lobby. No doubt the guys in security were having a laugh about it. As they exited the building, he saw Mac pulling up to the curb in his black Tahoe. He put his hand in the small of Emma's back, leading her toward the other man.

Mac was one of the few men Brant found himself looking up to. He was also one of the few people who made him want to run that extra mile on the beach in the mornings. Mac was all hard muscle, and leaving the military hadn't changed his dedication to physical fitness. In his line of work, he had to be observant, and Brant saw him take note of the possessive hand that he had on Emma's waist. Even though he didn't want to advertise their relationship to everyone at Danvers, he knew Mac could be trusted. The other man grinned at him before extending a hand. "Hey, man, we've run into each other a lot this week."

"Yes, we have." After Mac said hello to Emma, Brant asked, "Are you covering another shift today?" He was surprised and curious when Mac shifted uncomfortably.

"No . . . just picking someone up." When Brant heard footsteps behind them, he turned, fully expecting to see his sister. Instead of Ava, a stranger with long red hair walked to Mac's side. He was now closer to shocked when Mac slid his arm around the woman's shoulders and gave her a quick kiss. Mac's easygoing smile was back on his face, but Brant knew him well enough to see the strain behind it. "Brant, Emma, have you met Gwen Day? She works in marketing."

"Er . . . no, I haven't. Em?" Emma shook her head. After the introductions were made, a moment of awkward silence ensued. Brant was grateful when Emma stepped forward saying that she had to get home. Mac and Gwen walked toward his Tahoe while Emma took his hand and pulled him toward the parking garage.

"Yikes, was it my imagination or was that awkward as hell? I don't know Mac that well other than the few times he has been by to visit you, but I always kind of assumed that he was involved with Ava in some way."

Brant sighed as they reached Emma's car. "It's . . . complicated. Mac has been in love with her since we were kids, but Ava, well, she has issues. I always thought they would work it out in the end, though. I know she does love him in her own way. She just seems to have the Stone family curse of not being able to express herself." When Emma started chuckling, Brant nudged her, saying, "Hey, no comment necessary."

Emma smiled in return. "It looks like Mac is moving on. He wasn't groping her or anything, but that wasn't just a friendly embrace. Does your sister know?"

"I don't know," Brant admitted. "She has been acting funny lately, though. She and Mac are close in a distant way, if that makes sense, and I doubt that Mac could be dating and Ava not know about it. I should probably check in on her later."

Emma trailed her hand across his ass, murmuring, "Speaking of later . . ."

Here it was, Brant thought, the moment of truth. Did he lie to make this easier or man up and tell the truth? Oh, how he wanted to take the easy way out and lie. "Babe, I kind of promised Alexia that I would have dinner with her tonight. She wanted to thank me for letting her stay at my place."

When Emma just looked at him without saying anything, he stumbled on. "She's working things out with her fiancé, Carter. She's planning to move back in with him, so this is really more of a good-bye dinner." When he moved in to kiss her, she gave him a brief peck on the lips that was the equivalent of being stiff-armed. "I'll call you later?" *Shit, his statement had come out more like a question. Nothing like having some confidence.* She took her time getting in her car, almost as if she were waiting for him to add something more. When he didn't, she waved once as she backed out. He might not be that experienced in relationships, especially successful ones, but even he knew he was in trouble.

Chapter Eighteen

Emma slammed her apartment door behind her just to have the satisfaction of listening to it bang. She threw her handbag across the living room and gave in to the urge to stomp her feet. "Ugh!" she shouted to the empty apartment. When her cell phone rang, she actually thought for a moment that Brant had gotten the silent message she had been sending him. Seeing her mother's name on the caller ID, she knew there was no such luck.

"Hello, Mom."

"Well, aren't you just a ray of sunshine today, Emmie. What's wrong?"

Emma wedged the phone between her shoulder and neck while pulling an old bottle of wine from the refrigerator. If she was going to be dumped for another woman and have to talk to her mother tonight, she might as well have some alcohol in her system. She popped the cork and sniffed the bottle as her mother continued to badger her. Shrugging her shoulders, she poured a glassful and downed half of it in one sip.

When the line went silent, she knew she had missed answering a question. "What was that, Mom?"

"I asked how Brant was doing? Is he there now?"

"No," Emma muttered. "He has a date."

"Pardon?"

Rolling her eyes, Emma said, "I said he is working late."

"Oh," her mother laughed, "I thought you said something else. Honey, like I said, we just love him. He seems to adore everything about you. But my offer of a breast job is still on the table if you need it. It's the best thing I ever did for myself." Emma wondered idly if that included her marriage and motherhood, but she wasn't brave enough to ask.

Deciding to change the subject, she asked, "How's Boston doing? Is he on the chain gang yet?"

"Very funny; he is doing fine. Your uncle is confident that he can finish up some community service as long as he keeps out of trouble."

"If that's the case, maybe you should suggest he change his major? Something like computer science might be less encouraging to him than botany."

Her mother gave a disgusted snort before saying, "Honey, I think you need some sleep. You seem grumpy. Do you have PMS?"

Emma rolled her eyes. Boston was the baby of the family and if he got busted for growing a pot farm in their parents' bathroom, her mother would still defend him. Emma was starting to wonder if Boston was actually the slacker he pretended to be. Maybe it had served him well all of these years. *Poor Boston, it's just who he is.* She was fast coming to the conclusion that poor Boston might be the smartest one in the family.

She had to laugh when her mother said that her friend Doris had asked about buying a dime bag from Boston strictly for medicinal purposes . . . yeah, right.

When she finally managed to end the call, she checked her messages to make sure she hadn't missed one from either Brant or Suzy. She had left a few messages for Suzy during the day and had heard nothing back. That was really strange, considering that Jason and Gray also seemed to have been missing from work. Claire usually dropped in at some point during the day, but since Jason hadn't been at the office, she hadn't seen Claire either. She really missed Suzy's encouragement and would have loved to share this latest development with her. She needed someone to tell her if she was wrong to be hurt that she had been excluded once again by Brant. First the business dinner when the others had been taking their wives, and now he was having some thank-you dinner with Alexia? He had made no mention of inviting Emma along. Was it silly that being excluded once again hurt her feelings?

Last night had been so amazing. It was the first time they had been free to really explore each other. Their first time together in the hotel in Miami had been fast and furious, and their other encounters at her parents' house had been explosive but rushed. She had also held back to some degree for fear of being heard. Last night, though, had been something else entirely. The first time had been fast, but the second time had been a slow and gradual build of passion. They had made love, not just had sex, and for the first time, Emma knew the difference between the two. She had felt cherished afterward as she had lain in Brant's arms listening to the steady beat of his heart. He had stroked her hair with one hand while the other hand had drawn lazy circles against her side. She had slept curled into his side, with his arm anchoring her.

The uptight man that she had sniped with for so long had turned out to be so much more than that. He still had his moments when glimpses of the old Brant showed through, but she knew the fires that raged beneath the calm surface. He took her breath away when he touched her. She didn't want to drive him away by acting like a jealous girlfriend. He had been honest enough to tell her about Alexia staying with him and also about him having dinner with her tonight. She didn't think he was hiding anything. The only thing that bothered her was not knowing if Alexia was hiding something. Emma was in love with Brant and last night had just confirmed it. If she needed to be patient to win him, then she would, but if she needed to fight, then Alexia Shaw had better watch out. You didn't grow up as the daughter of Kat Davis without learning a thing or two.

Chapter Nineteen

Brant stumbled to the kitchen looking for the Tylenol bottle. Last night he had drunk entirely too much, which was unusual for him, especially during the week. Dinner with Alexia had started off so awkwardly that he had turned to alcohol to relax. Alexia had stuck to water, which was part of her postrehab treatment plan. By the end of the evening, he vaguely recalled that they had been joking around about old times. He suspected the Jack and Coke had something to do with that. Luckily, Alexia had driven them home afterward and other than a good-night kiss that made things uncomfortable for a brief moment, the evening had been fine. He had fallen into bed around midnight and he wasn't sure, but he thought he might have had phone sex with Emma before he went to sleep. A quick look at his cell phone confirmed that he had called her. Well, at least she wasn't likely to believe that he had been sleeping with Alexia while talking dirty to her. He shook his head in amazement—phone sex? What had happened to his perfectly ordered life? He couldn't find it in himself to regret the change. Life was better than it had been in a long time.

He grabbed a bottle of water from the refrigerator and downed it in one long guzzle. He tossed it in the trash can and grimaced as it popped back out and onto the floor. Shit. He'd never been one to have overflowing trash cans, but since Alexia had been staying with him, the condition of his house had gone downhill. She was a messy guest who didn't do much cleaning up after herself. The trash bag had slipped into the can and he mumbled a string of profanities as he slid his hand down the side, trying to pull the plastic back up.

He was shocked when he felt arms sliding around his waist and someone purred, "Good morning," against his back.

Jerking around, he gaped at Alexia standing closely behind him. "Lex . . . What are you doing?"

She smiled, reaching out to touch his arm. "Just saying good morning, silly. How did you sleep?"

"Er . . . fine, thanks. And you?" Something about the way she was looking at him made him uncomfortable. He turned to finish wrestling the bag from the trash can, figuring it was probably just his imagination. She was leaving today, right?

"I slept great after our dinner." Again, she reached out to touch him and this time, he knew something was definitely up. "Thank you for listening to me last night. I know it seems crazy after all this time and everything that happened, but we need to know before the moment is lost, right?"

What in the hell was she talking about? Apparently, he had been privy to this conversation last night, but damned if he could remember much about it. Why had he let himself have that last Jack and Coke? He remembered bits and pieces about her wanting to go back to school. That had to be it. "Um . . . yeah, of course." *That's it. Try to keep your answers general so she won't know that you're winging it.* When she beamed her approval at his reply, he figured he was convincing enough. Time to get out of here before she put him in the hot seat again. "I'm . . . I've got to get ready for work."

"Oh, of course." He was just turning away when she threw her arms around his neck, hugging him tightly. "I'm so happy we've decided to see if there is still something between us. I'll call Carter today and tell him that I need more time." She shyly gave him a light kiss on the mouth. He had never been more grateful that she was a timid person because otherwise he had a feeling that kiss would have involved tongue.

"Lex . . . I . . ." Shit, he was scrambling, trying to figure out what to say without hurting her feelings. "Damn, I'm just going to be honest here. I don't remember agreeing to anything last night. I had too much to drink and a lot of the evening is just a blur for me. I mean, you're engaged to Carter and I'm . . . seeing someone."

She took his hand, leading him to the small table in the breakfast nook. "I guess I did do a lot of the talking last night," she admitted. "You did mention that you were seeing someone. The whole evening just felt so easy with you, so natural, and I know you felt it too.

"Being with you again has made me realize how much I gave up and that scares me. I love Carter, but you were my first love, Brant, and a part of me has never let that go. Don't you think we both owe it to ourselves to make sure we're with the right people? What if everything that's happened to throw us back together is for a reason? Maybe in the end, we were always meant to find each other again."

My God, how did he answer that? Sitting here beside her as he had done so many times in the past was making him think of things that he hadn't in years. After everything that had happened between them, hadn't he at times missed having her in his life? But if that was a thought he was even entertaining, where did that leave things with Emma?

Standing abruptly, he said, "Alexia . . . I need some time to think about this." Without waiting for a reply, he took off to his bedroom. Frankly, he couldn't take anything else this morning. He didn't handle emotional upheaval well and this far surpassed that.

Brant made his way to his bedroom and slumped on the bed. He had thought that chapter of his life was over for good, yet here she was. He hadn't allowed himself to really think about her in those terms knowing she was engaged to another man, but now . . . he was confused as fuck. He needed some space away from here to think. His perfectly sane, rational life had been blown all to hell. Two women? Stuff like that just didn't happen to him.

When Jason called asking if he could take over

Gray's travel obligations, he jumped at the chance. He would be traveling with Mark DeSanto and as luck would have it, Mark needed to leave today. Yeah, he knew running wouldn't solve his problems, but it would damn sure give him space to breathe.

Emma was surprised to find that she had arrived at the office ahead of Brant. She had even stopped at Starbucks to pick up coffee for them both on the way. She smiled when she put his cup on his desk. Love, it appeared, was turning her into a better person. Sure, they still found ways to nag each other during the day but mainly because it was a form of foreplay for them. She didn't want nice Brant; she wanted the smart-ass that turned her on with just one sarcastic curl of his full lips.

She had just settled in at her desk when she noticed the message light blinking on her phone. She was surprised to hear Brant's voice telling her that he was running late but would be there for his ten o'clock appointment. Why hadn't he just called her cell phone? She pulled it from her handbag to make sure she hadn't missed his call. When her phone showed no missed calls, she shrugged. He had probably called the office first, thinking she was there. It would have been silly to place another call, right?

Emma had been working steadily for an hour when she looked up to see Ella open the door. She dropped the pen she had been holding and grinned at her friend. "Hey, Els, what brings you to my side of the building?"

Ella's pregnancy was more noticeable now and she looked so freaking adorable with her small baby bump. Even though she had never really thought about having kids, Emma had to admit to feeling a pang of longing at how her friend glowed. She had tamed the wild Stone brother and she had never looked happier. Emma was thrilled for Ella and envious all at the same time. She wondered idly if that made her a horrible person. When Ella settled into a chair in front of her desk, Emma realized that she had been so occupied thinking of all that was going right for Ella that she had missed the signs that there was also something wrong. It was there in the worry lines around her mouth, her eyes and in the smile that didn't fully reach her eyes. "Is . . . something wrong?"

Ella sighed and rubbed her eyes. Emma sat up straighter in her chair. Were those tears in her friend's eyes? "I just talked to Beth. I know you had been trying to reach Suzy yesterday. I think we all had at some point. It's not like her to just not show up, right? I was worried when I found out that Gray, Jason and Claire all seemed to have disappeared as well. Beth tried to call them several times during the day. We were both concerned. When Beth arrived this morning, she pulled me aside to let me know what had happened."

Emma wondered if Ella was aware that she had placed a protective hand over her stomach before continuing. "Suzy was pregnant. I don't know all of the details, but the pregnancy was ectopic and she had to have emergency surgery to remove one of her tubes."

"Oh my God," Emma whispered. "She was pregnant? I had no idea. I didn't . . . She didn't tell me."

"She didn't tell anyone. She had lost other pregnancies, but she didn't want anyone to know. She didn't want anyone to feel bad that she was having problems." With those words, the tears that Ella had been holding back slid down her cheeks. Emma handed her a tissue. She remembered asking Suzy whether she had received the results yet and she had said no. Now Emma understood why she had seemed evasive. "I'm sorry for blubbering all over you; damn it, I never stop crying now."

"I think it's probably normal, and this is upsetting to me, too, so I understand how you feel."

"Yeah, but at least you're not over there leaking all over the place," Ella sobbed. "I accidentally washed Declan's white T-shirt with my red shirt and turned it pink last night. He laughed and I cried for an hour. He even insisted on wearing it to dinner afterward, which made me cry again because it was just so sweet of him."

Again, Emma felt a flicker of jealousy at the relationship between Declan Stone and his wife. What was wrong with her today? One of her best friends was in the hospital after losing another baby and all she could do was feel jealous of their other friend's good fortune? When had she ever been so petty? She couldn't be happier for Ella and her heart was broken for Suzy.

Was this what love turned you into? Someone who could concentrate only on her own problems and didn't care about anyone else? Geez, she was starting to feel like an emotional wreck. There was no need for Ella to feel bad about her own emotional displays. Emma was right there with her, only hers were manifested into something of the green variety. Where were all of the things that those damn Hallmark cards promised you? Instead of basking in her feelings, she had turned into an insecure, paranoid, jealous wreck. A shell of her former careful self, it seemed. Sure, Brant's ex-fiancée moving in with him completely out of the blue was enough to push almost any woman to the edge, but poor Ella hadn't committed any sins other than being happy. She really needed to get a grip. She had already been caught this week doing a drive-by of the object of her affection's house—where did it end? Ugh.

She walked around the desk and gave Ella a hug. "I remember Beth not too long ago complaining about crying in McDonald's when they brought the McRib back, so I think it's normal. Don't beat yourself up over it. Caring about people isn't a crime, so you shouldn't have to feel like it is." *Yeah, and I need to be more like Ella and stop thinking about myself.*

Mark DeSanto, Brant's ten o'clock appointment, walked in just ahead of Brant. Both she and Ella seemed to take a deep breath as the testosterone level in the room skyrocketed. She heard Ella make an appreciative sigh and she was right there with her. She was surprised when Mark walked over to her and threw an arm around her shoulders. "Ah, sweet Emma, it's been too long."

She laughed. "It's been what . . . a day?" She saw Brant frowning at them and wanted to stick her tongue out in response.

Mark gave her a sexy grin. "Even a day without seeing your face is too long." Mark had just turned to say hello to Ella when Brant motioned her impatiently into his office.

"I'm flying to Boston with Mark this morning. Gray is going to be out for a few weeks, so I'm taking over his obligations until then." He kept his head down as he continued to pack his briefcase. "Things are going to be tight time wise. I'll probably fly straight from Boston to Dallas instead of coming home for a day."

Surprised, Emma asked, "When are you going to be back?"

He shrugged his shoulders. "Probably the end of next week, but I don't know for certain. Gray had a full schedule and added to mine, I'll be traveling a lot in the next month."

Emma felt her heart fall. "Could I . . . I mean, do you need me to come with you?"

He stopped what he was doing to look at her. "I wish you could, Em, but I need you here. Also, Mark will be with me on this first leg and I don't think it would be a good idea."

Before she could say anything in response, Mark stepped in the doorway looking at his obviously expensive watch. "My pilot just texted to tell me that he's ready."

Impressed despite herself, Emma asked, "You have your own plane?"

Mark nodded. "I take a lot of last-minute trips and I like my privacy. I'd be happy to give you a ride sometime."

Emma looked at him suspiciously, wondering if there was a double meaning in that offer. From the look on Brant's face, she didn't think she was the only one wondering. Brant motioned Mark out with a clipped "Let's go." He squeezed Emma's hand as he passed. "I'll call you later." And then he was gone. She stared after him, disappointed. What had she expected really? A sweeping kiss in front of Mark?

Ella stood, jarring Emma from her trance. She felt bad that she had completely forgotten that the other woman was still there. "I've got to get back to my desk, but are you free tonight?"

Looking at the door again, Emma sighed and said, "Yeah, you could say that."

"Beth is coming over. Declan is taking Evan to a movie and out to dinner. Nick is taking Henry for dinner with his parents, so it would be just the girls." Giving her a look full of sympathy, she added, "You look like you need to vent."

Dropping her head, Emma said, "You have no idea."

Chapter Twenty

Brant relaxed back in the leather captain's chair in Mark's private plane. He looked around the cabin, impressed as always by the excesses of the wealthy. Jason Danvers was a rich man but still flew commercial. Danvers could easily afford to have his own private jet on call, but that wasn't how Jason operated and Brant respected him for it. The man might close a multimillion-dollar deal one morning and stop to get groceries for his wife on the way home that evening. Brant was wealthy in his own right as well but didn't live a flashy lifestyle. If there were two things he knew, money made life easier, but it also brought about its share of problems. When you had it, someone else always wanted it. Brant dropped his jacket on the sofa behind him and tried not to imagine how many women had been given more than a plane ride on it.

Mark settled in to the seat across from him, dropping his briefcase on the table in front of him before swiveling around. The plane taxied smoothly down the runway and was soon airborne. No matter how often he flew, Brant never got used to the feeling of his stomach dropping to his feet as the plane climbed.

"So what's happening with you and the luscious Emma?"

Brant scowled before he could stop himself. "I don't think that's any of your business, and I'd appreciate it if you would stop hitting on her."

Mark grinned, completely unperturbed by his unfriendly tone. "Ah, come on, brother, it's innocent enough."

With a grimace, Brant admitted, "It's . . . complicated right now."

Mark swirled the liquid in the bottom of the crystal glass he was holding, looking pensive. "It always is when a woman's involved. Just a word of friendly advice: If you like the girl, then claim her. The next man might not be as nice as I am."

"Nice? Give me a break, Mark; you and I both know that's not a word that describes you where women are concerned."

Mark raised a brow. "And yet there is never a shortage of willing participants. Do you know why?"

Brant waved a hand. "Do tell."

"It's because all of the nice guys like you stay safely on the fence, ensuring that there's never a shortage for bastards like me."

Brant turned to face the other man, annoyed enough to take the gloves off. "If you can't be with the one you love . . . get spanked by the one you're with? Is that saying about accurate?"

"You have no idea," Mark drawled.

"Oh, I think I do. You know, small towns, people talk. You're practically a legend." Brant knew he was taking things too far, but the stress of the last twenty-four hours, coupled with the threat of losing Emma to Mark, was more than he could take. His frustration was boiling over and Mark was an easy target.

"So how does someone get into that sort of thing? Not spanked enough as a child? Spanked too much? I've always been curious, so please enlighten me."

If Brant was expecting an explosion from the other man, he was sorely disappointed. Far from looking angry, Mark seemed greatly amused. He should have remembered that the guy loved nothing better than a good debate. Mark moved his briefcase unhurriedly off the table before propping his legs on it, crossing his feet at the ankles. "It sounds like you've given a lot of thought to my . . . lifestyle. As to how it started, pick your cliché, buddy. I've got mommy and daddy issues. Fuck—I'll even throw in some granddaddy issues just for good measure. I don't know that that means a damn thing, though. I just love women."

Brant couldn't contain his smirk. "You mean, you love to tie up women and whip them, don't you? That's a little different from showing a girl a good time, isn't it?"

Mark gave him an answering smirk before he spoke. "That depends on the woman. I'll just say, I've never had a woman who didn't want to come back for seconds; I just rarely serve them. It's not all black and white, my friend. I would think that with a brother like Declan and a sister like Ava, you'd know that better than anyone. It appears that your family keeps just as many secrets as mine."

"Fuck you," Brant murmured halfheartedly. He had a bad feeling that it was too late to warn the other man off his sister. The thought of Mark punishing his sister was more than he could bear to think of. Ava was just messed up enough to look for something like that over choosing a man who had loved and looked out for her for years. Damn it, he should have never started this conversation.

Mark chuckled. "This all started with a simple question. It's not my fault that you choose the hard way around answering. I won't pursue Emma. In avoiding the question, you told me all I needed to know. Don't screw around, though, if you care about her. Trust me, even the most faithful people get tired of someone who runs from the truth."

Brant looked at Mark in confusion, but the other man was back to staring in his drink, almost as if seeking answers to some unknown questions there. Maybe he was completely off base with his assumption that Mark's family caused him to be the way he was. Maybe it was much more basic, more simple. Could he have loved and lost someone? It happened every day and maybe Mark was no exception. He had been right about one thing, though. It would be so easy to lose Emma, especially with the uncertainty that Alexia had unleashed in his life. Just the thought of it was enough to make a surge of panic race through his system. He just prayed he could keep it all together until he had a clue as to what to do.

"I totally love you, Ella—you know that, right?"

Oh God, was she slurring already? Emma wondered. This was only her second—or was it third—drink? Beth had given them an update on Suzy earlier. The first round had been to ease some of the sadness they all felt for someone who was dear to each of them.

Beside her on the couch, Beth nodded her agreement. "Isn't she the best? She can't drink right now and she still fixed us this big-ass pitcher of margaritas. Who does that?"

Ella smiled indulgently at them. "You girls really needed it. You both looked like you were either fixing to cry or have a breakdown. You are much happier drunk."

Emma held her glass up in the air. "I'll drink to that. If Brant had never done me with his sexy-ass body, I wouldn't be in this condition. I would be happily hating him instead of remembering what a big . . ."

"Personality he has?" Beth added before falling over in laughter.

"It must run in the family because Declan has a really big . . . personality." When both Emma and Beth gaped at her, Ella's face flamed. "Well, he does," she murmured under her breath.

Beth took another sip from her glass, then added, "Nick's no slouch in that area either. When I finally got the release to have sex again after having Henry, I couldn't walk right for a week. Henry's staying the night with the grandparents tonight, too, so when I go home . . . oh yeah, baby."

Emma giggled. "I really should hate you right now. I don't even have a vibrator to go home to. The Miami airport kept my pink rabbit for evidence. I should have picked those pills off it and taken the damn thing with me. Of course, after the drug dog slobbered all over it, that would have been kind of gross."

"Did you want to . . . do it more when you were pregnant?" Ella asked Beth.

"Mm-hmm," Beth laughed. "I was constantly horny. Nick loved it."

"I'm not pregnant, but I am constantly horny between the hours of eight and five now," Emma moaned. "When Brant shows up in one of his uptight suits, I almost orgasm. Things were much easier before I knew what was under his clothes."

"I bet he feels the same way," Beth offered. "Men can't get caught in a stiff wind without getting hard. It must be torture for him to see you every day and not throw you down on the desk."

Emma fanned herself, saying, "Oh, how I wish he would."

"I still have that fantasy about Declan," Ella added. "I've always dreamed of him throwing me on top of my desk and taking what he wants. Of course, being that I work in reception where a hundred people walk back and forth during the day, we'd be sure to have an audience."

"At this point, I don't think I'd care if Jason Danvers himself watched Brant and me as long as I could have him."

Beth wiggled her brow suggestively. "Maybe you'd just like for Jason to join in. Come on, I wouldn't admit it to Claire but . . . haven't we all had a fantasy or two about that man?"

Emma raised her hand. "Guilty as charged."

When Ella looked around the room without answering, Beth said, "Oh, come on, Els, you can't tell me you've never had some dirty thoughts about Jason. Every woman who works for Danvers has had them. The whole rich, powerful man in charge thing is a real panty-dropper."

Emma snickered, nodding. Ella looked like a kid with her hand in the cookie jar when she asked, "You both promise you will never tell Claire I said this, right?" Emma crossed her chest before taking a vow of silence along with Beth. "I did have a crush on him when I first started. It was nothing like how I felt when I met Declan, but I would get to work early every day just so I could see him walk in the lobby and to the elevator. He had the best butt I had ever seen."

They all howled with laughter. Emma spilled some of her drink on her shirt and did her best to wipe it off with her hand. Beside her, Beth had slumped from her chair and onto the floor, still giggling. "All right, I've got one for you," Beth gasped out. "This is a pinkie-swear that you not tell anyone." When everyone agreed, Beth confessed, "Nick dances for me sometimes. I bought him a pair of red thong underwear for Valentine's Day and he likes to wear them and dance to the song 'Sexy and I Know It.' He thrusts his hips better than a Chippendale dancer."

"No-o-o," Ella sputtered.

"Oh yes." Beth smirked. "I even put dollar bills in his underwear sometimes. He's got this really dirty thing where he rubs his—" At that moment, the front door opened and they all jumped. Declan walked in with Nick not far behind him.

Ella bolted up from the couch looking flustered and guilty. "What are you doing home so early?" she stammered.

Declan walked over to his wife, curving an arm protectively around her waist. He gave her a hard kiss on the lips. "It's not early, baby. I'm actually running a little late because Evan wanted me to come in and see his new science kit. Nick was pulling in behind me when I got here."

"Oh," Ella said, clearly at a loss as to what to say next.

Emma jumped up and then grabbed the back of a chair when she swayed on her feet. "Whew, I think I should have skipped that last one. I need to head home."

"Oh no, you don't," Nick said. "We can't let you drive yourself home. Beth and I will drop you." Beth snuggled up against Nick, giving him a smacking kiss on his neck.

Great, Emma thought, now I have to watch them grope each other all the way home.

"I'll run Emma home," Declan offered. "I forgot Ellie's orange juice, so I need to go back out anyway."

"You're my hero." Emma beamed at him. When she saw Beth cup Nick's butt on the way out the door, she knew she had been saved from some awkward moments. She hugged Ella and stumbled toward the door. Declan embraced Ella once again, causing a lump to form in Emma's throat. You would have to be blind not to see how much he loved his wife. What would it feel like to have someone waiting for her at the end of the day?

Next Declan took Emma's arm and led her toward his truck. Just as she settled into the passenger seat and Declan closed the door, her phone rang. She rummaged through her handbag with what seemed like five thumbs before finally pulling it out. "Yes?"

"Em?" Her heart skipped as she heard Brant's voice on the other end.

"Hey! Where are you?"

"Er . . . Still in South Carolina. Greenville, actually. Mark needed to make a stop here before heading on to Boston. We're staying at the Hyatt on Main Street." He was quiet for a moment, then asked, "Where are you?"

"Oh, I'm with your brother. Did you want to talk to him?" Emma had just started to pass the phone to a surprised Declan when Brant said hurriedly, "No, but what are you doing with him? Is Ella with you?"

"Ella? No, she's at home. It's just Declan and me."

Brant almost sounded angry as he demanded, "What are you doing with him? It's midnight."

Surprised, Emma said, "Really? Wow, that *is* late. It's okay, though, because we're going to my place now."

"What the fuck!" Brant exploded.

Declan, obviously hearing his brother's loud curse, held his hand out for her phone.

Relieved, she handed it over. "Good luck, the stick's back up his ass tonight."

The corners of Declan's mouth twitched and it looked like he was trying hard not to laugh. He put the phone up to his ear. "Hello, brother." He listened for a moment before he said, "Will you chill out? She was with Ellie and Beth tonight at my house. I wasn't even home. She had a few drinks, so I didn't think she should be driving. I'm just dropping her off at home on the way to the store for Ellie." Declan finally ended the call and handed her the phone back. "You're supposed to call Daddy back when you get home."

For some reason, that struck Emma as funny and she laughed until tears ran down her cheeks. "God," she gasped out, "why couldn't I have slept with the funny brother? Whoops, maybe that came out wrong. I'm not saying you specifically, just that I could use a man with a sense of humor, you know?"

"Er . . . yeah, I think so." Instead of looking offended, he looked vastly amused. "I've been accused of having a stick up my ass a time or two, though. Most men lose their sense of humor when another man is driving their woman home in the middle of the night."

"That might be true if the same man didn't have his

old girlfriend living with him. Isn't that all brick houses and stones?"

Declan looked puzzled for a moment before saying, "Ah, I think you mean glass houses and stones. I'll admit that's a little fu . . . messed up, but there is one thing I can say with absolute certainty. If Brant's with you, then he isn't with her. I'm not just saying that because he's my brother either. He just isn't built that way. After Alexia took off, he stayed closed off for a long time. Brant is a stand-up guy. As messed up as it may be, if Alexia is having problems, then Brant will help her out, regardless of how she screwed him over in the past."

"I had a few stalker lapses but, strangely enough, I do trust him. I even love him most days, stick up his ass and all."

Declan chuckled. "Well, there you go. If you can love someone at his worst, then loving them at his best is a breeze."

Emma turned her head and without any of the jealousy she had felt earlier, she said, "Ella is a very lucky woman to have you."

Brant stalked around his hotel room scowling at his silent cell phone. How long did it take for Emma to get home from his brother's house? In the back of his mind, he knew he was being unreasonable. Declan was crazy about Ella, and so there was no one that Emma was safer with than his besotted brother. It still rankled him, though, that Declan was with her while he was miles away in a hotel room alone. Shit, like he had a right to be pissed. Hadn't he just gotten off the phone with Alexia? She had pretty much listed every good time they had ever had together. The one thing she hadn't touched on was how horribly things had ended between them. A part of him would always be tied to her, but since getting some distance between them, he was starting to feel more and more certain Alexia belonged in his past. Emma was his future. And damn it, he needed to hear her voice.

He looked down at his watch only to see that she had had more than enough time to make it home. He punched in her number and waited while the phone rang numerous times before an obviously sleepy Emma murmured, "Hmm?"

"Emma?"

"Hmm?"

"Why didn't you call me when you got home? You are home, aren't you?"

On a big yawn, she said, "Yep. All safe and sound."

He sighed in exasperation. "I was worried about you."

Her voice still sleepy, she cooed, "Ah, that's so sweet. I miss you. I wish you were here."

Brant dropped back on his bed, feeling the stress of the evening drain away. "I miss you, too, baby. Trust me, I'd much rather be with you than with Mark."

He smiled as Emma giggled. "You guys aren't spooning, are you?"

"God, no." Brant shuddered. "He's up in the penthouse suite probably doing unspeakable things to some woman he picked up in the bar while I'm down here where the poor people stay."

"So how's Boston?" Emma asked.

Brant could tell that she was struggling to stay awake. He'd love to be there curled around her while she slept. "I'm in Greenville, remember?"

"Oh yeah, that's right. When are you coming home?"

"Probably sometime next week."

"I'm going to miss you," Emma said.

"Me too, baby. Why don't you get some sleep and I'll call you tomorrow?"

"Mmm, 'kay. I love you." The breath hitched in his chest as she ended the call. He wondered for a moment if he was hearing things that weren't there. No, he knew what she had said. Surprisingly, he found himself hoping that she meant the words and that it wasn't just the result of too much alcohol. There were two women wanting to be a part of his life but there was only one from whom he wanted to hear words of love—the woman who had just spoken them to him.

Chapter Twenty-one

Emma looked in the mirror the next morning and gasped. She vaguely remembered someone having the bright idea of doing homemade tattoos the previous night. Shit, she was pretty sure she had started it. Right in the middle of her chest was a crooked heart with the word "Bran" in the middle of it. Oh my God, she'd even left the *T* off the end. Great, everyone knows you only eat bran when you have digestive issues.

Even after a scrubbing so hard she had taken off a few layers of skin, the Sharpie still prevailed. She picked a shirt that covered up most of her drunken body art and left for work. She went straight to Ella and Beth's floor to see their tattoos. Beth had to pull her into the office to show hers since it was on her breast. "Nick loved it. He said he would be turned on all day knowing it was there."

Ella pulled her shirt down, showing another crooked heart with "Declan" written in the center. "All right," Emma huffed, "why am I the only one with a misspelled name on my chest? Who did it?"

Beth looked guilty before raising her hand. "I think I did. Don't judge me, though. I had had way too much to drink by then." Turning to Ella, she said, "You weren't drunk, why didn't you stop us? Or at least encourage us to use something a little less permanent than a Sharpie?"

Shaking her head, Ella replied, "Hey, I tried to talk you out of it, but you were both bound and determined to go through with it, even when I pointed out that the marker was permanent. So . . . I did what any good friend would do, I joined you."

Emma grimaced. "Well, I'll go back over mine with some bleach and a loofah tonight. I'm sure it'll be gone in a few days . . . or weeks."

Suddenly, the mood sobered as Ella asked, "Have you heard from Gray? How is Suzy doing?"

"He said she's feeling better but would like for everyone to wait to visit. I wanted to go by there during lunch, but he told me she's not really ready for visitors yet," Beth finished, looking miserable. "Part of me wants to go anyway, but I know how my sister is. She likes time to think things through and I feel that, regardless of my wanting to see her, I need to give her space."

Emma put her arm around Beth, giving her a brief hug of understanding. "I would love to see her, too, but I think Gray knows what she needs now better than we do, so even though it's tough, let's do this for her." Before she could comment further, the phone on the desk rang and Beth jumped to get it. Emma walked out with Ella and they promised to have lunch the next week.

She took the elevator to her floor and felt a pang of disappointment knowing that Brant wouldn't be there waiting as he usually was.

She worked steadily through the morning and grabbed a quick sandwich for lunch, eating at her desk while playing Candy Crush. She was almost bored enough to call her mother—almost. Instead, she settled for her sister. She could still get the same gossip from Robyn but wouldn't be forced to answer a lot of awkward questions as she would with their mother.

Unfortunately, Robyn was too busy to do more than say hello and talk for a few minutes about her upcoming vacation to Sebastian Inlet on the other side of Florida. Her sister spent most of her spare time surfing, and Sebastian Inlet had some of the best waves in the state. Emma might be decent on a paddleboard, but she had never been graceful on a surfboard. Their brother, Boston, was a natural surfer with the whole surfer-dude stereotype to go along with it. Her siblings had been more blessed in the natural athleticism department than she had.

At that moment, she envied them both. She seemed to be doing a lot of that lately. Robyn worked and surfed. She dated but had no desire to be in a serious relationship with anyone. Boston . . . well, whatever he did, he seemed pretty happy with it. Emma, on the other hand, had slept with her boss, going so far as to have a fake relationship with him and then fallen in love with him. She now realized that she had probably been in love with him for a while. Her uptight, boring boss was so unpredictable now that she had no idea what he would do next. He was hot, then cold and just generally all over the place. His ex-fiancée was living with him and she had vague recollections of him calling last night, sounding pissed off that she had been with Declan. God, her life was a mess.

The weekend loomed long and lonely before her. That had never bothered her before, but with Brant gone and so much up in the air, it was hard to enjoy the thought of more time on her hands. She decided that she would stop at Walmart on the way home and splurge on some chick flicks and snacks. She would spend the weekend in style . . . on her couch . . . wearing pajamas . . . not brushing her hair . . . and not bathing. Solo girl time was just what she needed.

Emma's shopping cart was full and she was trying to decide between *The Proposal* and *Sweet Home Alabama* when she heard, "Ahem, death by chocolate—how original." Emma jerked her head up to see Brant's sister, Ava, standing on the other side of her cart. She liked Ava, but she could have lived without the tall, beautiful blonde witnessing her descent into the Lonely Friday Night Syndrome. Ava was probably on her way to some swanky party and had stopped at Walmart for breath mints. It was obvious from Emma's shopping cart that she was here to stock up for a long weekend. When Ava picked up the king-size Cadbury chocolate caramel bar from her cart and lifted a brow, Emma grabbed it back. "Back off, that's the last one and I'll fight you for it," she warned in a teasing tone.

Ava smiled. "It's all yours. So . . . no plans tonight?"

Emma gave her a sarcastic smile in return. "What gave that away?"

Instead of answering immediately, Ava studied her for a moment before asking, "Do you want to go somewhere and have a drink? I was planning to buy a bottle of wine and head home, but I'd rather have some company."

"Er . . . sure. That sounds good." Actually, Emma was about as excited over the prospect as she had been over her root canal, but they both knew that she had no other plans. Maybe it would be better than going home and gaining five pounds in one evening. Like her brother, Ava was generally reserved, but tonight she looked as lost as Emma felt. There were cracks showing in her cool veneer, and Emma was just curious enough to want to find out what was going on.

Ava pointed to her cart. "Do you need to make your purchases first?"

Feeling guilty, Emma looked around to see if the coast was clear before she slid her cart against the wall on the next aisle. If she were lucky, it would still be there when she came back after her drink. There was no way she could unload a hundred dollars' worth of food and movies in front of Ava. Luckily, other than the knowing grin that twisted her lips, she didn't comment. "Should I just meet you somewhere?"

She really didn't want this bonding experience to include a car trip together if she could avoid it. She could just imagine the look on Ava's face when she saw the less than perfect condition of her car. It may have been a few months—or years—since she had cleaned it out.

"Charlie's is just down the block. Why don't we walk?" Even better, Emma thought to herself. As soon as things became too awkward between them, she could escape back to Walmart, grab her shopping cart and continue on with her miserable evening. Perfect. She was absurdly grateful that she hadn't been home to change yet and still looked reasonably respectable.

Conversation was difficult due to the traffic rushing by, so Emma decided to forgo any small talk as they walked to the restaurant. When they were seated at a table and had ordered drinks, she found herself shifting uncomfortably under Ava's curious gaze. "So . . . um . . . do you come here often?" *Oh my God, did I really just ask her that? It sounds like I'm trying to pick her up. Why does she make me so nervous? Just think of her as Brant with a vagina.*

Looking amused, Ava said, "No, not really. Mac and I usually go to a small Irish bar close to my place when we want a drink."

"Was he busy tonight?"

Ava looked down, drawing circles on the smooth tabletop with her fingers. "He's always busy now. I should know that life moves on, and it seems so has he."

Emma wasn't sure how to respond. The other woman seemed so sad that she felt compelled to offer some comfort. She reached out and squeezed her hand. "I'm sorry, Ava. Were you . . . Did you break up?"

Ava looked surprised by the question. "There was nothing to break up. I never let us start dating. Mac is too good for that."

Confused, Emma asked, "Too good for what?"

"Me," Ava whispered. "He's too good for me." Emma was too surprised to comment. As she was thinking of a reply, Ava shook her head and locked her blue eyes on Emma. "So, you and Brant?"

Words of denial sprang to Emma's lips at once, but then she dismissed the notion just as quickly. Why bother? She doubted that Brant was giving his sister a play-by-play of their relationship status, but Ava was far from stupid. She had to know that something was going on. Besides, it might be a mistake, but she needed someone to talk to. Blowing a wisp of hair inelegantly out of her face, she said, "Yeah, I guess you could say that."

Ava surprised her again when she gave her a satisfied grin and said, "That's good; I'm glad. He's been alone for too long. He was never good at that, no matter how much he tried to convince everyone, including himself, that he was fine. Brant was meant to be married and have a family. He shouldn't have been saddled with so much responsibility so early on. Our parents were irresponsible and the old man was a sadistic bastard."

Despite herself, Emma was intrigued. Other than throwing out bits of information here and there, Brant wasn't the type to disclose a lot of personal stuff. She knew that his parents were killed in a plane crash and that his grandfather had raised them afterward. She also knew that Declan had been the wild child and had enlisted in the military at eighteen. "So . . . um . . . your grandfather was tough on you?"

Ava's laugh was devoid of any real humor. "He didn't care enough to be tough. Yeah, he expected certain things . . . certain behavior, but mainly he just wanted us to stay out of his hair. His household staff raised us. Of course, we were all teenagers when we came to live with him, so it wasn't like we were in diapers and dependent upon someone for all of our care. What we were was traumatized but he never considered that."

Emma felt tears prick her eyes and hastily wiped them away, knowing that Ava wouldn't appreciate the show of sympathy. "I'm sorry," she offered, not knowing what else to say.

Ava looked at her blankly for a moment before draining the last of her drink and standing abruptly. "I've got to be going if you're ready."

Emma stood and followed her out. They made their way back to Walmart in silence. Emma had lost the urge to go back inside for her shopping cart full of sugar and movies. Suddenly this seemed more like a bottle of Jack Daniel's kind of evening. When she stopped at her car, Ava turned and squeezed her shoulder. "I meant what I said. Brant needs you. Don't let him push you away." Then with those words, she was gone.

Emma drove home more confused than ever. Her cell phone started ringing just as she shut her apartment door behind her. She saw Brant's name on the ID and smiled. Apparently, she was irresistible to the Stone siblings tonight. "Hey you," she answered.

A moment of silence followed her playful greeting before Brant said, "Hey . . . Em." Emma thought he had been close to using an endearment, but had settled for shortening her name. "Where are you?"

"I just attempted to gorge on chick flicks and chocolate at Walmart but was saved by your sister. I'm home now."

Brant chuckled that sexy laugh that she loved so much. "I don't even know what that means, but I'm glad you're safe. So you saw Ava?"

"Yep, I ran across her in the store and we went for a drink. I . . . I don't think she was having a good evening."

"Why not?" Brant asked, concern evident in his voice.

"I'm not sure, but I think it has something to do with Mac and his new girlfriend."

"Shit," Brant sighed. "I figured that was going to hit her hard."

"I'm confused about that situation," Emma admitted. "If Mac cares about her and she obviously cares about him, then why can't they just admit it?"

"It sounds simple enough, doesn't it? Mac has never made a secret of how he feels for my sister, but Ava hasn't been able to accept it. I know you've heard enough to know that she had something happen to her when she was younger. She was . . . raped by her prom date. I don't want to go into everything that happened afterward, but I will say that Mac found her and a bond was formed between them. My grandfather handled everything terribly and Ava has spent the years ever since then angry and grieving."

"Oh my God," Emma breathed. "She said that Mac was too good for her. She blames herself, doesn't she?"

"Yeah," Brant bit out. "Everyone made damn sure of that. The bastard who did it never faced any consequences. I know regardless of what she says, Ava has done nothing but look over her shoulder since then. Luckily, Mac will always watch out for her even if he isn't with her."

They ended up talking for hours that night before finally giving in to the need to get some sleep.

That evening started a pattern that continued every night while Brant was away. Emma spoke to him a few times during the day on business matters but at night, it was all personal. They shared their earliest memories all the way up to the present. There was also a point each evening when their words turned teasing and sexual. Emma had never had phone sex, but when Brant asked her to touch herself and imagine it was his big hands sliding through her slick folds, she hadn't been able to resist. Their calls always ended with a release for them both. Somehow it felt like she was falling for him even harder during these regular nightly phone calls. When they were finally together again in person, she didn't think she would be able to resist ripping his clothes off regardless of where they were. God, she was so ready to have him back home.

Chapter Twenty-two

Brant was barely holding on by a thread. The physical toll from a combination of stress and sexual frustration was making it difficult to function, let alone not blow up at the smallest setback. He had been back in town for just a few days and already it was a few too many. Alexia had been waiting at the door when he'd gotten home and she'd done her best to remind him that he had once loved her. He needed to resolve things with her before he could move forward with Emma.

Emma was doing her part to make things damned difficult on him, although he knew it wasn't her fault. Since he had returned to Myrtle Beach, she looked better than he could remember, smelled better, and on those occasions when gravity brought them close enough to touch, she felt fucking amazing. He had been forced to lie to her and tell her that he had come down with a bug while he was away, that it probably wasn't anything serious, but he didn't want to risk giving her his sore throat. She had assured him that she was willing to risk it, but he had held firm. Somehow, it just didn't feel right to him to touch her, without having the situation with Alexia resolved. He had never been a man to string a woman along and this whole situation felt wrong to him. But he knew Alexia was fragile and the last thing he wanted was to send her spiraling backward.

After two days, though, the excuses were starting to wear thin, and every time he kept her at arm's length, he almost choked on the hurt in her eyes. He couldn't even blame her. At this point, he'd be damned skeptical, too. *Oh, let's see, ex-fiancée living with you, sudden business trip where you didn't come home when you could have and now doing the Texas Two-Step every time she comes too close. Yeah, nothing remotely unusual about any of that.* He found it hard to believe she was still speaking to him, much less still had the desire for anything more personal.

He knew he had brought this all on himself. Instead of using the distance between them to his advantage while he was away, what did he do? He called her every night and talked for hours with her about stuff he had never told anyone. Emma now knew more about him than his own family. And he couldn't deny that he had fallen impossibly in love with her on those nightly phone calls. They made unspoken promises to each other as they poured their souls out and then what? He came back into town and acted like it had never happened. But he just didn't know any other way to handle it. So he had buried himself in work, making things seem busier than they actually were. Add then the faked illness and here he was two days later trying to figure a way out of the shitstorm called his life.

Brant hadn't realized that he had been pacing in front of his desk until Emma burst into his office and wrapped herself around him. Instinctively, he embraced her, rocking back on his heels as the force of her momentum moved him. Suddenly, his frustration, fueled by a healthy amount of lust, caused the short fuse on his temper to ignite. He pushed Emma away from him, growling, "Damn it, Emma, can I please have one day at work without getting mauled? I can't do this with you right now!"

She jerked back from him as if he had slapped her. She even touched her face with a shaking hand, looking up at him in bewilderment. He reached for her just as she turned and raced out the door. A tendril of hair slipped through his fingers before she was gone, the outer door slamming behind her.

"Holy fuck." He pushed a trembling hand through his hair, cursing his lack of control. None of this was her fault and he had done nothing but heap abuse on her. He went back to his chair and sank down wearily. He would give her some time today because he knew he was the last person she wanted to see right now. He was tired of living in limbo. Alexia had thrown him for a serious curve, but it was Emma he wanted. He should have never let things get to this point. He'd talk to Alexia tonight. He would offer to find her a hotel, but that was it. He was ashamed that he had let something he now recognized as simple nostalgia almost ruin his future with Emma. He realized that his confusion was more panic than anything. He had been falling in love with Emma and Alexia had given him the perfect excuse to step back before he risked his heart again. The only problem was that it had been too late. Emma already owned his heart and he hoped that she would still want it after he told her everything.

By late afternoon, Brant had finished his last conference call of the day. When he heard a sound outside his closed door, he looked up eagerly, hoping it was Emma. She hadn't returned to the office after his asshole move that morning and he was worried about her. He had already left her several messages, but the calls were going straight to voice mail. Instead of Emma, Mark and Ava stood in his doorway. Privacy appeared to have taken a flying leap at Danvers lately. He frowned at Mark, wanting to make his disapproval of any social association with his sister known. "What's up?" he asked.

Ava cleared her throat to get his attention. "We just wanted to see if you wanted to grab a drink?" Before he could answer, Jason and Claire stepped into his now crowded office. Since office hours were officially over for the day, the head of Danvers and his wife were holding hands. Brant felt a pang that he was powerless to control. He needed to find Emma.

He started to clear his desk to do just that.

Claire stepped forward. "Brant, how is Emma doing? I guess it's too soon to know any type of arrangements yet, but we want to do something for her. All of us would like to be there for her."

Brant dropped the papers he was holding, looking at Claire in confusion. "What are you talking about? Arrangements for what?"

Jason stepped forward and put his arm around his wife. "Didn't Emma talk to you when she left today?"

"Er . . . we talked some this morning. She went home, though, hours ago." He didn't feel the need to elaborate as to why. "What's going on?"

"Beth came to my office and said that she had run into Emma in the lobby and that she was hysterical. Her sister . . ."

When Claire stopped, Jason stepped in for her. "I believe her sister has passed away. Beth insisted on taking her to the airport and helping her get a flight home. She tried to go with her, but there was only one seat available. We were all concerned and want to make sure that she arrived home safely."

"Oh my God!" Brant surged to his feet. "I didn't know. She came in here this morning and hugged me, but I thought . . . fuck . . . no . . . no . . . no! She needed me and I practically threw her out. NO!" His chest was tight, his heart was racing and there wasn't enough air in the room. He had never felt anything like this before. The concerned and shocked faces before him were starting to spin out of focus.

"Brant!" He vaguely heard Ava's voice before she was beside him. Before he knew it, he was sitting in his chair with his head between his legs. "Easy, slow breaths. Slow and steady." For what felt like hours, he focused on getting his breathing back under control. The heart attack that he'd thought he was having was looking more like his first panic attack. He had to get himself under control. This wasn't about him; it was about Emma. He had already let her down in the worst way imaginable today. It was time to find her.

Everyone gave him a wary look as he got unsteadily to his feet. "Mark, I need to go to Florida right now. . . ."

Without any questions, Mark pulled out his phone and they heard him instruct his pilot to fuel the jet. "You're all set. He was already staying near the airport, since I was planning to head out later tonight. He'll change his flight plan and be ready when you arrive. My car is downstairs. Ava and I will drop you."

Brant assured Jason and Claire that he would be in touch and followed Mark and Ava out. His head was reeling, but his usual sense of organization was kicking in. If he could just stay focused on the task of getting to Emma and block out the emotion, he could make it. If he stopped to think back on what he had done to her when she had come to him today, it would be all over.

He would fall apart and be useless to her. *I'm coming, baby, I'm coming.*

Emma had no idea how she had made it through the flight and the taxi ride to her parents' home. There had been no chance of being stopped by security or dogs this time, as she had nothing but her purse and the clothes on her back. *Robyn . . . Oh my God, Robyn.* It couldn't be true. When she walked in the door, her parents, Robyn and Boston would all be sitting there laughing and so relieved. It was just a misunderstanding. Some awful trick someone had played on them. In the part of her mind still capable of rational thought, she knew that no one would ever play this type of horrible joke on her family—she needed to believe that there was some hope, though. It was all that had kept her going since the call. She had fallen apart when her father told her the news. She had sat at her desk for a few moments before rushing to Brant. She had needed him to hold her, to tell her that everything was okay. When he had thrust her away from him and yelled at her, she had crawled into her shell and gone into survival mode.

Thank goodness for Beth. Without her, she would have driven herself to the airport and she was in no condition to do that. She vaguely remembered Beth arguing and pleading with the airline to let her have a seat on the plane. It didn't happen, though, and Emma was on her own. She had made it, though. She had broken all records for speed getting home to her family. Except now why was she standing at the front door, afraid to go in? *Because if you go in, then it's real*. Instead of opening the door, she dropped to the steps, needing just another moment. When the door opened behind her, she looked over in surprise as Boston lowered himself to the step beside her. She laid her head on his shoulder and murmured, "It's true, isn't it?"

He let out a breath that sounded more like a sob and said, "Yeah, she's gone, Em."

"What happened? Dad said that she drowned. How is that possible? Robyn could swim like a fish."

"She was surfing a new break with some of her friends. From what we've been told, the surf was pretty brutal and she wiped out over some coral. Her leash was tangled. She had taken a big hit to her head and they think she was too disoriented to free herself."

Emma could tell by the shaking of Boston's body against hers that he was crying. She turned and put her arms around him, burying her face against his big shoulders. They stayed that way until their father found them sometime later.

"Emmie, Boston, come on in. It's too hot to stay out here." Emma stood, looking at the strongest man she had ever known. He was pale, his normally tanned skin having taken on a sallow cast. He ruffled her hair as he usually did, but the gesture was more automatic than affectionate. He was a man operating on fumes, doing what he needed to do to survive.

She hugged him before asking, "Where is Mom?"

"She's in bed. I had to call Doc Janice out to give her something. She just completely lost it when we got the call. Maybe you could go up and check on her. She's calm now but just staring at the walls. I don't know what to do, where to start. Your uncle is handling the arrangements, but we need to go see Robyn. I don't know if your mother is able."

Boston, looking more sober than she had ever seen him, stepped up to lead their dad to the living room while Emma walked with a heavy heart toward her parents' room.

As her father had indicated, her mother was under the covers but instead of sleeping, she appeared to be staring at the wall. Emma sat next to her on the bed. "Mom?" Her mother gave her a blank look, leading her to wonder if perhaps she had been overmedicated.

"Mom, it's Em."

The glassy look seemed to leave as her mother said, "I believe I know who you are, honey. You know about your sister."

Emma nodded. "Yeah, I know."

"I tried to talk her out of going," her mother continued. "I just had a bad feeling about the trip. I know all you kids are great swimmers; your father and I made sure of that. I never worried about any of you being in the water. But I was nervous about Robyn surfing somewhere new. She knew the waters here like the back of her hand. She got it in her head that she wanted to start training somewhere more challenging. Some of her friends were encouraging her to enter the Wave Masters tournament. She felt like she needed more experience before the competition."

Emma pulled back the bed covers and crawled in next to her mother while she continued to talk. They wrapped their arms around each other and the tears came in a torrent. Emma found herself wondering if there would ever be a time again when the house would be filled with laughter. The sorrow hung heavily over them like a black cloud.

Chapter Twenty-three

At nine the next morning, Brant could no longer hold off on going to Emma's house. Despite his objections, Mark and Ava had insisted on accompanying him on the flight to Florida and to the hotel afterward. It was a little difficult to throw a man off his own plane, so he had been forced to settle for company that he hadn't really wanted. It was late by the time they landed in Pensacola and he had been reluctant to drop in on Emma and her family on the off chance that they were sleeping. Instead, Mark had ushered them to a waiting car at the airport and then to a local beachfront resort. Apparently, Ava and Mark had decided between them that Brant needed some moral support. What he actually needed was a good kick in the ass for the way he had fucked up his life so completely. He was pretty sure that Emma would be happy to provide him with that should she ever speak to him again after the way he had treated her.

He still couldn't believe what had happened. Had there ever been a worse time to completely lose it with someone? Of course, he had had no way of knowing that she had suffered such a tragic loss, but it didn't excuse him for taking his frustrations out on her. She had done nothing but take her cues from him. He had called her every night he had been out of town, and their conversations almost always had some kind of intimate content. He hadn't just been checking in on things at the office. In fact, their evening talks hadn't related to business at all, and they both knew it.

He had called Alexia from the airport and done what he should have done from the beginning. He had told her that he loved Emma. He had asked that she make other arrangements for somewhere to stay immediately. He ended the call by apologizing for letting things get as far as they had. True, they hadn't had sex or anything approaching a physical relationship, but he had let things coast between them as he struggled to accept the depth of his feelings for Emma. He was at fault for creating this whole mess the minute he had allowed Alexia to stay with him. He had no idea if Alexia planned to return to Carter, but hoped she would give herself time to find out who she was and what she really wanted without a man making her decisions.

He picked up the keys that Mark had dropped off a few moments ago. Mark thought it would be wise to have a car in case Emma wasn't comfortable with him staying. What the other man had meant, of course, was that he thought she would kick Brant out on sight.

Brant had to smile when he made it to the parking

area and found the rental car. Mark had just said that it was a silver sedan with his name on it. He hadn't questioned how that was possible until he saw the silver Mercedes sitting in the first parking space with a sign across the windshield that said BRANT STONE. Leave it to Mark to rent a Mercedes. Luckily, the hotel was also on Santa Rosa Island where Emma's parents lived, so after taking a moment to familiarize himself with his surroundings, he was on his way. The drive took less than five minutes. No doubt Mark had planned it that way.

He pulled into the driveway at the Davis house just as Boston walked through the side yard, holding a cigarette—or what Brant hoped was just a cigarette. They met on the sidewalk. Brant noted the younger man's fatigue as he dropped the cigarette to the ground and squashed it under the foot of his flip-flop. Brant didn't know why he did it, other than that Boston looked like he needed it, but he pulled him into a hug instead of a handshake. Boston returned the embrace before pulling back. "Hey, man, I wondered where you were."

"Hey, Boston, I came as soon as I found out. How's everyone holding up?" Unlike their previous meeting, Brant thought Boston looked painfully sober now. Losing his sister seemed to have matured him almost overnight.

"About like you'd expect. Mom is completely zoned out on something, Dad is trying to act normal, and Em is trying to pretend that she isn't hiding out in the bathroom to cry. The neighbors and Mom's crazy friends have brought enough food by to feed an army. Every time they come, they try to force-feed me. It's quiet now, but the crowd will be here soon."

Confused, Brant asked, "The crowd?"

"Oh yeah." Boston grimaced. "From the moment we found out, there has been someone here. It was like a revolving door yesterday, and I don't expect today to be any better. The service is tomorrow afternoon. It's one of those all-in-one where the visitation is right before the funeral."

"Is there anything I can do for you or your family?" Brant asked.

"No, thanks, man. Just um . . . take care of Em, okay?"

Brant nodded in response and followed the younger man into the house.

Kat and Ken Davis were sitting side by side on the sofa in the living room. Brant thought fleetingly that Boston wasn't the only one who had aged overnight. Kat Davis looked pale and lifeless. The vivacious woman that he'd met a few weeks ago seemed to have disappeared and in her place was a woman ravaged by grief. Ken Davis also seemed to have lost his happy, relaxed air. The love was still obvious in his face as he looked at his wife, but now that emotion was also tinged with devastation and concern.

They were in the midst of every parent's nightmare: outliving a child. Since Emma was nowhere in sight, Brant stood there uncertainly, not wanting to intrude on a private moment. Then Boston spoke up behind him. "Hey, look who I found outside."

Kat stood up, walking over to him slowly. She put her hand on his arm before pulling him into a hug. He returned the embrace gently. "I'm so glad you're here; Em needs you." Kat stepped back, wiping her eyes. Ken stood next to his wife, extending his hand.

"I'm glad you could make it, Brant. I believe Emmie's upstairs in her room if you want to go see her." The doorbell sounded in the foyer, and Boston turned to answer it as Brant made his way slowly up the stairs. He stood outside Emma's door uncertainly. Maybe he had been wrong to come. He didn't want to be the cause of more stress in her life, but God, he needed to be here for her. If she asked him to leave, he would, he vowed, regardless of what he wanted.

He knocked on the door and when he heard her voice, he opened it. It took him a moment to locate her in the darkened room. The bed was empty as well as the chair. He finally saw her sitting against the wall of the window seat. She was facing away from him and he stood waiting for her cue. Finally, she asked, "Why are you here, Brant?"

He lowered himself to the seat beside her so he could study her face. Much like her parents, hers was also pale and somber. Her hair was mussed as if she had drawn a hand through it many times, and her eyes were red-rimmed and swollen, giving truth to Boston's statement of her crying in the bathroom. "I'm sorry, Em . . . I came as soon as I found out."

In a voice completely devoid of humor, she asked, "Aren't you afraid I'm going to maul you again?"

"Em," he breathed, "I'm so sorry. There has been a lot going on that I should have told you about. It's no excuse, but I'm so damn sorry." When she looked at him in shock, clearly believing the worst, he hastened to add, "Shit, not what you're thinking. I don't want to throw all of this on you now, but I promise you, you're it for me."

She looked away again and Brant had no idea whether she believed a word out of his mouth. He knew they needed to talk, but it was hardly the appropriate time. For now all he wanted was to be there for Emma and her family, if she would let him.

There would be time later to find out where they stood. Right now, he would do the only thing he could . . . he would love her.

Chapter Twenty-four

Emma sat between her brother and Brant during her sister's funeral. The visitation hour had been brutal. Standing next to her sister's casket while everyone repeated over and over again how wonderful she looked was almost more than Emma could bear. Only Brant's hand holding hers had kept her grounded in place. Without him, she would have bolted from the room. Her mother had stood beside her, chatting through her drug-induced fog, anchored firmly by Emma's father while Boston had shifted from foot to foot uncomfortably on Brant's other side. As soon as it ended, Emma had escaped to the restroom for a few moments to compose herself before walking back out to find Brant waiting for her. He took her hand, not saying a word, and led her toward the chapel.

She had been surprised to see her friends and co-workers from Danvers sitting a few rows behind the family pews. Suzy, Ella, Beth and Claire had all stood to hug her while Jason, Gray, Nick and Declan conveyed their sympathies with a brief embrace. Claire had apologized that they hadn't arrived early enough to attend the visitation. Emma was further surprised when Mark DeSanto and Ava Stone walked up behind them. They both hugged her as well, and Emma felt her eyes starting to burn with tears at the show of support from her friends. She had never expected to see familiar faces this far from Myrtle Beach, and she was touched that so many had made the trip. She was also glad to see Suzy looking so well after everything she had been through recently. That she would be here now meant so much to her.

As the rest of the family started to take their places, Brant had put his arm around her, steering her toward their pew. "Come on, honey, the service is starting." Her legs had locked in place for a moment—she didn't want to do this. She didn't want to say this final good-bye. Her friends looked on in sympathy, seeming to read her thoughts. Brant had leaned down to whisper in her ear, "It's okay, just lean on me." Her brain seemed to obey those words and her feet started slowly moving forward. They slid into the pew beside Boston and Emma allowed Brant to draw her firmly into his side. He had promised her yesterday to give her anything she needed and he was doing it so far. She would have never made it without him today. She wondered idly if he knew that.

Emma had perfected a process for surviving funerals when she was little and it automatically kicked in when the opening prayers began. First she started by counting the light fixtures in the chapel, then the windows, then the pews, then the people. When that was finished, she started all over again. She had made numerous passes around the room when she looked up to see Brant watching her. At some point, he had started following her eyes and she could have sworn that he knew exactly what she was doing. Next to her, Boston, too, stared off into the distance. Farther down the pew, she saw tears trailing silently down her mother's cheeks as she stared sightlessly ahead, and her father, who had been strong through the entire process, looked more in need of his wife's support than at any other time since Robyn had passed.

Emma almost made it through the entire service without breaking down. Her mother had insisted on the final songs, and Emma should have anticipated how difficult it would be to hear them. Her mother wanted Robyn remembered for who she was and what she loved. The lights in the chapel dimmed and images started flickering on the screen in the front of the chapel. The song "There You'll Be" by Faith Hill played first as images flashed by of Robyn holding a surfboard when she was barely old enough to walk.

If you could show a life in pictures, then their mother had certainly managed to do it. Emma had always hated having so many pictures taken by their parents. Now, as she saw her sister's life played out before her eyes—even though it was incredibly painful to witness—she was happy that their mother had never let an important moment pass without capturing it. When the last song, "If I Die Young" by The Band Perry, started playing, their father finally broke down and hastily left the chapel. The song had been a favorite of Robyn's, and their mother had wanted it included even though it wasn't exactly a traditional funeral song. Neither Emma nor her father had thought it was appropriate for a funeral, but her mother was adamant and Boston, of course, sided with her.

Now, to Emma, it felt like her sister was in the room for the first time. Sobs could be heard from all over the chapel as the slide show ended. She hadn't even realized that she was quietly crying until Brant pressed a tissue in her hand. On her other side, Boston wasn't doing much better. She gripped his hand tightly as Brant squeezed hers in return. *I love you, sis, and I always will,* she whispered in her mind.

She remembered Brant telling her that morning, "This is the worst day you'll ever live through. You may not believe it now, but there will never be another day like today. Each new day will be better than this one." She clung to those words like a promise as they left the chapel for the burial. For once she hadn't argued with him because she wanted him to be right with all of her heart.

At last the house was quiet and everyone was gone. Emma sank gratefully into the tub of steaming water that Brant had insisted on running for her before going back downstairs to check on her parents. She suspected that he was really intent on cleaning up any messes left by the barrage of people who had visited earlier.

As the water eased some of her tension from the day, Emma's mind started to drift. To say that she had been surprised by Brant the last few days was an understatement. Despite how mad and disappointed she was in him when she arrived in Florida, she had to admit that he had been the glue that had held all of them together. She had never doubted his organizational skills; the man had some serious OCD about stuff like that. Those same traits had been her family's saving grace. She figured he had taken one look at them when he arrived and realized that he needed to take control. Her father, who could usually be counted on to keep an even keel, had looked to Brant for assistance with making the funeral arrangements. Both her mother and Boston had looked to him for everything from their clothing for the service to the gathering of friends and family at the house before and after the service. Emma had just needed his support. He knew when she wanted to be alone, when she needed to cry and when she just needed to talk. He had been their rock and regardless of what happened next, she would always love him for that.

She knew that he needed to return home soon, and she felt a pang at the thought of him leaving. Her friends from Danvers had dropped by the house after the service. Jason and Claire had pulled her aside and told her to take the time that she needed with her family and assured her that her job would be waiting when she was ready. She had been truly touched. She counted Claire as a friend but hadn't often been in a social setting with Jason. When she had started to thank him, calling him Mr. Danvers, since he was, after all, the president of the company, he had gently stopped her, insisting that she call him Jason. Truthfully, she had been tongue-tied to have their support. She had promised Suzy that they would catch up soon. Her friend looked wonderful after her ordeal, but you could hardly miss the protective arm that her husband, Gray, kept around her.

Emma shivered, realizing that the water had grown cold. She had been so lost in thought she hadn't noticed that almost an hour had passed. She stepped out of the bath, toweling off before grabbing her robe. In the bedroom, she dressed for comfort in a long T-shirt before sliding into bed. She was still staring at the ceiling when Brant walked in. She hadn't protested the first night when he had stripped down to his boxers and crawled into bed, pulling her against his chest. She needed him and they both knew it.

Obviously thinking she was asleep, he crept quietly across the darkened room, going into the bathroom. She heard the shower running and a while later, the bed shifted as he settled in beside her. Without hesitation, she curled onto her side and he settled his big body around hers. "I thought you were asleep," he murmured against her head.

Suddenly snuggling back against him with all of the unknowns between them seemed wrong. Despite her mental and physical exhaustion, she needed to know what had been going on with him for the past few weeks. Pulling away, she reached over and snapped on the bedside light. They both blinked like owls for a moment until they adjusted to the artificial glow. Brant gave her a wary look before rolling over onto his back. He ran his hand through his hair, a habit that she had come to recognize was caused by stress.

She settled back against the headboard and said, "I need to know, Brant." He pulled himself into a sitting position beside her, not bothering to ask what she was talking about.

Without hesitating, he started to speak. "You know that Alexia and I were once engaged." At her nod, he continued on. "When she came to see me weeks ago, I was shocked. She and I hadn't stayed in touch at all after we parted. Alexia was very quiet and shy when we met. Her father and I were business acquaintances. We fell in love, or what I thought was love, and were soon engaged. Looking back now, I can see that she was never truly happy. Her father was very controlling, so she basically traded one prison for another one with more freedom. Things took a real nosedive when she made a new friend who was heavily into the drugs and party scene. Without betraying Alexia's trust too heavily, I'll just say that Alexia got involved with the wrong sorts of people and ended up using pretty heavily. She left me standing in a parking lot after dinner one night and took off. That was the last time I saw her until she showed up in my office that day."

"My God," Emma whispered in surprise. "She looked fine when I met her."

"She is . . . now," Brant agreed, "but it took her a couple of years and hitting rock bottom to get to that point. She has just recently finished a stint in a rehabilitation facility for drug abuse. The doctor who helped her get treatment is also her fiancé. She came to town to visit her parents and tell them about what had been happening with her. They really didn't know the level of her addiction or where she had been since leaving home. I guess they didn't take it well and were more worried about appearances than their daughter. Her fiancé, Carter, was completely against her visiting her parents and possibly seeing old friends who were bad influences this soon after treatment. They had a fight before she left and after her parents turned her away, she didn't feel that she had anywhere else to turn. She wanted somewhere away from all of the pressure, to regroup. I think she also feared relapsing if she was left on her own for too long."

Emma found herself running a hand through her hair in much the same nervous gesture that Brant had used earlier. His story explained why Alexia was staying with him but didn't explain why he had been pulling away from her. She feared that there was an explanation she wasn't going to want to hear. Choosing her words carefully, she asked, "Is she still staying with you?"

"No, I asked her to leave before I came here to you. Em . . . something happened while she was staying with me that I haven't told you about."

She nodded her head for him to continue, even

though she wasn't sure she wanted to know. If he had slept with Alexia, she didn't think she could get past it . . . not now.

When he remained quiet, she prodded him softly. "Please tell me, Brant. I can't stand not knowing."

Clearing his throat, he said, "Remember the night I went out to dinner with her? I called you afterward. I'm sure you noticed on the phone that I'd had too much to drink." When she agreed that she had, he continued on. "Well, the next morning she thanked me for agreeing to see if there were still romantic feelings between us. She needed to know before making a final commitment to Carter. I didn't know what in the hell she was talking about. The only thing I remembered encouraging her to do was go back to school. I . . . just, fuck, I panicked. When Gray needed someone to cover his travel for a while, I jumped at it. I was scared because I was falling in love with you and there she was, making me doubt myself. Making me question my feelings. I realized after you left that the only thing I was really afraid of was loving and losing you. I never felt about Alexia the way I feel about you. She simply brought all of my fears to the surface. I was terrified of making a mistake and being destroyed by it again."

"That's why you were pulling away from me," Emma added. "I guess you being sick was just an excuse too. But did you sleep with her?"

"No! Hell no, I didn't. There really wasn't anything physical involved. The day she told me that I'd agreed to see where things went, I left town. Things with

Alexia were never like they are between you and me. She isn't someone to initiate physical contact beyond a hug."

Stiffening, Emma asked, "Are you saying I'm all over you?"

"Shit, no, baby. Well, I mean, yes, I want you all over me every moment of the day. I can't keep my hands off you. I don't feel like that toward her; I never did."

"I knew in my gut that something was wrong when you avoided me like the plague after you returned home from your trip. I thought you were sleeping with her."

Brant took her hand before saying, "I didn't sleep with Alexia. I know how this looks, but I swear nothing happened between us other than what I've told you."

Emma sighed, partly relieved and partly hurt. "I believe you; but damn it you've had me on a complete emotional roller coaster. I thought we crossed into a new place in our relationship while you were away. Our phone calls every night made me believe that we were on the same page. Then you came home and immediately started pushing me away. I was totally confused. I thought you wanted Alexia and were just afraid to admit it to me. It was almost like going on a date with someone who never calls again and you're left wondering what went wrong."

Brant pulled her into his arms, holding her close. "Oh, baby, I'm so sorry. I know I made a fucking mess out of everything. I know you weren't completely comfortable with her staying with me and I don't blame you. I'd have been a mess if the circumstances were reversed. Hell, I almost cussed my happily married brother out for taking you home that night."

A little chuckle escaped Emma's lips before reality returned. "I just . . . It's hard for me to get past the fact that you kept all of this from me. I know we hadn't officially made any promises to each other, but you hurt me, Brant."

"Emma, I lo—"

She put her finger to his lips, stopping what she knew was coming. "Please don't. Not right now. I need some time to process everything. I never want to look back and think that you said that to me for the first time under duress." She reached over and clicked off the lamp before turning back to him. "No words tonight, just take me away for a while."

Without comment, Brant pulled her into his arms and even though she didn't think it was possible, within moments there was nothing on her mind but him. His arms holding her, his body possessing hers and his mouth laying siege to every inch of skin she exposed. Where she would have rushed to completion, he gentled her, drawing more waves of pleasure from her body. No words of love were spoken, no promises made. Instead, she felt Brant use his body to show her a love that took her breath away.

Afterward, she lay spent across his chest, feeling their hearts hammer in tempo. She drifted away as she felt his lips brush her forehead. The first real sleep she had had in days claimed her.

When Emma woke in the morning, Brant's side of the bed was already cold and she knew without looking around the room that his suitcase was gone. On his pillow, written on a scrap piece of paper that he had obviously found in the room, was a note: "Flying back with Mark and the others this morning. Don't want to leave, but giving you the time you need. I'll be waiting, baby. Love, B." For the first time since the nightmare had begun, she cried herself dry, to a point where there were no tears left. She didn't try to make herself stop or put a time limit on her grief; she cried until it wasn't possible to cry anymore.

Chapter Twenty-five

Brant was hardly surprised to see the crew from Danvers along with Mark and Ava at the airport. Of course Mark would have offered them a ride back to Myrtle Beach on his plane. He was hardly in the mood to socialize after leaving Emma behind, but maybe it was for the best. Less time to brood could only be a good thing.

Everyone kept the conversation light as they were cleared for takeoff. When the plane reached its cruising altitude, the flight attendant Mark had hired for the return trip took drink orders. Mark ordered a scotch and soda and Brant requested the same. It was still early, but damn, he needed a drink. Suzy looked at him sympathetically before dropping her hand briefly over his. "She'll be home soon." He stared at her for a moment, seeing not the beautiful and intimidating woman before him but, surprisingly, an ally.

He looked around, thankful that no one seemed to be paying any attention to their conversation. "Do you think so?" he asked, needing some reassurance.

Suzy studied him for a moment. "Yeah, I do. Whatever else is happening or has happened between you two, you were meant to be together from the moment you met." In typical Suzy fashion, she added, "You two generated enough sparks together to singe my damn eyebrows off."

He chuckled, surprising both himself and Suzy. "Thank you." He smiled. "You have no idea how much I needed that."

"Oh, I think I do," she replied, "and you're welcome." Brant looked away as Gray claimed his wife's attention. Jason and Claire sat beside them. Jason idly twirled a lock of his wife's hair as if he needed to stay connected while he discussed business with Declan. Ella was curled against her husband, who kept a protective arm around her while she slept against his shoulder.

Brant was glad to see his brother so at peace after years of searching for something that never seemed to be there. Looking at Ella, Brant thought he finally understood what Declan had been so desperate to find . . . it was her. When at last Brant's gaze landed on Mark and Ava, he was more puzzled than angry. Hell no, he didn't want Mark involved with his sister, but that wasn't the vibe he was getting from them. In a weird way, it looked more like some kind of friendship than anything romantic or, God forbid, sexual. It was a strange concept to think of Mark having a straight friendship with someone as attractive as Ava.

Brant was relieved when Jason drew him into a discussion of a new customer and forced his mind away from Emma and onto business. Maybe it was obvious to the other man that he needed a break from all the thoughts racing through his head.

Emma fixed herself a cup of coffee, taking a much-needed sip before walking through the open double doors and onto the deck. The day so far was unusually mild for Florida. Her mother was already sitting on a patio chair and Emma took the one next to her. They sat in companionable silence for a few moments, sipping their coffee and watching the waves break in the ocean. Emma suspected that they were both imagining Robyn riding the waves and throwing up a hand in greeting when she spotted them watching her. Sadly, the memory of it was all they had now. Her mother was the first to break the silence. "I heard Brant leave this morning. Did he have to get back home?"

"Yeah. He was catching a flight with the others from Danvers."

"I see." Her mother took another drink of coffee. "Why didn't you go back with him?"

Surprised, Emma said, "Why would I do that? I couldn't just leave you guys to handle everything. Jason told me to take all the time I needed." Emma almost cringed, knowing she sounded defensive.

Showing some of her former spark, her mother turned to her with a knowing expression on her face.

"Honey, I'm not blind. You looked like someone had kicked your cat when Brant showed up here. Now, I'm thinking that someone in a relationship wouldn't be surprised if the other person came in those circumstances. Are you and Brant having problems?"

Emma sighed. She was just too damn tired to continue the charade. If nothing else, she was sure that she could distract her mother for a while with her straight-out-of-a-book tale of blackmail, lust, mixed signals and finally love, so she confessed everything . . . well, some things in less detail than others, but she gave her the gist of what had been going on.

Sometime later, her mother flopped back against her chair, saying, "Wow, you could have just answered with 'It's complicated.'"

Emma started laughing. "Are you kidding, it was worth the embarrassment just to see your mouth hanging open. Admit it, Mom, you didn't think I had it in me."

"Honey, I knew you had it in you; after all, you have my blood in your veins. I just wondered when you would realize it. One thing you didn't say, though, during your story. Do you love Brant?"

Without hesitation, Emma said, "Yes. No matter how much he drives me crazy at times, I absolutely love him. I think I have from the moment he gave me his first disapproving frown. He had no idea that those frowns turned into the highlight of my day."

"Well then, I repeat, why are you still here?"

Emma took her mother's hand. "He hurt me and I

need some time to come to terms with that. And more important, I would never leave you here to go through Robyn's apartment and her things alone. I love Brant, but my family comes first right now. He'll wait for me, Mom. If I know nothing else, I know that."

Chapter Twenty-six

In the end, it was eighteen days later when Emma returned home to Myrtle Beach. Suzy had agreed to pick her up at the airport. She hadn't told Brant that she was coming home; she wanted to surprise him. True to his word, he had stepped back and given her the time she needed. If it hadn't been for her friends letting her know that, other than working twelve-hour days, he was fine, she probably would have broken down and called him much sooner. She knew it was silly, but she just couldn't risk having long telephone conversations with him again and then coming home to find a completely different Brant. She was still traumatized from the pain of receiving the cold shoulder from him before Robyn's accident.

She spotted Suzy immediately in the airport arrivals area. There was no way to miss the striking redhead with the impossibly high heels. Emma was thrilled to see her friend looking so happy and healthy. Suzy had told her on the phone that they were planning to adopt and that they had taken their first step in the process this week: a home study. Emma was confident that the agency would see that Suzy and Gray would be wonderful parents. She had little doubt that her tough-talking friend would melt when she held her child in her arms for the first time. They threw their arms around each other, hugging like it had been months instead of a couple of weeks. Suzy pulled back, looking at her. "Babe, it's so good to have you back. We've all missed you."

Emma felt her eyes tearing. She was so appreciative to have such a close group of friends. She hadn't really had that since college. "I missed you guys, too. How is everyone doing?" As they made their way to baggage claim and then out to the parking area, Suzy gave her a rundown.

"Well, Ells, bless her heart, looks bigger every time I see her. Don't you dare tell her I said that, though, because I don't want her to start crying. She's got the most adorable waddle now." Emma thought it spoke volumes about Suzy that she could mention Ella's pregnancy so easily.

"Beth and Nick are fighting with Hermie over his pacifier. Between you and me, I'd say the kid will still be using it when he's eighteen. There is no way they are going to lose sleep every night; they'll keep giving in. Jason and Claire are actually going on a solo vacation next week, if you can believe it. This will be the first since Chrissy was born. I took Claire to Victoria's Secret yesterday and let me just say . . . Jason is gonna be a happy man when he gets back."

When Emma struggled to contain her laughter, Suzy said, "I also talked to Ava about what we discussed and she is on board so we're all set."

"Oh Suzy, thank you! I can't believe how the timing worked out."

When Suzy stopped at a red light, she turned to study Emma. "Are you really sure you want to do this? It's going to be an adjustment for you."

"I know," Emma admitted, "and I'm not thrilled about it, but it's the right thing to do . . . the only thing really. Is he at the office?"

Suzy nodded. "Yep, I checked on my way out. As far as Gray knows, he doesn't have any meetings planned off-site today so you should be good to go. I don't suppose I could listen at the door, could I?"

"Sure," Emma agreed, "as long as I can listen at your door the next time Gray visits you."

"Well, hell, you could have just said no. I'm trying to be good anyway. I don't think voyeurism would look good on our adoption application, so you're safe."

Emma felt her palms start to sweat as they pulled into the circular drive in front of the Danvers headquarters. Alarmed, she turned to Suzy. "What are you doing?"

"I'm being a good friend and letting you out at the door. You'll just torture yourself all the way through the parking lot otherwise."

"But . . . what about my luggage?"

"We'll deal with it later." Flashing her a grin, Suzy added, "Now get out of my car."

Emma reluctantly opened the door and stepped out. She stood near the front door uncertainly for a few moments before blowing out a long breath. *Oh good grief, what the hell is wrong with me? Get it together, Emma!* Throwing her shoulders back, she charged forward, not giving herself time to think. In record time, she was standing in front of her office door. She opened it quietly and was relieved to see Brant's office door closed. When she heard his deep voice, her resolve wavered and she wanted nothing more than to launch herself into his arms. *Yeah, like that worked out so well last time.*

She kept an eye on the blinking light of the phone line he was using and eased into her chair in front of the computer. She quickly found the form that she was looking for and filled it out. The printer sounded like a wrecking ball as it spit the paper out. A quick look showed her that he was still on the phone. As she stood holding the form uncertainly, she heard him moving around his office and saw that the call had ended. *Shit, shit! Everyone always said if you were nervous, imagine the other person naked . . . Oh yeah, that would really help.* The decision was taken out of her hands when Brant's door suddenly flew open and he walked out with his head bent. He was an inch from plowing her down before he looked up.

The look on his handsome face was almost comical. If she had any doubts that he knew she was coming home today, they were extinguished now. His mouth opened and closed and even more surprising, Brant

Stone started stuttering when he tried to speak. "Em . . . you . . . I didn't . . . when . . . ?"

She looked into the face of the man she loved and her fingers twitched with the urge to touch him. He looked so tired, but God, he was beautiful. When he started to reach for her, she put the paper she had just printed into his outstretched hands and stepped back. Puzzled, he looked at her, then at the paper. "Are you kidding me? Em . . . I waited, I've been waiting . . . I thought you understood. I thought you could forgive me. Baby, I lo—"

Once again, she put her hand over his mouth to stop his declaration. "Brant, this is the last transfer request I will ever submit to you. You've turned me down time and again. My reason is completely valid and if you won't sign the form this time, I'll have to find another job."

He ran an agitated hand through his hair. "Em, please don't do this. We'll go talk to Alexia together; she'll tell you that nothing happened between us." By this time, he was waving the form frantically, not bothering to finish reading it.

"Brant . . ." He continued to talk, forcing her to raise her voice. "BRANT!" God, she really hoped the offices had good soundproofing. When he stopped to gape at her in midsentence she said, "Read the damn form . . . please." He gave her a perplexed look, no doubt thinking she was trying to torture him, but obligingly held the paper up and started scanning it. She saw the exact moment when he got to her reasons for transferring.

"You're requesting a transfer because you're 'in love

with your pigheaded boss' and can't imagine being able to keep your hands off him during business hours. You are requesting a move to Ava Stone's office and also requesting 'someone really old' to replace you in Mr. Stone's office."

She couldn't keep the grin off her face as he looked at her, his shock finally giving way to a look of utter happiness. "You're going to drive me crazy," he sighed happily.

"Always," she answered.

"Could I please tell you that I love you now without you putting your hand over my mouth?" Brant joked happily.

"Well, I think you just did, but go ahead."

Brant pulled her into his arms, kissing her until she was gasping for breath before pulling back. "I love you, Emma Davis. I even love your smart little mouth."

Giving him a wicked look, she murmured, "Oh, I think you will find all manner of things that you love about my mouth . . . starting as soon as we get out of here. How long until you can leave?"

Brant gave her another kiss, resting his hand on her ass. "Fuck it. I've worked damn near around the clock for weeks. I think they can manage without me for an afternoon." Emma giggled, pulling his hand away from her butt before they walked out into the hall.

As the doors of the empty elevator closed behind them, Brant leaned against her, running his lips down her neck. "You and Ava working together? Baby, you just jumped from the frying pan into the fire."

Much later that night she would remember those words and wonder what she had gotten herself into. But first they were lucky enough to make it to Brant's house without being arrested, and nothing else mattered beyond the man worshipping her with his eyes and his body.

The grief of losing Robyn so suddenly was still there—the pain still felt raw and probably would for a long time to come—but with Brant in her life, she finally had someone to share both the good and the bad moments. She suspected that he was right. Every passing day would get a little easier and, with him by her side, one day she would be able to look back with him happily on the times she had shared with her sister. Robyn would have wanted it that way.

Epilogue

Emma turned into the driveway of the house that she shared with Brant. They had decided to move in together almost immediately and, since he lived on the beach, it hadn't been a tough decision for her. She parked beside the sports car that he let her drive on rare occasions. She usually got a charge out of him sitting in it beside her, gritting his teeth and trying to act like he trusted her with his baby. *Men and their toys.*

The last three months with Brant had been close to paradise. The verbal sparring was still there, which made the sex afterward only that much more amazing. Her uptight man had no reservations between the sheets . . . at all. He had even managed to shock her a few times. If variety was the spice of life, then things would never be boring with Brant Stone.

Emma looked around when she opened the door, not seeing Brant in the living room. As she always did, she started talking to him because inevitably he came out and picked up the conversation. He seemed to hear her no matter where he was in the house. "Hey, baby.

I'm sorry I'm so late getting home, but your demon sister was out of her mind today. I bet you were laughing your ass off when you signed that transfer to her office. If Mac doesn't break up with his girlfriend soon, I'm going to have to find another job."

When Brant still hadn't appeared, she walked toward the bedroom, stopping in surprise at the closed door. What was he doing in there? She flung the door open and stood in the doorway gaping. Holy shit. "What're you . . . Oh wow, Mr. December," she exclaimed. Lying on the bed, in re-creation of his Mr. December pose complete with Santa hat and boughs of holly, was the man she adored. When he swiveled his hips, she noticed that something sparkled on his . . . yule log, and she started laughing.

"Um . . . baby, you're going to have to cut out the laughing or the ring is going to lose its suspension. Thanks to you being late getting home, it's been a . . . challenge to keep it up there for so long."

"Oh my God," Emma gasped out as she dropped down on the bed beside him. "If this is what I think it is, then it's the most original proposal . . . ever!" Brant looked at her, the grin slipping from his face. Suddenly, he jumped from the bed, untying the ribbon from his . . . yule log and catching the ring as it fell. Emma stared at him in shock as he jerked on some clothing and grabbed her hand. Her head was spinning as he pulled her from the house and to the beach. When he dropped to one knee in front of her, she looked at him in shock.

"Em, baby, I love you. I just . . . had a flash of what we would tell our kids one day when they wanted to know how Daddy proposed to Mommy and I couldn't do it." He took her hand in his, clearing his throat. "Emma, from the moment you first walked through the door at the office, my life has never been the same. You've shown me that not everything has to be taken so seriously. I can't imagine a future without you in it. Will you marry me and save me from a future of . . . well, being myself?"

Emma felt tears rolling down her cheeks as she whispered, "Yes." Then Brant slid the ring onto her finger. She had no idea what it even looked like because she couldn't see through the tears filling her eyes. "That was so beautiful. I love you, Brant."

He hugged her to him, saying against the top of her head, "I love you more." She pulled back from him and finally took a good look. By now, he was used to her laughing at unusual times, so he looked only mildly curious when she burst out laughing.

She reached up and tugged the Santa hat from his head. "I guess I should have said, 'I love you, Mr. December.'"

He gave her the sexy grin that made her skin burn and picked her up effortlessly into his arms.

"I believe we need to deal with the boughs of holly and my yule log . . . now." The sound of their laughter filled the air as Brant rushed back toward the house with her cradled in his arms. Fittingly, his proposal was just like their love story—one of a kind.

Acknowledgments

To my dear friends: Amanda Lanclos and Heather Waterman with Crazy Cajun Book Addicts. Thanks for all that you do. I love you guys so much! Also, to my very special ladies: Tracey Quintin, Lisa Salvary, Shelley Lazar, Lorie Gullian, Sharon Cooper, Melissa Lemons, Tracy Gaylord, Amy Minor and Marion Archer. I am blessed to have you as friends. To my wonderful Facebook group, Sydney's Seductresses, how I wish I could list each and every one of you. You make every day special for me and I consider you all dear friends.

As always, to my editor at Penguin, Kerry Donovan, and my agent, Jane Dystel. These two ladies work tirelessly behind the scenes to make each new book possible.

A special note of thanks to Noël Kristan Higgins. You take my best and make it better.

Also to: Tianna Croy and Tasha Whitbread. Thank you, ladies, for all of your help.

Don't miss the next book in the bestselling
Danvers series from Sydney Landon,

ALWAYS LOVING YOU

Available from Signet Eclipse in February
wherever books and e-books are sold.

"Oh my God, what's he done now?"

Ava scowled at her assistant and future sister-in-law,
Emma Davis, as she settled into a seat in front of her
desk. Ava had been a vice president at Danvers International since she and Brant had sold their family business to Jason Danvers. Truthfully, she enjoyed the work
as well as the challenge of something new.

Ava gave an unladylike snort at Emma's question
and resigned herself to playing twenty questions. There
was no way her nosy assistant was going to let her off
without explaining her shittier-than-usual mood. She
gave her best innocent look and said, "I have no idea
what you're talking about. Don't you have some work
to do in your own office?"

Emma merely smirked at Ava's disgruntled expression, knowing by now that her bark was worse than her

bite. Ava would never let the other woman know it, but she had grown to love her dearly since Emma had gotten engaged to her brother Brant. Between Emma and her other brother Declan's wife, Ella, family occasions were no longer akin to a gathering at the morgue. Emma and Ella had breathed some much-needed life into the Stone family. "Nah, I'm on a break, so I have time."

Rolling her eyes, Ava said, "A break, huh? You seem to have a lot of those." Secretly, Ava knew why Brant had enjoyed arguing with Emma when she had been his assistant before their engagement. It was just freaking fun. Emma was actually fabulous at her job and took a lot of the workload from Ava's shoulders.

"All right, enough of this stalling crap. What's happening with Mac? I take it you've spoken to him again, even though he's been avoiding you, since you're suddenly acting like someone with a monthlong case of PMS."

Putting all pretense aside, Ava said, "Yeah I ran into him and . . . her in the parking garage yesterday."

"Oh shit! Did you, like . . . speak to the tramp?"

Ava smiled even though she felt the need to defend the woman who'd stolen her sorta man. "I don't think she's a tramp, Em. Mac wouldn't be interested in anyone like that."

Emma shook her head in disgust. "You're totally missing the point here. This woman is messing with your guy. We don't take that lightly. Until we get rid of her, she is the 'tramp' to us. So . . . how did it go?"

Ava tried to hide her pain as she relayed her run-in

with Mac. "Well, he was walking . . . her to the car when I saw them. He helped her inside and kissed her, and then she drove off. He saw me and we talked for a minute. That's it."

"Ava, why do you put yourself through all this? If you leveled with Mac about how you really feel, he'd probably kick . . . the tramp to the curb faster than you could say bye-bye. He loves you. According to your family, he's never made any secret of that fact. And . . . you love him. Are you really going to let . . . her have him?"

It all sounded so simple when Emma put it like that, but the reality was completely different. After years of being terrified of intimacy and feeling as if she wasn't good enough for Mac, Ava had finally decided to do everything she could to overcome her fears. She had purchased every self-help book that she could find and was seriously considering going to a therapist. She was so very tired of being afraid all of the time. Just when she was on the brink of confessing to Mac how screwed-up she really was and how she felt about him, he had pulled the rug out from under her. Apparently, they had both arrived at the same conclusion—that they needed to move on and stop tiptoeing around each other. Only she had wanted to move toward him, but unfortunately, his moves had taken him away from her.

Since then, she had been reeling in shock. What now? He had been her reason for finally getting her shit together. He had waited for her all of these years, and just when she thought they might be on the same page, he was gone. Just like that. He'd freaking left her behind. And damn it, she couldn't even blame him, which was the worst part. "Em, it's not that simple. What am I supposed to say? 'Oh, Mac, please toss your new girlfriend aside. I've decided that although I'm too fucked-up to have a relationship with you myself, I can't let anyone else have you? I'm going to need you to masturbate and remain true only to me.'"

Emma cocked a brow before saying, "Well, that wasn't quite what I had in mind, other than the tossing of the new girlfriend. Seriously, though, grow a pair or whatever the female equivalent of that is and take Mac back."

Ava reluctantly smiled. "So you're going the tough-love route today, huh? Given up coddling the poor, messed-up girl?" She saw the look of sympathy that Emma tried to hide as she stood, turning toward the door.

"You're one of the strongest people I know, Ava. I have no idea what it's been like for you all of these years. However, I know if you lose Mac, you'll never move forward. He's your white knight, but this time you're going to have charge to his rescue. You need to save the both of you from living a life without 'the one.'"

When the door closed behind the other woman, Ava turned to stare out the window. The beach town was bustling with the last of the summer crowd before cooler weather took over. She hardly noticed, though, as her friend's words echoed through her head. Was she strong enough to finally show Mac how she felt? God, where did she even start? He wouldn't even agree to have a drink with her last night, so it was unlikely he was up for an impromptu date. Emma would probably laugh her ass off if she knew that at this moment, Ava was sitting at her desk googling 'how to show a man that you love him.' Great, number one was just telling him. Fucking Google. Always making everything sound so simple.

When Ava entered her empty apartment, feeling lonelier than ever, she was no closer to a solution than she had been. Embarrassingly enough, she'd even resorted to stopping at the store on the way home and buying almost a hundred dollars' worth of magazines. If there was anything pertaining to men or love, she bought it. Walking into her kitchen, she pulled out the bottle of wine she had also purchased. You had to love today's conveniences. You could now buy everything short of a car at Walgreens. She'd even paused by the condom aisle as if trying to think positively that she might need them soon. Yeah . . . that really looked likely.

Popping the cork on the bottle, she filled a glass nearly to the brim and walked back to the couch with her overflowing bag. The first magazine cover promised twenty sexual moves that would drive her man crazy. She laughed under her breath. She'd have to actually have a man for that to work. She had bought it, though, just in case she ever moved on to the next level. Setting it aside, the headline on the next one immediately caught her eyes: *Want to catch his attention? Unleash your inner daredevil!* Okay, maybe she could work with that. Flipping the magazine open, she found the page number on the contents page and went to the article. The picture showed a woman about her age holding a motorcycle helmet in one hand and a pair of skates in the other hand. Ava grabbed a notepad and a pen off the coffee table. Her brother Brant was an organizational freak and she was more like him than she cared to admit. How many women would buy a magazine for help with landing their man and take notes along the way? She was even tempted to highlight relevant paragraphs but suppressed the urge.

Hours and almost one bottle of wine later, she had filled her notepad with suggestions from the ten magazines she had spent the evening scouring. The overall advice was the same in all of them, except for the one encouraging her to be a daredevil. Shit, it was either that or start dressing like a slut and making sexual advances toward Mac. One even suggested in a roundabout way that she invite her man to her house for dinner, wear a dress and sit in front of him. Then, after a few moments of small talk, she was to open her legs and start touching herself. According to the author of the article, it would have him eating out of the palm of her hand . . . or eating *something* for sure. She could feel herself blush furiously just thinking about doing that. Mac would probably have her committed. *Poor Ava's finally snapped.*

She wanted Mac in every way, but damn it, she was

essentially a twenty-eight-year-old virgin. She had never had a real sexual relationship with a man. Like most single women her age, she had needs and desires. Her vibrator took the place of a real man in her bed, and she had learned to live with that. It was the safe way out. When she needed to take the edge off, she used it. Sometimes—most of the time—it was Mac's name that she called as she reached orgasm.

She didn't know how to function outside of that, though. She could probably talk to her sister-in-law Ella if she could muster up the courage. Ella had confided that she had been a virgin when she met Declan. That was where their similarities stopped, though. Ella might have lived a sheltered life before meeting Ava's brother, but she hadn't spent her life running from past trauma. She wasn't scared of intimacy or afraid she'd freak out during sex and humiliate herself.

Part of her knew that Mac would take care of her and help her overcome her fears, but the other part didn't want him to know how messed up she was. His opinion of her mattered. She wanted him to see her as strong and confident, not scared and insecure. God, what would he think if he found out that she had picked men up in bars for years, paying them to come home with her for a few hours, just to keep up the pretense that she was normal? She knew it would sound bad, but it seemed to make people look at her with less pity when they believed that she was dating. Normal, unattached women her age had sex, right? She wasn't normal, and she wasn't having sex, but it was all about perception. If you threw people a few tidbits here and there, they would draw their own conclusions. In this case, the assumptions were wrong.

Ava had spent years believing that one day she would cross some invisible line and she would be worthy of Mac. It was kind of like holding on to an outfit in a smaller size, thinking you'll lose weight and fit into it in the future. Well, fast-forward ten years and the damn outfit still didn't fit and she was no closer to making it happen. She was still dreaming of the day when it would all come together and she woke up normal, in love, and with Mac.

Looking down at the magazines spread over her couch and coffee table, she felt a wave of despair. This was it? All that was standing between her and losing Mac to another woman was a bunch of magazine articles? Self-help and advice for the romantically hopeless. Shit, short of the boob job, she planned to try some of the other suggestions. What did she have to lose? Mac was probably with Gwen tonight, maybe having sex. While she was sitting home alone, just like always. When had she given up? At what point had she stopped trying to get better and accepted herself as broken beyond repair? Had her friendship with Mac unwittingly become a replacement for a real relationship with him? While he was in the military, there hadn't been any real pressure. Actually, it had made it easier for her to communicate with him, knowing he was too far away to drop by unexpectedly. She had seen him when he was home on leave, and they had written and talked on the phone, but she hadn't seen him every day. When he'd finally come home for good, they had just fallen into the routine of spending most of their spare time together. They went for drinks, had dinner, hung out at each other's apartments and attended family events together. They were more of a couple than many married people she knew. They were almost back to where they had been before her attack, only now they were both very much adults.

Mac had never been one to verbalize his feelings, but he showed her in a million different ways that he cared for her. In the last year, though, it was as if his patience was wearing thin. His touches had gone from fleeting to lingering. A few months ago, before he had started dating Gwen, he'd kissed her. Not the usual brief peck either. There had been lips and tongue involved and . . . she'd freaked out. They'd been watching a movie at her place, and she'd been curled up next to him, half asleep. When she felt his hands sliding through her hair, stroking her neck, she had nestled closer, instinctively seeking the comfort of his touch. When he lowered his mouth to hers, she had allowed it, more curious than anything. But things had quickly escalated. She had found herself returning his kiss, tangling her tongue with his. Desire had raced through her veins until he pulled her closer, embracing her solidly against his hard chest. Then she'd panicked. She couldn't breathe; she had to get away. So she had jumped from his arms to the other side of the room to put as much distance as possible between them.

Things had gotten awkward after that. He had apologized that night, and she had thought things were okay until he started pulling away. Day by day, she lost him. Then he was dating someone else right in front of her for the first time since they were teenagers. Oh, she knew that Mac had sex; she wasn't that naive. But he didn't have relationships, and she had never seen him out on a regular date. Ava had always came first with him—but no longer. Now Gwen was the priority, and she felt a very distant second, if even that. He'd given up on her that night just as plainly as if he had said it aloud.

He was no longer content to wait around; he wanted more out of life. He wanted the fairy-tale happy ending. He wasn't going to be satisfied with half measures; it was going to take more to get him back. And scariest of all, she knew he wasn't coming back to a friends-with-no-benefits relationship. In order to get Mac, she would have to become part of his fairy tale. She would have to put the ugliness of her past behind her and become his freaking Cinderella.

She put in her purse the notes that she had made while reading the magazines. "Okay, *Cosmo*, let's give it our best shot."

About the Author

Sydney Landon is the *New York Times* and *USA Today* bestselling author of *Weekends Required, Not Planning on You*, and *Fall for Me*. When she isn't writing, Sydney enjoys reading, swimming and being a minivan-driving soccer mom. She lives in Greenville, South Carolina, with her family.

Also available from *New York Times*
and *USA Today* bestselling author

Sydney Landon

THE DANVERS NOVELS

Weekends Required

Claire Walters has worked for Jason Danvers as his assistant for
three years, but he never appreciated her as a woman—until the
day she jumps out of a cake at his friend's bachelor party...

Not Planning on You

Suzy Denton thought she had it all: a great job as an event
planner and a committed relationship to her high school
sweetheart. But life is never quite so simple...

Fall For Me

All her life, Beth Denton battled both her weight and her
controlling parents. And now that she's declared victory, she's
looking for one good man to share the spoils of war...

Fighting For You

Ella Webber has spent years uncomfortable around the opposite
sex, but as soon as she meets the handsome Declan Stone, she's
smitten. But can she persuade Declan that they're a
perfect match?

Available wherever books are sold or at
penguin.com

sydneylandon.com